P9-DDS-592

U

Updike, John

Problems and other
stories

80-1931   11/22

Two Weeks

PROBLEMS
and Other Stories

John Updike

PROBLEMS
and Other Stories

Alfred A. Knopf   New York

1979

u

THIS IS A BORZOI BOOK
PUBLISHED BY ALFRED A. KNOPF, INC.

Of these twenty-three stories, seventeen first appeared in *The
New Yorker.* "Minutes of the Last Meeting" was first published
in *Audience;* "Believers" in *Harper's Magazine;* "Augustine's Concubine" in *The Atlantic Monthly;* "Nevada" and "The Faint" in
Playboy; and "Transaction" in *Oui.*

The quotations from St. Augustine's *Confessions* in "Believers"
and "Augustine's Concubine" are as translated by Edward B.
Pusey; those from Plato's *Critias* in "Atlantises," as translated by
R. G. Bury. The quotations concerning science in "Here Come
the Maples" are from a talk by Professor Steven Weinberg, "The
Forces of Nature," given before the American Academy of Arts
and Sciences and reprinted in that organization's January 1976
Bulletin (Vol. XXIX, No. 4). © 1976 by The American Acad-
emy of Arts and Sciences. Reprinted with permission of Mr.
Weinberg and the Bulletin.

Library of Congress Cataloging in Publication Data
Updike, John.
Problems and other stories. I. Title.
PZ4.U64Pr [PS3571.P4] 813'.5'4 79–1480
ISBN 0-394-50705-3

Manufactured in the United States of America
Published October 29, 1979
Second Printing Before Publication

Author's Note

SEVEN YEARS since my last short-story collection? There
must have been problems. One of these stories remembers
a time when we were advised to love America or leave it.
Another predicts eternal stasis for an Ethiopia that shortly
thereafter underwent a revolution. A third refers to the
fad of transactional analysis. Tales involving Henry Bech,
and all but two about that perennial couple the Maples,
are not included. The stories appear in the order in which
they were written, from 1971 to 1978; the collection as a
whole, with the curve of sad time it subtends, is dedicated
lovingly to Elizabeth, David, Michael, and Miranda.

Contents

PROBLEMS
and Other Stories

Commercial

It COMES ON EVERY NIGHT, somewhere in the eleven o'clock news. A CHILD runs down a STAIRCASE. A rotund ELDERLY WOMAN stands at the foot, picks up the CHILD, gives him a shake (friendly), and sets him down. There is MUSIC, containing the words "laughing child," "fur-lined rug," etc.

The STAIRCASE looks unexpectedly authentic, oaken and knobby and steep in the style of houses where we have childhoods. We know this STAIRCASE. Some treads creak, and at the top there is a branching many-cornered darkness wherein we are supposed to locate security and sleep. The wallpaper (baskets of flowers, at a guess, alternating with ivied medallions) would feel warm, if touched.

The CHILD darts offscreen. We have had time to register that it is a BOY, with long hair cut straight across his forehead. The camera stays with the ELDERLY WOMAN, whom by now we identify as the GRANDMOTHER. She gazes after the (supposedly) receding BOY so fondly we can imagine "(gazes fondly)" in the commercial's script.

The second drags; her beaming threatens to become

blank. But now, with an electrifying touch of uncertainty, so that we do not know if it was the director's idea or the actress's, GRANDMOTHER slowly wags her head, as if to say, *My, oh my, what an incorrigible little rascal, what a lovable little man-child!* Her heart, we feel, so brims with love that her plump body, if a whit less healthy and compact, if a whit less compressed and contained by the demands and accoutrements of GRANDMOTHERLINESS, would burst. GRANDMOTHERLINESS massages her from all sides, like the brushes of a car wash.

And now (there is so much to see!) she relaxes her arms in front of her, the fingers of one hand gently gripping the wrist of the other. This gesture tells us that her ethnic type is Anglo-Saxon. An Italian mama, say, would have folded her arms across her bosom; and, also, wouldn't the coquetry of Mediterranean women forbid their wearing an apron out of the kitchen, beside what is clearly a front STAIRCASE? So, while still suspended high on currents of anticipation, we deduce that this is not a commercial for spaghetti.

Nor for rejuvenating skin creams or hair rinses, for the camera cuts from GRANDMOTHER to the BOY. He is hopping through a room. Not quite hopping, nor exactly skipping: a curious fey gait that bounces his cap of hair and evokes the tender dialectic of the child-director encounter. This CHILD, who, though a child actor acting the part of a child, is nevertheless also truly a child, has been told to move across the fictional room in a childish way. He has obeyed, moving hobbled by self-consciousness yet with the elastic bounce that Nature has bestowed upon him and that no amount of adult direction can utterly squelch. Only time can squelch it.

We do not know how many "takes" were sifted through to get this second of movement. Though no child in reality (though billions of children have crossed millions of rooms) ever moved across a room in quite this way, an impression of CHILDHOOD pierces us. We get the message: GRANDMOTHER'S HOUSE (and the montage is so swift we cannot itemize the furniture, only concede that it appears fittingly fusty and congested) is cozy, safe—a place to be joyful in. Why? The question hangs.

We are in another room. A kitchen. A shining POT dominates the foreground. The BOY, out of focus, still bobbing in that unnatural, affecting way, enters at the background, comes forward into focus, becomes an alarmingly large face and a hand that lifts the lid of the POT. STEAM billows. The BOY blows the STEAM away, then stares at us with stagily popped eyes. Meaning? He has burned himself? There is a bad smell? The director, offscreen, has shouted at him? We do not know, and we are made additionally uncomfortable by the possibility that this is a spaghetti commercial after all.

Brief scene: GRANDMOTHER washing BOY's face. Bathroom fixtures behind. Theme of heat (cozy HOUSE, hot POT) subliminally emerges. Also: suppertime?

We do not witness supper. We are back at the STAIRCASE. New actors have arrived: a tall and vigorous YOUNG COUPLE, in stylish overcoats. Who? We scarcely have time to ask. The BOY leaps (flies, indeed; we do not see his feet launch him) upward into the arms of the MAN. These are his PARENTS. We ourselves, watching, welcome them; the depth of our welcome reveals to us a dread within ourselves, of something morbid and claustral in the old HOUSE, with its cunningly underlined snugness and its lonely

PROBLEMS

household of benevolent crone and pampered, stagy brat. These other two radiate the brisk air of outdoors. To judge from their clothes, it is cold outside; this impression is not insignificant; our sense of subliminal coherence swells. We join in the BUSTLE of WELCOME, rejoicing with the YOUNG COUPLE in their sexual energy and safe return and great good fortune to be American and modern and solvent and fertile and to have such a picture-book GRANDMOTHER to babysit for them whenever they partake of some innocent infrequent SPREE.

But whose mother is GRANDMOTHER, the FATHER's or the MOTHER's?

All questions are answered. The actor playing the YOUNG FATHER ignores GRANDMOTHER with the insouciance of blood kinship, while the actress playing the YOUNG MOTHER hugs her, pulls back, reconsiders, then dips forward to bestow upon the beaming plump cheek a kiss GRAND-MOTHER does not, evidently, expect. Her beaming wavers momentarily, like a candle flame when a distant door is opened. The DAUGHTER-IN-LAW again pulls back, as if coolly to contemplate the product of her affectionate in-spiration. Whether her tense string of hesitations was spun artfully by an actress fulfilling a role or was visited upon the actress as she searched her role for nuances (we can imagine how vague the script might be: *Parents return. Greetings all around. Camera medium tight*), a ticklish closeness of maneuver, amid towering outcroppings of good will, has been conveyed. The FAMILY is complete.

And now the underlying marvel is made manifest. The true HERO of these thirty seconds unmasks. The FAMILY fades into a blue cartoon flame, and the MUSIC, no longer buried by visual stimuli, sings with clarion brilliance, "NATURAL GAS is a Beauti-ful Thing!"

: 6 :

Commercial

. . .

A MAN, discovered in BED, beside his WIFE, suffers the remainder of the NEWS, then rises and turns off the TELEVISION SET. The screen palely exudes its last quanta of daily radiation. The room by default fills with the dim light of the MOON. Risen, the MAN, shuffling around the BED with a wary gait suggestive of inelasticity and an insincerely willed silence, makes his way into the bathroom, where he urinates. He does this, we sense, not from any urgent physical need but conscientiously, even Puritanically, from a basis of theory, to clear himself and his conscience for sleep.

His thoughts show, in vivid montage. As always when hovering above the dim oval of porcelain, he recalls the most intense vision of beauty his forty years have granted him. It was after a lunch in New York. The luncheon had been gay, prolonged, overstimulating, vinous. Now he was in a taxi, heading up the West Side Highway. At the 57th Street turnoff, the need to urinate was a feathery subliminal thought; by the Seventies (where Riverside Drive begins to rise like an airplane), it was a real pressure; by the Nineties (Soldiers' and Sailors' Monument crumbling, Riverside Park a green cliff looming), it had become a murderous imperative. Mastering shame, the MAN confessed his agony to the DRIVER, who, gradually suspending disbelief, swung off the highway at 158th Street and climbed a little cobblestone mountain and found there, evidently not for the first time, a dirty triangular garage. Mechanics, black or blackened, stared with white eyes as the strange MAN stumbled past them, back through the oily and junk-lined triangle to the apex: here, pinched between obscene frescoes, sat the most beautiful thing he ever saw. Or would ever see. It was a TOILET BOWL, a

TOILET BOWL in its flawed whiteness, its partial wateriness, its total receptiveness: in the harmonious miracle of its infrangible and unvariable *ens*. The beautiful is, precisely, what you need at the time.

Quick cameo mug shots of Plato, Aquinas, Santayana, and other theorists of beauty, X'ed in rough strokes to indicate refutation.

Brief scene: MAN brushing teeth, rinsing mouth, spitting. Cut to MOON, impassive.

Return to MAN. He stands before the bathroom cabinet, puzzling. He opens the door, which is also a mirror. Zoom to tiny red BOX. What is in the BOX? Something, we sense, that he resists because it does not conform to his ideal conception of healthy normality. He closes the door.

He sniffs. As he has been standing puzzling, the odor of his own body has risen to him, a potato-ish reproachful odor. When he was a child living, like the CHILD in the commercial, with adults, he imagined that adults emitted this odor on purpose, to chasten and discipline him. Now that it is his own odor, it does not seem chastening but merely nagging, like the pile of SLIT ENVELOPES that clutter the kitchen table every afternoon. Quick still of ENVELOPES. Replay of CHILD running down STAIRCASE to awaiting arms. We are, subliminally, affected.

Shuffling (in case he stubs his toe or steps on a pin), the MAN returns from the bathroom and proceeds around the BED. The TELEVISION SET is cold now. The MOON is cold, too. As if easing a read letter back into a slit envelope, he eases himself back into BED beside his WIFE. He sneaks his hand under her nightie and rubs her back; it is a ritual question. In ritual answer, the WIFE stirs in her sleep, awakens enough to realize that the room is cold, presses her body tight against that of the MAN, and falls again asleep. Asleep again. Again again. Asleep.

Now his half of the BED has been reduced to a third—a third, furthermore, crimped and indented by oblivious elbows and knees. The MAN's eyes close but his EARS open wider, terrible eyes from which lids have been scissored, vast deep wells hungry for the whispers and crackles of the WORLD. He buries his EARS alternately in the pillow, but cannot staunch both at once. He thinks of masturbating, but decides there is not enough room.

A radiator whistles: steam heat, oil-fired. Would natural gas be noiseless? A far car whirs. Surf, or wind, murmurs; or can it be a helicopter?

Now the CAT—a new actor!—mews a foot below the MAN's face. Svelte and insistent, the CAT wants to go out. The MAN, almost gratefully, rises. Better action than nothing, he thinks—in this a typical citizen of our fagged era. The CAT's whiskers, electric, shivering, tingle like frost on the MAN's bare ankles.

Together MAN and CAT go down a STAIRCASE. No oaken knobs here. The style is bare, modern. The MAN touches the wall: chill plaster.

The MAN opens the front door. GRASS, TREES, SKY, and STARS, abruptly framed, look colorless and flat as if, thus surprised, they had barely had time to get their outlines together. The STARS, especially, appear perfunctory: bullet holes in a hangar roof. The CAT darts offscreen.

We are back in the BED. The MAN turns the pillow over, to explore with his cheek its dark side. Delicately, yet borrowing insistence from the CAT's example, he pushes his WIFE's body toward her side of the BED, inch by inert inch. Minutes of patient nudging are undone when, surfacing toward consciousness, she slumps more confidingly into him. Does she wake, or sleep? Is her reclamation of two-thirds of the BED an instinctive territorial assertion of her insensate body, or is it the product, cerebral enough, of a calculation scribbled on the wavering marital ground between them? Here the MAN, our inadequate HERO, seems to arrive at one of those fumbling-points that usefully distract the brain with the motions of thinking while the body falls into thoughtless bliss. Hopeful pits and bubbles and soft, stretching aches develop within him, forerunners of merciful dissolution.

Abrupt cut: within a child's room, the HAMSTER, yielding to some sudden fantasy of speed and space, accelerates within his unoiled running-wheel. The clatter is epic; the HAMSTER twirls the world on a string.

We are back in the bathroom. The MAN imagines he must urinate again. The shadowy porcelain oval again reminds him of absolute beauty. A forlorn sense of surrender suffuses the aroma of overripe potatoes. He is removing the little red BOX from the cabinet whose door is a mirror. He takes two small objects from this BOX. Zoom. They are little balls of WAX. Why? What on EARTH?

Back in the bedroom. The MOON in the window has shrunk in size. In contracting, it has gained heat; its pallor looks hot, almost solar.

The MAN inserts himself back into the BED. He inserts the wax EAR PLUGS into his ears. The sharp bright wires of noise etched on darkness dull down into gray threads, an indistinct blanket. He grows aware, sensate, of the tangible blanket, as a source of goodness, a SKY tangent to him. His WIFE mysteriously, voluntarily shifts her weight toward the wide horizon where all pressures meet in a dull wedge.

A subterranean whistling noise dawns upon him as the sound of his own breathing. He has buried himself, his *ens*. The cave of his skull furs with nonsense. *Pan, fade, dissolve.* That is how it happens every night.

One question remains. What is being advertised? (1) Ear plugs (2) Natural gas (3) Lucifer's fall (4) Nothing.

Minutes of the
Last Meeting

THE CHAIRMAN OF THE COMMITTEE again expressed his desire to resign.

The Secretary pointed out that the bylaws do not provide for resignation procedures, they provide however for a new slate of officers to be presented annually and a new slate of officers was being accordingly presented.

The Chairman responded that however on the new slate his name was again listed as Chairman. He said he had served since the founding of the Committee and sincerely felt that his chairmanship had become more of a hindrance than a help. He said that what the Committee needed at this point was new direction and a refined sense of purpose which he could not provide, being too elderly and confused and out of sympathy with things. That the time had come either for younger blood to take over the helm or possibly for the Committee to disband.

The Secretary pointed out that the bylaws do not provide for disbandment.

In answer to a query from the Chairman, Mrs. Hepple on behalf of the Nominating Sub-Committee explained that the Sub-Committee felt as a whole that the Chairman was invaluable in his present position, that support in the wider community would be drastically weakened by his resignation, and that the nomination of two vice-chairmen and the creation of appropriate sub-committees would effectively lighten his work load.

The Chairman asked how often the Nominating Sub-Committee had met. Mrs. Hepple responded that due to the holiday season they had convened once, by telephone. There was laughter. In the same humorous spirit the Chairman suggested that the only way he could effectively resign would be to shoot himself.

Mr. Langbehn, one of the newer members, said before presuming to participate in this discussion he would be grateful for having explained to him the original purposes and intents of the Committee.

The Chairman answered that he had never understood them and would be grateful himself.

Miss Beame then volunteered that though the youngest Founder present she would offer her impressions, which were that at the founding of the Committee their purpose was essentially the formal one of meeting to give approval to the activities of the Director. That without the magical personality and earnest commitment of the Director they would not have been gathered together at all. That beyond appointing him Director the bulk of the business at the first meeting had centered upon the name of the Committee, initially proposed as the Tarbox Betterment Committee, then expanded to the Committee for Betterment and Development of Human Resources. That the Director had felt that the phrase Equal Opportunity should also be included, and perhaps some special emphasis on youth as well, without appearing to exclude the senior citizens of the community. Therefore the title of Tarbox Committee for Equal Development and Betterment for Young and Old Alike was proposed and considered.

Dr. Costopoulos, a Founder, recalled that the Director did not however wish the Committee to appear to offer itself as a rival to already extant groups like the Golden Agers and the Teen Scene and had furthermore regretted in the official committee title any indication of a pervasive ecological concern. So a unanimous vote was taken to leave the name of the Committee temporarily open.

Mrs. Hepple added that even though the Director had been rather new in town it all had seemed a wonderful idea. He was the kind of young man who made things happen, she added.

Mrs. MacMillan, a new member, asked where the Director was.

Miss Beame explained that the Director had vanished after the founding meeting.

Leaving behind a cardboard suitcase and an unpaid phone bill, the Chairman volunteered. There was laughter.

The Secretary pointed out that the bylaws perfectly clearly specify the purpose of the Committee and read excerpts spelling out that "no political candidates or partisan causes should be publicly espoused," "no stocks or bonds were to be held with the objective of financial profit or gain," and "no gambling or licentious assignation would be permitted on any premises leased or owned entirely or in part by the said Committee."

Mr. Langbehn asked to see the bylaws.

The Secretary graciously complied.

Mr. Langbehn claimed after examination that this was

a standard form purchasable in any office supplies or stationery store.

Mrs. Hepple said she didn't see that it made any difference, that here we all are and that is the main point.

Mrs. MacMillan inquired as to why the Committee kept meeting in the absence of the Director.

The Treasurer interrupted to ask the evening's Hostess, Mrs. Landis, if it weren't time for refreshments to be served.

The Reverend Mr. Trussel asked if he might attempt to elucidate the question asked by the good Mrs. MacMillan. He said that at first the Committee had met in the expectation that the Director would reappear and then, in later sessions, as a board of inquiry into where the Director had gone. Finally, they had continued to meet because, in his opinion, they had come to love and need one another.

Miss Beame said she thought that was a touching and true description.

Mrs. Hepple said she didn't see where any of it mattered at this point because not only were most of the Founders in attendance but many new members as well. That the membership had grown instead of withering away as one would suppose if the Committee were entirely dependent upon the Director who for that matter she had quite forgotten what he looked like.

Mr. de Muth volunteered that he had come on to the Committee in his capacity as a social science teacher because he understood at that time there had been under consideration a program to arrange a lecture series or series of happenings on the theme of betterment of resources at the public schools.

Mr. Tjadel said he had come on in his capacity as a tree surgeon because of the ecology angle.

Mrs. MacMillan said she had been given the impression her interest in oral contraception might be applied by the Committee to the town drinking water.

The Chairman stated it was all a muddle and again offered his resignation.

The Secretary pointed out that all of these projects had been under consideration and as far as she was concerned still were.

Mr. Langbehn began to speak.

The Treasurer interrupted to compliment Mrs. Landis on the quality of her refreshments.

Mr. Langbehn thanked all present for bearing with him and filling him in so thoroughly. He said that though none of the projects described had apparently come to fruition he nevertheless did not feel that the members of the Committee including himself should entertain the fear that their efforts were in vain. That on the contrary they had created much talk and interest in the wider community and that just the fact that they continued to attract to membership such distinguished and personable citizens as those present negated any idea of failure. [Several sentences missed here due to accident spilling glass.—SEC.] That what was needed was not any long-term narrowing of the horizons established by the Director but a momentary closer focus upon some doubtless limited but feasible short-term goal within the immediate community.

Mrs. Hepple suggested that a dance or rummage sale be held to raise funds so such a goal might be attacked.

Miss Beame thought that a square dance would be better than a black-tie dance so as to attract young people.

The Chairman moved that the bylaws be amended so as to permit the Committee to disband.

No one seconded.

Mr. Tjadel said he didn't see why there was all this worrying about human resources, in his opinion they had fine human resources right here in this room. If the trunk is solid, he said, the branches will flourish. There was laughter and applause.

The Treasurer volunteered that in his opinion this was the best meeting yet and that to make itself more effective the Committee should meet more often.

Miss Beame said her heart went out to the Chairman and she thought his wishes should be respected.

Reverend Mr. Trussel moved that the board of officers as presented by the Nominating Sub-Committee be accepted with the proviso that the Chairman be nominated as Chairman *pro tem* and that to assist his labors further a Sub-Committee on Goals and Purposes be created, with Mr. Langbehn and Miss Beame as co-chairpersons.

Mrs. Hepple and others seconded.

The affirmative vote was unanimous, the Chairman abstaining.

Believers

THE WOMAN NEXT TO HIM at the party is sipping ginger ale, though he knows her to be a devoted drinker of vodka martinis. He points at the sparkling beverage and says, "Lent?" She nods. Her eyes are calm as a statue's. He knows her to be a believer. So is he. Let us christen him Credo.

Credo is in the basement of a church. He is on the church Church Heritage Committee, along with four old ladies. Their problem is, they are going to move to a new church, of white plastic, and what shall they do with all this old religious furniture? It has been accumulating for centuries: box pew doors and tin foot warmers from the edifice of 1736; carpeted kneeling stools and velvet collection bags from the edifice of 1812; a gargantuan Gothic deacon's bench, of pinnacled oak, from the edifice of 1885. It would strain seventeen laymen to lift and move it; there must have been giants in those days. Giants of faith.

One of the old ladies mounts up onto its padded arms. Puffs of dust sprout beneath her feet. She retrieves something—a kind of jewel—from the pinnacle of the ornate bench back. They pass it around. It is a little brown photograph embedded in cracked glass, of a Victorian child wearing a paper crown. "Maybe some church just starting up would like to buy it all," the first lady says.

"One of those new California sects," the second amplifies.

"Never," says Credo. "Nobody wants this junk."

"At least," the third lady begs, "let's get an antique dealer to appraise the picture frames." Behind an old spinet and cartons of warped hymnals they have uncovered perhaps forty picture frames, all empty. "People will pay a fortune for such things nowadays."

"What people?" Credo asks. He cannot believe it. The basement seems airless; he cannot breathe. The ancient furnace comes on. Its awakening shudder shakes loose flakes of asbestos packing from the pipes; like snow the flakes drift down onto old hymnals, picture frames, piano stools, broken Sunday-school chairs, attendance charts with pasted-on gold stars coming unstuck, old men's-club-bowling-league bowling shoes, kneeling stools worn like ox yokes, tin foot warmers perforated like cabbage graters. God, it is depressing. God.

The fourth old lady has brought a paper shopping bag. Out of it she pulls dustrags, a bottle of Windex, a rainbow of Magic Markers, some shipping tags in two colors—green for preserve, red for destroy. "Let's make some decisions," she says briskly. "Let's separate the sheep from the goats."

Credo is visiting with his minister. The minister is very well informed. He says, "The Dow Jones was off two point three today, that's one less soprano pipe on our new fiberglass organ." The minister's wife brings them in tea and honey. The jar of honey glows in a shaft of dusty parsonage sunlight. The minister's wife's hair is up in a towering beehive; she is a voluptuous blonde. Credo's wife is a mousy brunette. *Buy now, pay later,* he thinks, piously sipping.

Credo surveys the new church. The glistening bubble-shaped shell of white plastic holds a multitude of pastel rooms. He served on the New Creation Committee, which worked with the team of architects; the endless meetings and countless blueprints have become reality. There are many petty disappointments. The altar spot has been rheostatted in sync with the pulpit spot. The pre-pressed steeple weeps in a storm. The Sunday-school room dividers scrape and buckle when pulled into place. The organ sounds like fiberglass. The duct blower blows down the wrong duct and keeps extinguishing the pilot light in the wall oven. The proportions of the boiler room do not uplift the heart. The foundation slab is already cracking. Credo follows the sinuous crack with his eyes. The earth, of course, slumps and shrugs; the continental plates are sliding. Yet somehow one expects that it will hold firm beneath a church. Yet by this pattern miracles would become everyday and a tyranny. Yet the Lisbon earthquake, he reflects, his faith sliding.

He reads St. Augustine. It is too hot, too radiant, blinding, and wild. *Is there indeed, O Lord my God, aught in me that can contain Thee? do then heaven and earth, which Thou hast made, and wherein Thou hast made me, contain Thee? or, because nothing which exists could exist without Thee, doth therefore whatever exists contain Thee? Since, then, I too exist, why do I seek that Thou shouldest enter into me, who were not, wert Thou not in* me? Why? It is too serious, frightening, and exciting; Credo has to get up and dull himself with a drink so he can continue reading. Augustine scribbles on a dizzying verge: he nearly indicts God for his helplessly damned infancy, for his schoolboy whippings; then pulls back, blames himself, and exonerates the Lord. . . . *let not my soul faint under Thy discipline, nor let me faint in confessing unto Thee all Thy mercies, whereby Thou hast drawn me out of all my most evil ways, that Thou mightest become a delight to me above all the allurements which I once pursued.* . . . It is too terrific, there is no relenting; Credo makes another drink, stares out the window, lets in the cat, asks a child how his day went at school, anything for relief from this whirlwind . . . *is not all this smoke and wind? and was there nothing else whereon to exercise my wit and tongue? Thy praises, Lord, Thy praises might have stayed the yet tender shoot of my heart by the prop of Thy Scriptures; so had it not trailed away amid these empty trifles, a defiled prey for the fowls of the air. For in more ways than one do men sacrifice to the rebellious angels.* He cannot go on, he has waited four decades to read this, his heart cannot withstand it. It is too strict and searing, fierce and judicious; nothing alloyed can survive within it. Credo reads *The New York Times* Sunday magazine supplement instead. "China: Old Hands and New." "The Black Bourgeoisie Flees the Ghetto." "I Was a Marigold Head." He flips through *Sports Illustrated, Art News, Rolling Stone.* He puts St. Augustine back on the shelf, between Marcus Aurelius and Boethius. The book is safe there. He will take it down again, when he is sixty-five, and ready. *These things Thou seest, Lord, and holdest Thy peace; long-suffering, and plenteous in mercy and truth. Wilt Thou hold Thy peace for ever?*

．　．　．

Credo is in a motel. He has brought a shaker of vodka and vermouth and ice, and a can of ginger ale, just in case. The woman with him cannot be tempted. It is still Lent. She sips from the can, and he from the shaker; they take off each other's clothes. Her body is radiant, blinding, strict, serious, exciting. They admire each other, they make of one another an occasion for joy. Because they are believers, their acts possess an immense dimension of glory, of risk; they are flirting with being damned, though they do not say this. They say only gracious things, commensurate with the gratitude and exaltation they feel. To arouse her again, he quotes St. Augustine: *If bodies please thee, praise God in occasion of them, and turn back thy love upon their Maker lest in these things which please thee, thou displease.*

Credo is in a hospital. He has had an accident, and then an operation. As the drugs in his blood ebb, pain rises beneath him like a poisonous squid rising beneath a bather floating gently in the ocean. It seizes his knee. It will not let go. By the luminescent watch on the night table it is two hours before he can ring the nurse and receive his next allotment of Demerol. A single window shows a dead city, lit by street lights. Credo prays. Aloud. It is a long conversational prayer, neither apologetic nor dubious; his pain has won him a new status. He speaks aloud as if on television, giving the dead-of-the-night news. Abruptly, his chest breaks out in a sharp sweet copious sweat. He miraculously relaxes. The squid lets go, falls back, into unknowable depths. The nurse when she comes finds Credo asleep. It is morning. Up and down the hall, rosary beads click.

He is sitting on a subway, jiggling and swaying opposite other men jiggling and swaying. Back to work, though he

limps now. He will always limp. The body does not forgive, only God forgives. Between two stops, the subway
surfaces over a bridge, into the light. Below, a river
sparkles as if not polluted; sailboats tilt in the shining wind.
Credo is reminded of that passage in the Venerable Bede,
when, arguing for conversion to Christianity, an ealdor-
man likens our life to the flight of a sparrow through the
bright mead-hall. "Such appears to me, king, this present
life of man on earth in comparison with the time which is
unknown to us, as though you were sitting at the banquet
with your leaders and thanes in winter and the fire was
lighted and your hall warmed, and it rained and snowed
and stormed outside; and there should come a sparrow
and quickly fly through the house, come in through one
door and go out through the other."

In this interval of brightness Credo notices a particular
man opposite him, a commonplace, weary-looking man, of
average height and weight, costumed unaggressively, yet
with something profoundly uncongenial and *settled* about
his mouth, and an overall look of perfect integration with
the heartless machine of the world. Credo takes him for an
atheist. He thinks, Between this innocuous fellow and
myself yawns an eternal abyss, because I am a believer.

The subway, rattling, plunges back underground. Or, it
may be, as some extreme saints have implied, that beneath the majesty of the Infinite, believers and non-believ-
ers are exactly alike.

The Gun Shop

BEN'S SON MURRAY looked forward to their annual Thanksgiving trip to Pennsylvania mostly because of the gun. A Remington .22, it leaned unused in the old farmhouse all year, until little Murray came and swabbed it out and begged to shoot it. The gun had been Ben's. His parents had bought it for him the Christmas after they moved to the farm, when he was thirteen, his son's age now. No, Murray was all of fourteen, his birthday was in September. Ben should have remembered, for at the party, Ben had tapped the child on the back of the head to settle him down, and his son had pointed the cake knife at his father's chest and said, "Hit me again and I'll kill you."

Ben had been amazed. In bed that night, Sally told him, "It was his way of saying he's too big to be hit anymore. He's right. He is."

But the boy, as he and Ben walked with the gun across the brown field to the dump in the woods, didn't seem big; solemn and beardless, he carried the freshly cleaned rifle under his arm, in imitation of hunters in magazine illustrations, and the barrel tip kept snagging on loops of matted orchard grass. Then at the dump, with the targets of tin cans and bottles neatly aligned, the gun refused to fire, and Murray threw a childish tantrum. Tears filled his eyes as he tried to explain: "There was this little *pin*, Dad, that fell out when I cleaned it, but I put it back in, and now it's not *there!*"

Ben, looking down into this small freckled face so earnestly stricken, couldn't help smiling.

Murray, seeing his father's smile, said "*Shit.*" He hurled the gun toward an underbrush of saplings and threw himself onto the cold leaf mold of the forest floor. He writhed there and repeated the word as each fresh slant of injustice and of embarrassment struck him; but Ben couldn't quite erase his own expression of kindly mockery. The boy's tantrums loomed impressively in the intimate scale of their Boston apartment, with his mother and two sisters and some fine-legged antiques as audience; but out here, among these mute oaks and hickories, his fury was rather comically dwarfed. Also, in retrieving and examining the .22, Ben had bent his face close into the dainty forgotten smell of gun oil and remembered the Christmas noon when his father had taken him out to the barn and shown him how to shoot the virgin gun; and this memory prolonged his smile.

That dainty scent. The dangerous slickness. The zigzag marks of burnishing on the bolt when it slid out, and the amazing whorl, a new kind of star, inside the barrel when it was pointed toward the sky. The snug, lethally smart clicks of re-assembly. He had not known his father could handle a gun. He was forty-five when Ben was thirteen, and a schoolteacher; once he had been, briefly, a soldier. He had thrown an empty Pennzoil can into the snow of the barnyard and propped the .22 on the chicken-house windowsill and taken the first shot. The oil can had jumped. Ben remembered the way his father's mouth, seen from the side, sucked back a bit of saliva that in his concentration had escaped. Ben remembered the less-than-deafening slap of the shot and the acrid whiff that floated from the bolt as the spent shell spun away. Now, pulling the dead trigger and sliding out the bolt to see why the old gun was broken, he remembered his father's arms around him, guiding his hands on the newly varnished stock and pressing his head gently down to line up his eyes with the sights. "Squeeze, don't get excited and jerk," his father had said.

"*Get* up," Ben said to his son. "Shape up. Don't be such a baby. If it doesn't work, it doesn't work; I don't know why. It worked the last time we used it."

"Yeah, that was last Thanksgiving," Murray said, surprisingly conversational, though still stretched on the cold ground. "I bet one of these idiot yokels around here messed it up."

"Idiot yokels," Ben repeated, hearing himself in that phrase. "My, aren't we a young snob?"

Murray stood and brushed the sarcasm aside. "Can you fix it or not?"

Ben slipped a cartridge into the chamber, closed the bolt, and pulled the trigger. A limp click. "Not. I don't understand guns. You're the one who wants to use it all the time. Why don't we just point our fingers and say *Bang?*"

"Dad, you're quite the riot."

They walked back to the house. Ben lugged the disgraced gun while Murray ran disdainfully ahead. Ben noticed in the dead grass the rusty serrate shapes of strawberry leaves, precise as fossils. When they had moved here, the land had been farmed out—"mined," in the local phrase—and the one undiscouraged crop consisted of the wild strawberries running from ditch to ridge on all the sunny slopes. At his son's age, Ben hated the strawberry leaves and the rural isolation they ornamented; it surprised him, gazing down, to have their silhouettes fitting so exactly a shape in his mind. The leaves were still here, and his parents were still in the square sandstone farmhouse. His mother looked up from the sink and said, "I didn't hear the shots."

"There weren't any, that's why."

Something pleased or amused in Ben's voice tripped Murray's temper again; he went into the living room and kicked a chair leg and swore. "Goddam thing *broke*."

"That's no reason to break a chair," Ben shouted after him. "That's not our furniture, you know."

Sally froze, plate in one hand and dish towel in the other, and called weakly, "Hey."

"Well, hell," he said to her, "why are we letting the kid terrorize everybody?"

He chased the boy into the living room. His murderous mood met there the torpor that follows a feast. The two girls, in company with their grandfather, were watching the Gimbels parade on television. Murray, hearing his father approach, had hid behind the chair he had kicked. A sister glanced in his direction and pronounced, "Spoiled." The other sniffed in agreement. One girl was older than Murray, one younger; all of his life he would be pinched between them. Their grandfather was sitting in a rocker, wearing the knit wool cap that made him feel less cold. Obligingly he had taken the chair with the worst angle on the television screen, watching in fuzzy

foreshortening a flicker of bloated animals, drum major-
ettes, and giant cakes bearing candles that were really girls
waving.

"He's not spoiled," Ben's father told the girls. "He's like
his daddy, a perfectionist."

Ben's father since that Christmas of the gun had become
an old man, but a wonderfully strange old man, with a
long yellow-white face, a blue nose, and the erect carriage
of a child who is straining to see. His circulation was poor,
he had been hospitalized, he lived from pill to pill, he had
uncharacteristic quiet spells that Ben guessed were sei-
zures of pain; yet his hopefulness still dominated any room
he was in. He looked up at Ben in the doorway. "Can you
figure it out?"

Ben said, "Murray says some pin fell out while he was
cleaning it."

"It *did,* Dad," the child insisted.

Ben's father stood, prim and pale and tall. He was
wearing a threadbare overcoat, in readiness for adventure.
"I know just the man," he said. He called into the kitchen,
"Mother, I'll give Dutch a ring. The kid's being frus-
trated."

"Aw, that's O.K., forget it," Murray mumbled. But his
eyes shone, looking up at the promising apparition of his
grandfather. Ben was hurt, remembering how his own
knack, as father, was to tease and cloud those same eyes.
There was something too finely tooled, too little yielding
in the boy that Ben itched to correct.

The two women had crowded to the doorway to inter-
vene. Sally said, "He doesn't *have* to shoot the gun. I hate
guns. Ben, why do you always inflict the gun on this
child?"

"I don't," he answered.

His mother called over Sally's shoulder, "Don't bother people on Thanksgiving, Murray. Let the man have a holiday."

Little Murray looked up, startled, at the sound of his name pronounced scoldingly. He had been named for his grandfather. Two Murrays: one small and young, one big and old. Yet alike, Ben saw, in a style of expectation, in a tireless craving for—he used to wonder for what, but people had a word for it now—"action."

"This man takes never a holiday," Ben's father called back. "He's out of this world. You'd love him. Everybody in this room would love him." And, irrepressibly, he was at the telephone, dialling with a touch of frenzy, the way he would scrub a friendly dog's belly with his knuckles.

After a supper of leftover turkey, the men went out into the night. Ben drove his father's car. The dark road carried them off their hill into a valley where sandstone farmhouses had been joined by ranch houses, aluminum trailers, a wanly lit Mobil station, a Pentecostal church built of cinder blocks, with a neon JESUS LIVES. JESUS SAVES must have become too much of a joke.

"The next driveway on the left," his father said. The cold outdoor air had shortened his breath. No sign advertised a gun shop; the house was a ranch, but not a new one—one of those built in the early Fifties, when the commuters first began to come this far out from Alton. In order of age, oldest to youngest, tallest to shortest, they marched up the flagstones to the unlit front door; Ben could feel his son's embarrassment at his back, deepening his own. They had offered to let little Murray carry the gun, but he had shied from it. Ben held the .22 behind him, so as not to terrify whoever answered his father's ring at the door. It was a fat woman in a pink wrapper. Ben saw that there had been a mistake, this was no gun shop, his father had humiliated him once again.

But no, she said, "Hello, Mr. Trupp," giving it that affectionate long German *u;* in Boston people rhymed the name with "cup." "Come in this way I guess; he's down there expecting everybody. Is this your son now? And who's *this* big boy?" Her pleasantries eased their way across the front hall, with its braided rug and enamelled plaque of blessing, to the cellar stairs.

As they clattered down, Ben's father said, "I shouldn't have done that, that was a headache for his missus, letting us in, I wasn't thinking. We should have gone to the side, but then Dutch has to disconnect the burglar alarm. Everybody in this county's crazy to steal his guns. When you get to be my age, Ben, it hurts like Jesus just to *try* to think. Just to *try* not to annoy the hell out of people."

The cellar seemed bigger than the house. Cardboard cartons, old chairs and sofas from the Goodwill, a refrigerator, stacked newspapers, shoot posters, and rifle racks lined an immense cement room. At the far end was a counter and behind it a starkly lit workshop with a lathe. Little Murray's eyes widened; his boyhood had known no gun shops. Whereas in an alley of Ben's boyhood there had been a mysterious made-over garage called "Repair & Ammo." Sounds of pounding and grinding came out of it, the fury of metals, and on dark winter afternoons, racing home with his sled, Ben would see blue sparks shudder in the window. But he had never gone in. So this was an adventure for him as well. There was that about being his father's son: one had adventures, one blundered into places, one *went* places, met strangers, suffered rebuffs, experienced breakdowns, exposed oneself in a way that Ben, as soon as he was able, made impossible, hedging his life with such order and propriety that no misstep could occur. He had become a lawyer, taking profit from the losses of others, reducing disorderly lives to legal folders. Even in his clothes he had retained the caution of the Fifties, while his partners blossomed into striped shirts and bell-bottomed slacks. Seeing his son's habitual tautness relax under the spell of this potent, acrid cellar, Ben felt that he had been much less a father than his own had been, a father's duty being to impart the taste of the world. Golf lessons in Brookline, sailing off Maine, skiing in New Hampshire—what was this but bought amusement compared to the improvised shifts and hazards of poverty? In this cave the metallic smell of murder lurked, and behind the counter two men bent low over something that gleamed like a jewel.

Ben's father went forward. "Dutch, this is my son Ben and my grandson Murray. The kid's just like you are, a perfectionist, and this cheap gun we got Ben a zillion years ago let him down this afternoon." To the other man in this lighted end of the cellar he said, "I know your face, mister, but I've forgotten your name."

The other man blinked and said, "Reiner." He wore a Day-Glo hunting cap and a dirty blue parka over a clean shirt and tie. He looked mild, perhaps because of his spectacles, which were rimless. He seemed to be a customer, and the piece of metal in the gunsmith's hand concerned him. It was a small slab with two holes bored in it; a shiny ring had been set into one of the holes, and Dutch's gray thumb moved back and forth across the infinitesimal edge where the ring was flush with the slab.

"About two-thousandths," the gunsmith slowly announced, growling the *ou*'s. It was hard to know whom he was speaking to. His eyelids looked swollen—leaden hoods set slantwise over the eyes, eclipsing them but for a glitter. His entire body appeared to have slumped away from its frame, from the restless ruminating jowl to the undershirted beer belly and bent knees. His shuffle seemed deliberately droll. His hands alone had firm shape—hands battered and nicked and so long in touch with greased machinery that they had blackened flatnesses like worn parts. The right middle finger had been shorn off at the first knuckle. "Two- or three-thousandths at the most."

Ben's father's voice had regained its strength in the warmth of this basement. He acted as interlocutor, to make the drama clear. "You mean you can just tell with your thumb if it's a thousandth of an inch off?"

"Yahh. More or less."

"That's incredible. That to me is a miracle." He explained to his son and grandson, "Dutch was head machinist at Hager Steel for thirty years. He had hundreds of men under him. Hundreds."

"A thousand," Dutch growled. "Twelve hunnert during Korea." His qualification slipped into place as if with much practice; Ben guessed his father came here often.

"Boy, I can't imagine it. I don't see how the hell you did it. I don't see how any man could do what you did; my imagination boggles. This kid here"—Murray, not Ben—"has what you have. Drive. Both of you have what it takes."

Ben thought he should assert himself. In a few crisp phrases he explained to Dutch how the gun had failed to fire.

His father said to the man in spectacles, "It would have taken me all night to say what he just said. He lives in

New England, they all talk sense up there. One thing I'm grateful the kid never inherited from me, and I bet he is too, is his old man's gift for baloney. I was always embarrassing the kid."

Dutch slipped out the bolt of the .22 and, holding the screwdriver so the shortened finger lay along a groove of the handle, turned a tiny screw that Ben in all his years of owning the gun had never noticed. The bolt fell into several bright pieces, tinged with rust, on the counter. The gunsmith picked a bit of metal from within a little spring and held it up. "Firing pin. Sheared," he said. His mouth when he talked showed the extra flexibility of the toothless.

"Do you have another? Can you replace it?" Ben disliked, as emphasized by this acoustical cellar, the high hungry pitch of his own voice. He was prosecuting.

Dutch declined to answer. He lowered his remarkable lids to gaze at the metal under his hands; one hand closed tight around the strange little slab, with its gleaming ring.

Ben's father interceded, saying, "He can make it, Ben. This man here can make an entire gun from scratch. Just give him a lump of slag is all he needs."

"Wonderful," Ben said, to fill the silence.

Reiner unexpectedly laughed. "How about," he said to the gunsmith, "that old Damascus double Jim Knauer loaded with triple FG and a smokeless powder? It's a wonder he has a face still."

Dutch unclenched his fist and, after a pause, chuckled.

Ben recognized in these pauses something of courtroom tactics; at his side he felt little Murray growing agitated at the delay. "Shall we come back tomorrow?" Ben asked.

He was ignored. Reiner was going on, "What was the make on that? A twelve-gauge Parker?"

"English gun," Dutch said. "A Westley Richards. He paid three hunnert for it, some dealer over in Royersford. Such foolishness, his first shot yet. Even split the stock." His eyelids lifted. "Who wants a beer?"

Ben's father said, "Jesus, I'm so full of turkey a beer might do me in."

Reiner looked amused. "They say liquor is good for bad circulation."

"I'd be happy to sip one but I can't take an oath to finish it. The first rule of hospitality is, Don't look a gift horse in the face." But an edge was going off his wit. After the effort of forming these sentences, the old man sat down, in an easy chair with exploded arms. Against the yellowish pallor of his face, his nose looked livid as a bruise.

"Sure," Ben said. "If they're being offered. Thank you."

"Son, how about you?" Dutch asked the boy. Murray's eyes widened, realizing nobody was going to answer for him.

"He's in training for his ski team," Ben said at last.

Dutch's eyes stayed on the boy. "Then you should have good legs. How about now going over and fetching four cans from that icebox over there?" He pointed with a loose fist.

"Refrigerator," Ben clarified.

Dutch turned his back and fished through a shelf of grimy cigar boxes for a cylinder of metal that, when he held it beside the fragment of firing pin, satisfied him. He shuffled into the little room behind the counter, which brimmed with light and machinery.

As the boy passed around the cold cans of Old Reading, his grandfather explained to the man in the Day-Glo hunting cap, "This boy is what you'd have to call an ardent athlete. He sails, he golfs, last winter he won blue medals at, what do they call 'em, Murray?"

"Slaloms. I flubbed the downhill, though."

"Hear that? He knows the language. If he was fortunate enough to live down here with you fine gentlemen, he'd learn gun language too. He'd be a crack shot in no time."

"Where we live in this city," the boy volunteered, "my mother won't even let me get a BB gun. She hates guns."

"The kid means the city of Boston. His father's on a first-name basis with the mayor." Ben heard the strained intake of breath between his father's sentences and tried not to hear the words. He and his son were tumbled together in a long, pained monologue. "Anything competitive, this kid loves. He doesn't get that from me. He doesn't get it from his old man, either. Ben always had this tactful way of keeping his thoughts to himself. You never knew what was going on inside the kid. My biggest regret is I couldn't teach him the pleasure of working with your hands. He grew up watching me scrambling along by my wits and now he's doing the same damn thing. He should have had Dutch for a father. Dutch would have reached him."

To deafen himself Ben walked around the counter and into the workshop. Dutch was turning the little cylinder on a lathe. He wore no goggles, and seemed to be taking no measurements. Into the mirror-smooth blur of the spinning metal the man delicately pressed a tipped, hinged cone. Curls of steel fell steadily to the scarred lathe table. Tan sparks flew outward to the radius perhaps of a peony. The cylinder was becoming two cylinders, a narrow one emerging from the shoulders of another. Ben had once worked wood, in high-school shop, but this man could shape metal. He could descend into the hard heart of things. Dutch switched off the lathe, with a sad grunt pushed himself away, and comically shuffled toward some other of his tools. Ben, fearing that the love he felt for this man might burst his face and humiliate them all, turned back toward the larger room.

Reiner had undertaken a monologue of his own. ". . . you know your average bullet comes out of the barrel rotating; that's why a rifle is called that, for the rifling inside, that makes it spin. Now what the North Vietnamese discovered, if you put enough velocity into a bullet beyond a critical factor it tumbles, end over end like that. The Geneva Convention says you can't use a soft bullet that mushrooms inside the body like the dumdum, but hit a man with a bullet tumbling like that, it'll tear his arm right off."

The boy was listening warily, watching the bespectacled man's soft white hands demonstrate tumbling. Ben's father sat in the exploded armchair, staring dully ahead, sucking back spittle, struggling silently for breath.

"Of course now," the lecture went on, "what they found was best over there for the jungle was a plain shotgun. You take an ordinary twenty-gauge, maybe mounted with a short barrel, you don't have visibility more than fifty feet anyway, a man doesn't have a chance at that distance. The spread of shot is maybe three feet around." With his arms Reiner placed the circle on himself, centered on his heart. "It'll tear a man to pieces like that. If he's not that close yet, then the shot pattern is wider and even a miss is going to hurt him plenty."

"Death is part of life," Ben's father said, as if reciting a lesson learned long ago.

Ben asked Reiner, "Were you in Vietnam?"

The man took off his hunting cap and displayed a bald head. "You got me in the wrong rumpus. Navy gunner, World War Two. With those forty-millimeter Bofors you could put a two-pound shell thirty thousand feet straight up in the air."

Dutch emerged from his workshop holding a bit of metal in one hand and a crumpled beer can in the other. He put the cylindrical bit down amid the scattered parts of the bolt, fumbled at them, and they all came together.

"Does it fit?" Ben asked.

Dutch's clownish loose lips smiled. "You ask a lot of questions." He slipped the bolt back into the .22 and turned back to the workshop. The four others held silent, but for Ben's father's breathing. In time the flat spank of a rifle shot resounded, amplified by cement walls.

"That's miraculous to me," Ben's father said. "A mechanical skill like that."

"Thank you very much," Ben said, too quickly, when the gunsmith lay the mended and tested .22 on the counter. "How much do we owe you?"

Rather than answer, Dutch asked little Murray, "Didja ever see a machine like this before?" It was a device, operated by hand pressure, that assembled and crimped shotgun shells. He let the boy pull the handle. The shells marched in a circle, receiving each their allotment of powder and shot. "It can't explode," Dutch reassured Ben.

Reiner explained, "You see what this here is"—holding out the mysterious little slab with its bright ring—"is by putting in this bushing Dutch just made for me I can reduce the proportion of powder to shot, when I go into finer grains this deer season."

Murray backed off from the machine. "That's neat. Thanks a lot."

Dutch contemplated Ben. His verdict came: "I guess two dollars."

Ben protested, "That's not enough."

Ben's father rescued him from the silence. "Pay the man what he asks; all the moola in the world won't buy God-given expertise like that."

Ben paid, and was in such a hurry to lead his party home he touched the side door before Dutch could switch off the burglar alarm. Bells shrilled, Ben jumped. Everybody laughed, even—though he had hated, from his schoolteaching days, what he called "cruel humor"—Ben's father.

In the dark of the car, the old man sighed. "He's what you'd have to call a genius and a gentleman. Did you see the way your dad looked at him? Pure adoration, man to man."

Ben asked him, "How do you feel?"

"Better. I didn't like Murray having to listen to all that blood and guts from Reiner."

"Boy," Murray said, "he sure is crazy about guns."

"He's lonely. He just likes getting out of the house and hanging around the shop. Must give Dutch a real pain in the old bazoo." Perhaps this sounded harsh, or applicable to himself, for he amended it. "Actually, he's harmless. He says he was in Navy artillery, but you know where he spent most of the war? Cruising around the Caribbean having a sunbath. He's like me. I was in the first one and my big accomplishment was surviving the flu in boot camp. We were going to board in Hoboken the day of the Armistice."

"I never knew you were a soldier, Grandpa."

"Kill or be killed, that's my motto."

He sounded so faraway and fragile, saying this, Ben told him, "I hope we didn't wear you out."

"That's what I'm here for," Ben's father said. "We aim to serve."

The Gun Shop

In bed, Ben tried to describe to Sally their adventure, the gun shop. "The whole place smelled of death. I think the kid was a little frightened."

Sally said, "Of course. He's only fourteen. You're awfully hard on him, you know."

"I know. My father was nice to me, and what did it get him? Chest pains. A pain in the old bazoo." Asleep, he dreamed he was a boy with a gun. A small bird, smaller than a dot in a puzzle, sat in the peach tree by the meadow fence. Ben aligned his sights and with exquisite slowness squeezed. The dot fell like a stone. He went to it and found a wren's brown body, neatly deprived of a head. There was not much blood, just headless feathers. He awoke, and realized it was real. It had happened just that way, the first summer he had had the gun. He had never forgiven himself. After breakfast he and his son went out across the dead strawberry leaves to the dump again. There, the dream continued. Though Ben steadied his trembling, middle-aged hands against a hickory trunk and aimed so carefully his open eye burned, the cans and bottles ignored his shots. The bullets passed right through them. Whereas when little Murray took the gun, the boy's freckled face gathered the muteness of the trees into his murderous concentration. The cans jumped, the bottles burst. "You're killing me!" Ben cried. In his pride and relief, he had to laugh.

How to Love America and Leave It at the Same Time

ARRIVE IN SOME TOWN around three, having been on the road since seven, and cruise the main street, which is also Route Whatever-It-Is, and vote on the motel you want. The wife favors a discreet back-from-the-road look, but not bungalows; the kids go for a pool (essential), color TV (optional), and Magic Fingers (fun). Vote with the majority, pull in, and walk to the office. Your legs unbend weirdly, after all that sitting behind the wheel. A sticker on the door says the place is run by "The Plummers," so this is Mrs. Plummer behind the desk. Fifty-fiveish, tight silver curls with traces of copper, face motherly but for the brightness of the lipstick and the sharpness of the sizing-up glance. In half a second she nails you: family man, no trouble. Sweet tough wise old scared Mrs. Plummer. Hand over your plastic credit card. Watch her give it the treatment: people used to roll their own cigarettes in machines with just that gesture. Accept the precious keys with their lozenge-shaped tags of plastic. Consider the

career of motelkeeper: selling what shouldn't be buyable—
rest to the weary, bliss to the illicit, space to the living.
Providing television and telephones as threads to keep us
in touch with the unreal worlds behind, ahead. Shelter, the
oldest commodity.

Untie the bags from the roof of the car. Your legs still
feel weird, moving. The kids have the routine down pat:
in three minutes in and out of their room and into the
pool. Follow at a middle-aged pace, taking care not to dis-
array the suitcase in removing the bathing suits. The wife
looks great, momentarily naked, but she claims she has a
headache, after all those miles.

Wait until the kids get bored with yelling and splashing. Then, beside the pool, it is crystalline. Soak in the
sun. Listen to the town. You have never heard of the town
before: this is important. Otherwise, there are expectations,
and a plan. This is not to say the town need be small.
America conceals immense things. Here are thousands of
busy souls as untangent to you as individual rocks on the
moon. Say the town is in California, on the dry side of the
Sierras; though it could as well be in Iowa, or Kentucky,
or Connecticut. Out of nowhere, here it has arrived. Listen. The wavelets in the pool lap the tile gutter. The rush
of traffic along Route Whatever-It-Is doesn't miss you; it
sings, sighs, cruises, hurls multitudes, passes as a river.
Nearer by, car tires chew the gravel, creeping closer.
Look. Two long-haired children in patched jeans, their
clothes full of insignias, pale, scarcely older than your own
children, emerge, with a reluctance somehow loving, from
a crumpled green Volkswagen, and walk to the motel
office. A far-off door slams. Retreating tires chew the
gravel smaller and smaller. In the other direction, a laundry
cart rattles. And beyond all this, enclosing it, like a trans-

parent dome, an indecipherable murmur, like bees in the eaves or the continual excited liquid tremolo of newly hatched birds hidden in a tree trunk, waiting to be fed.

A siren sounds.

It sounds distant, then proximate, then distant again, and lower-pitched. This cry of emergency cuts through the afternoon like a crack in crystal. Disaster, here? An accident up the road, that might have been you, had you pressed on? A heart attack, high in the mountains? Relax. Let the lordly sun dry the drops of water on your chest. Imagine an old Californian, with parched white beard and a mountain goat's unfriendly stare, his whole life from birth soaked in this altitude, this view, this locality until an hour ago unknown and after tomorrow never to be known again—imagine him dead, his life in a blood-blind moment wrenched from his chest like a root from a tummock. The thought, curiously, is no more disturbing than the chuckling rush of traffic, than the animal ripple of the kids having returned their bodies to the pool, than the remote distinct voice that now and then, for reasons of its own, monotonously recites numbers into a kind of megaphone, an amplification system. "Fifteen . . . twenty . . ." Something to do with the disaster? An air alert? The voice drones on, part of the peace. Further sirens bleat, a black police car and a square white truck with blue flashers smoothly rip by, between the motel and the Mexican restaurant across Route Whatever-It-Is.

Beyond the restaurant's red tile roof lies a tawny valley; beyond it, a lesser range of mountains, gray, but gray multitudinously, with an infinity of shades—ash, graphite, cardboard, tomcat, lavender. Such beauty wants to make us weep. If we were crystal, we would shatter. The amplified voice goes on, "Twenty . . . thirty . . ." The kids begin to squabble. You have had enough sun. Time to reconnoitre.

The wife says her headache is better but she will stay in the motel room, to give herself a shampoo. Walk, family man, with the kids, out from the parking lot and down the main street. The heat from the sidewalk swims across your shins. The high mountain sun gives a tinny thin coating of glory to the orange Rexall signs, the red tongues of the parking meters, the pink shorts of girls whose brown backs are delicately trussed by the strings of minimal halters, the Army-surplus green being worn alike by over-muscled youths and squinting bent geezers. They drift, these natives, in their element. Love them because they are here. There is no better reason for love. They squint through you. To acquire substance, enter a store and buy something. Discover that the town offers postcards of itself; it is self-conscious, commercial, enterprising. It contains many sporting-goods stores, veritable armories in the war against the wilderness—fishing rods, ski poles, hunting slingshots, collapsible rafts, folding tents, backpack racks, freeze-dried fruits in aluminum wrap, fanciful feathered fishing flies in plastic capsules, tennis rackets, tennis shirts, tennis balls the colors of candy. Your boys are enchanted, your girls are bored. Purchase five postcards, some freeze-dried pears for tomorrow's long drive through the desert, and exit. Out on the hot pavement, the little girl's sandals flop. She has been begging for new ones every day. Her hair is still wet from the motel pool. Take her into a shoe store. Solemnly the salesman seats her, measures her foot size. Marvel at the way in which his hand deigns to touch this unknown child's sticky bare foot. Alas.

What he has in her size she does not like, and what she likes he does not have in her size. Express regret and leave. Crossing the dangerous thoroughfare, you take her hand, a touch more tender with her, having witnessed the tenderness of others. Across the street, in a little main square pared to insignificance by successive widenings of the highway, an old covered wagon instead of a statue stands. Think of those dead unknown—plodding flights of angels —who dared cross this land of inhuman grandeur without highways, without air-conditioning, without even (a look underneath confirms) shock absorbers, jolting and rattling each inch, in order to arrive here and create this town, wherein this wagon has become a receptacle for (a look inside discovers) empty cans of Polar Bear Beer, Diet Pepsi, and Mountain Dew.

America is a vast conspiracy to make you happy.

Or, alternatively, get into the car at the motel and drive around the back streets: a wooden church, a brick elementary school with basketball stanchions on a pond of asphalt, houses spaced and square-set and too clean-looking. There is something sterilizing about the high air here. The lawns look watered, like putting greens. They contrast vividly with spaces of unkempt parched hay. The houses out of their rectilinear, faintly glistening fronts strive to say something, a word you are anxious to hear, and would drive forever to hear finally. But the kids are bored, and beg to go "home." Home is the motel.

The wife's hair is springy and fragrant from her shampoo. The pool is deserted and looks chill. Evening shadows have slid down from the mountain. The sun sets in the west, everywhere. The gray range to the east basks in light like an intricate bone. Where shall we eat? Discuss. The kids want a quick clean hamburgery place, with Formica tables and clear neutral windows giving on the stream of traffic that ties them securely to the future. You and the wife want something enclosed, with regional flavor and a liquor license. Perhaps the kids win, and you sit there looking out through the windows thinking, This is America, a hamburger kingdom, one cuisine, under God, indivisible, with pickles and potato chips for all. What you see through the clear windows looks blanched without sunglasses, which you have worn all day, assigning the landscape you were driving through an unnatural postcard brilliance, the blue sky dyed cobalt, the purple mesas and orange rocks tinted as if by the pastel artist who timidly sells bad portraits at a country fair.

Or perhaps you talk the kids into the Mexican restaurant, and as they sit in candlelight struggling with their tacos and enchiladas you sip your salt-rimmed Margarita and think, This is America, where we take everything in, tacos and chow mein and pizza and sauerkraut, because we are only what we eat, we are whatever we say we are. When a Japanese says "Japanese," he is trapped on a little definite racial fact, whereas when we say "American" it is not a fact, it is an act, of faith, a matter of lines on a map and words on paper, an outline it will take generations and centuries more to fill in. And, yes, the waitress bringing the sherbet and the check appears to illustrate these meditations, for she is lovely and young and deracinated, one of the breed our coast-to-coast desert has engendered, her bones grown straight on bland food, her fertility encased in the chemical Saniwrap of the Pill, her accent pleasantly presupposing nothing, her skin tanned dark as an Indian's but her eyes blue and her hair sun-blond and loose down her back in Eve's timeless fall.

Be careful crossing the highway. In the motel parking lot, before you can reach the anonymity of your room, Mrs. Plummer, hustling from her car to the office clutching papers in her hand, has to cross your path, and smiles. This slightly spoils it. She knows you. You know her. When innocence ends, plans must be made. First, sleep. Then, early in the morning, when the traffic is spotty and the sun is feeble in the east, move on.

Nevada

POOR CULP. His wife, Sarah, wanted to marry her lover as soon as the divorce came through, she couldn't wait a day, the honeymoon suite in Honolulu had been booked six weeks in advance. So Culp, complaisant to the end, agreed to pick the girls up in Reno and drive them back to Denver. He arranged to be in San Francisco on business and rented a car. Over the phone, Sarah mocked his plan—why not fly? An expert in petroleum extraction, he hoped by driving to extract some scenic benefit from domestic ruin. Until they had moved to Denver and their marriage exploded in the thinner atmosphere, they had lived in New Jersey, and the girls had seen little of the West.

He arrived in Reno around five in the afternoon, having detoured south from Interstate 80. The city looked kinder than he had expected. He found the address Sarah had given him, a barn-red boardinghouse behind a motel distinguished by a giant flashing domino. He dreaded yet longed for the pain of seeing Sarah again—divorced, free of him, exultant, about to take wing into a new marriage.

But she had taken wing before he arrived. His two daughters were sitting on a tired cowhide sofa, next to an empty desk, like patients in a dentist's anteroom.

Polly, who was eleven, leaped up to greet him. "Mommy's left," she said. "She thought you'd be here hours ago."

Laura, sixteen, rose with a self-conscious languor from the tired sofa, smoothing her skirt behind, and added, "Jim was with her. He got really mad when you didn't show."

Culp apologized. "I didn't know her schedule was so tight."

Laura perhaps misheard him, answering, "Yeah, she was really uptight."

"I took a little detour to see Lake Tahoe."

"Oh, Dad," Laura said. "You and your sight-seeing."

"Were you worried?" he asked.

"Naa."

A little woman with a square jaw hopped from a side room behind the empty desk. "They was good as good, Mr. Culp. Just sat there, wouldn't even take a sandwich I offered to make for no charge. Laura here kept telling the little one, 'Don't you be childish, Daddy wouldn't let us down.' I'm Betsy Morgan, we've heard of each other but never met officially." Sarah had mentioned her in her letters: Morgan the pirate, her landlady and residency witness. Fred Culp saw himself through Mrs. Morgan's eyes: cuckold, defendant, discardee. Though her eye was merry, the hand she offered him was dry as a bird's foot.

He could only think to ask, "How did the proceedings go?"

The question seemed foolish to him, but not to Mrs. Morgan. "Seven minutes, smooth as silk. Some of these judges, they give a girl a hard time just to keep themselves from being bored. But your Sary stood right up to him. She has that way about her."

"Yes, she did. Does. More and more. Girls, got your bags?"

"Right behind the sofy here. I would have kept their room one night more, but then this lady from Connecticut showed up yesterday could take it for the six weeks."

"That's fine. I'll take them someplace with a pool."

"They'll be missed, I tell you truly," the landlady said, and she bent down and kissed the two girls. This had been a family of sorts, there were real tears in her eyes; but Polly couldn't wait for the hug to pass before blurting to her father, "We had pool privileges at the Domino, and one time all these Mexicans came and used it for a *bath-room!*"

They drove to a motel not the Domino. Laura and he watched Polly swim. "Laura, don't you want to put on a suit?"

"Naa. Mom made us swim so much I got diver's ear."

Culp pictured Sarah lying on a poolside chaise longue, in the bikini with the orange and purple splashes. One smooth wet arm was flung up to shield her eyes. Other women noticeably had legs or breasts; Sarah's beauty had been most vivid in her arms, arms fit for a Greek statue, rounded and fine and firm, arms that never aged, without a trace of wobble above the elbow, though at her next birthday she would be forty. Indeed, that was how Sarah had put the need for divorce: She couldn't bear to turn forty with him. As if then you began a return journey that could not be broken.

Laura was continuing, "Also, Dad, if you *must* know, it's that time of the month."

With clumsy jubilance, Polly hurled her body from

the rattling board and surfaced grinning through the kelp of her own hair. She climbed from the pool and slap-footed to his side, shivering. "Want to walk around and play the slots?" Goose bumps had erected the white hairs on her thighs into a ghostly halo. "Want to? It's fun."

Laura intervened maternally. "Don't *make* him, Polly. Daddy's tired and depressed."

"Who says? Let's go. I may never see Reno again." The city, as they walked, reminded him of New Jersey's little municipalities. The desert clarity at evening had the even steel glint of industrial haze. Above drab shop fronts, second-story windows proclaimed residence with curtains and a flowerpot. There were churches, which he hadn't expected. And a river, a trickling shadow of the Passaic, flowed through. The courthouse, Mecca to so many, seemed too modest; it wore the disheartened granite dignity of justice the country over. Only the Reno downtown, garish as a carnival midway, was different. Polly led him to doors she was forbidden to enter and gave him nickels to play for her inside. She loved the slot machines, loved them for their fruity colors and their sleepless glow and their sudden gush of release, jingling, lighting, as luck struck now here, now there, across the dark casino. Feeling the silky heave of their guts as he fed the slot and pulled the handle, rewarded a few times with the delicious spitting of coins into the troughs other hands had smoothed to his touch, Culp came to love them, too; he and Polly made a gleeful hopeful pair, working their way from casino to casino, her round face pressed to the window so she could see him play, and the plums jerk into being, and the bells and cherries do their waltz of chance, 1-2-3. One place was wide open to the sidewalk. A grotesquely large machine stood ready for silver dollars.

Polly said, "Mommy won twenty dollars on that one once."

Culp asked Laura, who had trailed after them in disdainful silence, "Was Jim with you the whole time?"

"No, he only came the last week." She searched her father's face for what he wanted to know. "He stayed at the Domino."

Polly drew close to listen. Culp asked her, "Did you like Jim?"

Her eyes with difficulty shifted from visions of mechanical delight. "He was too serious. He said the slots were a racket and they wouldn't get a penny of his."

Laura said, "I thought he was an utter *pill*, Dad."

"You don't have to think that to please me."

"He *was*. I told her, too."

"You shouldn't have. Listen, it's her life, not yours." On the hospital-bright sidewalk, both his girls' faces looked unwell, stricken. Culp put a silver dollar into the great machine, imagining that something of Sarah had rubbed off here and that through this electric ardor she might speak to him. But the machine's size was unnatural; the guts felt sluggish, spinning. A plum, a bar, a star. No win. Turning, he resented that Polly and Laura, still staring, seemed stricken for *him*.

Laura said, "Better come eat, Dad. We'll show you a place where they have pastrami like back East."

As Route 40 poured east, Nevada opened into a strange no-color—a rusted gray, or the lavender that haunts the corners of overexposed color slides. The Humboldt River, which had sustained the pioneer caravans, shadowed the expressway shyly, tinting its valley with a dull green that fed dottings of cattle. But for the cattle, and the cars that brushed by him as if he were doing thirty and not eighty miles an hour, and an occasional gas station and cabin café promising SLOTS, there was little sign of life in Nevada. This pleased Culp; it enabled him to run off in peace the home movies of Sarah stored in his head. Sarah pushing the lawn mower in the South Orange back yard. Sarah pushing a blue baby carriage, English, with little white wheels, around the fountain in Washington Square. Sarah, not yet his wife, waiting for him in a brown-and-green peasant skirt under the marquee of a movie house on 57th Street. Sarah, a cool suburban hostess in chalk-pink sack dress, easing through their jammed living room with a platter of parsleyed egg halves. Sarah after a party, drunk in a black-lace bra, doing the Twist at the foot of their bed. Sarah in blue jeans crying out that it was nobody's *fault*, that there was nothing he could *do*, just let her *alone;* and hurling a quarter pound of butter across the kitchen, so the calendar fell off the wall. Sarah in miniskirt leaving their house in Denver for a date, just like a teen-ager, the sprinkler on their flat front lawn spinning in the evening cool. Sarah trim and sardonic at the marriage counsellor's, under the pressed-paper panelling where the man had hung not only his diplomas but his Aspen skiing medals. Sarah some Sunday long ago raising the shades to wake him, light flooding her translucent nightgown. Sarah lifting her sudden eyes to him at some table, some moment, somewhere, in conspiracy—he hadn't known he had taken so many reels, they just kept coming in his head. Nevada beautifully, emptily poured by. The map was full of ghost towns. Laura sat beside him, reading the map. "Dad, here's a town called Nixon."

"Let's go feel sorry for it."

"You passed it. It was off the road after Sparks. The next real town is Lovelock."

"What's real about it?"

"Should you be driving so fast?"

In the back seat, Polly struggled with her needs. "Can we stop in the next real town to eat?"

Culp said, "You should have eaten more breakfast."

"I hate hash browns."

"But you like bacon."

"The hash browns had touched it."

Laura said, "Polly, stop bugging Daddy, you're making him nervous."

Culp told her, "I am *not* nervous."

Polly told her, "I can't keep holding it."

"Baby. You just went less than an hour ago."

"I'm nervous."

Culp laughed. Laura said, "You're not funny. You're not a baby anymore."

Polly said, "Yeah and you're not a wife, either.

Silence.

"Nobody said I was."

Nevada spun by. Sarah stepped out of a car, their old Corvair convertible, wearing a one-piece bathing suit. Her hair was stiff and sun-bleached and wild. She was eating a hot dog loaded with relish. Culp looked closer and there was sand in her ear, as in a delicate discovered shell.

Polly announced, "Dad, that sign said a place in three miles. 'Soft Drinks, Sandwiches, Beer, Ice, and Slots.' "

"Slots, slots," Laura spit, furious for a reason that eluded her father. "Slots and sluts, that's all there is in this dumb state."

Culp asked, "Didn't you enjoy Reno?"

"I hated it. What I hated especially was Mom acting on the make all the time."

On the make, sluts—the language of women living together, it occurred to him, coarsens like that of men in the

Army. He mildly corrected, "I'm sure she wasn't on the make, she was just happy to be rid of me."

"Don't kid yourself, Dad. She was on the make. Even with Jim about to show up she was."

"Yeah, well," Polly said, "you weren't that pure yourself, showing off for that Mexican boy."

"I wasn't showing off for any bunch of spics, I was practicing my diving and I suggest you do the same, you toad. You look like a sick frog, the way you go off the board. A sick *fat* frog."

"Yeah, well. Mommy said you weren't so thin at my age yourself."

Culp intervened: "It's *nice* to be plump at your age. Otherwise, you won't have anything to shape up when you're Laura's age."

Polly giggled, scandalized. Laura said, "Don't flirt, Dad," and crossed her thighs; she was going to be one of those women, Culp vaguely saw, who have legs. She smoothed back the hair from her brow in a gesture that tripped the home-movie camera again: Sarah before the mirror. He could have driven forever this way; if he had known Nevada was so easy, he could have planned to reach the Utah line, or detoured north to some ghost towns. But they had made reservations in Elko, and stopped there. The motel was more of a hotel, four stories high; on the ground floor, a cavernous dark casino glimmered with the faces of the slots and the shiny uniforms of the change girls. Though it was only three in the afternoon, Culp wanted to go in there, to get a drink at the bar, where the bottles glowed like a row of illumined stalagmites. But his daughters, after inspecting their rooms, dragged him out into the sunshine. Elko was a flat town full of space, as airy with emptiness as a honeycomb. The broad street in front of the hotel held railroad tracks in its center. To Polly's amazed delight, a real train—nightmarish in scale but docile in manner—materialized on these tracks, halted, ruminated, and then ponderously, thoughtfully dragged westward its chuckling infinity of freight cars. They walked down broad sunstruck sidewalks, past a drunken Indian dressed in clothes black as his shadow, to a museum of mining. Polly coveted the glinting nuggets, Laura yawned before a case of old-fashioned barbed wire and sought her reflection in the glass. Culp came upon an exhibit, between Indian beads and pioneer hardware, incongruously devoted to Thomas Alva Edison. He and Sarah and the girls, driving home through the peppery stenches of carbon waste and butane from a Sunday on the beach at Red Bank, would pass a service island on the Jersey Turnpike named for Edison. They would stop for supper at another one, named for Joyce Kilmer. The tar on the parking lot would sting their bare feet. Sarah would go in for her hot dog wearing her *dashiki* beach wrapper—hip length, with slits for her naked arms. These graceful arms would be burned pink in the crooks. The sun would have ignited a conflagration of clouds beyond the great Esso tanks. Here, in Elko, the sun rested gently on the overexposed purple of the ridges around them. On the highest ridge a large letter E had been somehow cut, or inset, in what seemed limestone. Polly asked why.

He answered, "I suppose for airplanes."

Laura amplified, "If they don't put initials up, the pilots can't tell the towns apart, they're all so boring."

"I like Elko," Polly said. "I wish we lived here."

"Yeah, what would Daddy do for a living?"

This was hard. In real life, he was a chemical engineer for a conglomerate that was planning to exploit Colorado shale. Polly said, "He could fix slot machines and then at night come back in disguise and play them so they'd pay him lots of money."

Both girls, it seemed to Culp, had forgotten that he would not be living with them in their future, that this peaceful dusty nowhere was all the future they had. He took Polly's hand, crossing the railroad tracks, though the tracks were arrow-straight and no train was materializing between here and the horizon.

Laura flustered him by taking his arm as they walked into the dining room, which was beyond the dark grotto of slots. The waitress slid an expectant glance at the child, after he had ordered a drink for himself. "No. She's only sixteen."

When the waitress had gone, Laura told him, "Everybody says I look older than sixteen; in Reno with Mom, I used to wander around in the places and nobody ever said anything. Except one old fart who told me they'd put him in jail if I didn't go away."

Polly asked, "Daddy, when're you going to play the slots?"

"I thought I'd wait till after dinner."

"That's too long."

"O.K., I'll play now. Just until the salad comes." He took a mouthful of his drink, pushed up from the table, and fed ten quarters into a machine Polly could watch. Though he won nothing, being there, amid the machines' warm and impetuous colors, consoled him. Experimenting, he pressed the button marked CHANGE. A girl in a red uniform crinkling like embers came to his side inquisitively. Her face, though not old, had the Western dryness—eyes smothered in charcoal, mouth tightened as if about to say,

I thought so. But something sturdy and hollow-backed in her stance touched Culp, gave him an intuition. Her uniform's devilish cut bared her white arms to the shoulder. He gave her a five-dollar bill to change into quarters. The waitress was bringing the salad. Heavy in one pocket, he returned to the table.

"Poor Dad," Laura volunteered. "That prostitute really turned him on."

"Laura, I'm not sure you know what a prostitute is."

"Mom said every woman is a prostitute, one way or another."

"You know your mother exaggerates."

"I know she's a bitch, you mean."

"Laura."

"She *is*, Dad. Look what she's done to you. Now she'll do it to Jim."

"You and I have different memories of your mother. You don't remember her when you were little."

"I don't want to live with her, either. When we all get back to Denver, I want to live with *you*. If she and I live together, it'll always be competing, that's how it was in Reno; who needs it? When *I* get to forty, I'm going to tell my lover to shoot me."

Polly cried out—an astonishing noise, like the crash of a jackpot. "*Stop* it," she told Laura. "Stop talking big. That's all you do, is talk big." The child, salad dressing gleaming on her chin, pushed her voice toward her sister through tears: "You want Mommy and Daddy to fight all the time instead of love each other even though they *are* divorced."

With an amused smile, Laura turned her back on Polly's outburst and patted Culp's arm. "Poor Dad," she said. "Poor old Dad."

Their steaks came, and Polly's tears dried. They walked out into Elko again and at the town's one movie theater saw a Western. Burt Lancaster, a downtrodden Mexican, after many insults, including crucifixion, turned implacable avenger and killed nine hirelings of a racist rancher. Polly seemed to be sleeping through the bloodiest parts. They walked back through the dry night to the hotel. Their two adjoining rooms each held twin beds. Laura's suitcase had appeared on the bed beside his.

Culp said, "You better sleep with your sister."

"Why? We'll have the door between open, in case she has nightmares."

"I want to read."

"So do I."

"You go to sleep now. We're going to make Salt Lake tomorrow."

"Big thrill. Dad, she mumbles and kicks her covers all the time."

"Do as I say, love. I'll stay here reading until you're asleep."

"And then what?"

"I may go down and have another drink."

Her expression reminded him of how, in the movie, the villain had looked when Burt Lancaster showed that he, too, had a gun. Culp lay on the bedspread reading a pamphlet they had bought at the museum, about ghost towns; champagne and opera sets had been transported up the valleys, where now not a mule survived. Train whistles at intervals scooped long pockets from the world beyond his room. The breathing from the other room had fallen level. He tiptoed in and saw them both asleep, his daughters. Laura had been reading a book about the persecution of the Indians and now it lay beside her hand. How short her fingernails seemed! Relaxed, her face revealed its freckles, its plumpness, the sorrowing stretched smoothness of the closed lids. Polly's face wore a film of night sweat on her brow; his kiss came away tasting salty. He did not kiss Laura, in case she was faking. He switched off the light and stood considering what he must do. A train howled on the other side of the wall. The beautiful emptiness of Nevada, where he might never be again, sucked at the room like a whirlpool.

Downstairs, his intuition was borne out. The change girl had noticed him, and said now, "How's it going?"

"Fair. You ever go off duty?"

"What's duty?"

He waited at the bar, waiting for the bourbon to fill him; it couldn't, the room inside him kept expanding, and when she joined him, after one o'clock, sidling up on the stool (a cowboy moved over) in a taut cotton dress that hid the tops of her arms, the blur on her face seemed a product of her inner chemistry, not his. "You've a room?" As she asked him that, her jaw went square: Mrs. Morgan in a younger version.

"I do," he said, "but it's full of little girls."

She reached for his bourbon and sipped and said, in a voice older than her figure, "This place is lousy with rooms."

Culp arrived back in his own room after five. He must have been noisier than he thought, for a person in a white nightgown appeared in the connecting doorway. Culp could not see her features, she was a good height, she reminded him of nobody. Good. From the frozen pose of her, she was scared—scared of him. Good.

"Dad?"

"Yep."

"You O.K.?"

"Sure." Though already he could feel the morning sun's grinding on his temples. "You been awake, sweetie? Sorry."

"I was worried about you." But Laura did not cross the threshold into his room.

"Very worried?"

"Naa."

"Listen. It's not your job to take care of me. It's my job to take care of you."

Son

HE IS OFTEN UPSTAIRS, when he has to be home. He prefers to be elsewhere. He is almost sixteen, though beardless still, a man's mind indignantly captive in the frame of a child. I love touching him, but don't often dare. The other day, he had the flu, and a fever, and I gave him a back rub, marvelling at the symmetrical knit of muscle, the organic tension. He is high-strung. Yet his sleep is so solid he sweats like a stone in the wall of a well. He wishes for perfection. He would like to destroy us, for we are, variously, too fat, too jocular, too sloppy, too affectionate, too grotesque and heedless in our ways. His mother smokes too much. His younger brother chews with his mouth open. His older sister leaves unbuttoned the top button of her blouses. His younger sister tussles with the dogs, getting them overexcited, avoiding doing her homework. Everyone in the house talks nonsense. He would be a better father than his father. But time has tricked him, has made him a son. After a quarrel, if he cannot go outside and kick a ball, he retreats to a corner of the house and reclines on the beanbag chair in an attitude of strange—infantile or leonine—torpor. We exhaust him, without meaning to. He takes an interest in the newspaper now, the front page as well as the sports, in this tiring year of 1973.

He is upstairs, writing a musical comedy. It is a Sunday in 1949. He has volunteered to prepare a high-school assembly program; people will sing. Songs of the time go through his head, as he scribbles new words. *Up in de mornin', down at de school, work like a debil for my grades.* Below him, irksome voices grind on, like machines working their way through tunnels. His parents each want something from the other. "Marion, you don't understand that man like I do; he has a heart of gold." His father's charade is very complex: the world, which he fears, is used as a flail on his wife. But from his cringing attitude he would seem to an outsider the one being flailed. With burning red face, the woman accepts the role of aggressor as penance for the fact, the incessant shameful fact, that *he* has to wrestle with the world while she hides here, in solitude, at home. This is normal, but does not seem to them to be so. Only by convolution have they arrived at the dominant/submissive relationship society has assigned them. For the man is maternally kind and with a smile hugs to himself his jewel, his certainty of being victimized; it is the mother whose tongue is sharp, who sometimes strikes. "Well, he gets you out of the house, and I guess that's gold to you." His answer is "Duty calls," pronounced mincingly. "The social contract is a balance of compromises." This will infuriate her, the son knows; as his heart thickens, the downstairs overflows with her hot voice. "*Don't* wear that smile at me! And *take* your hands off your hips; you look like a fairy!"

Their son tries not to listen. When he does, visual details of the downstairs flood his mind: the two antagonists, circling with their coffee cups; the shabby mismatched furniture; the hopeful books; the docile framed photographs of the dead, docile and still like cowed students. This matrix of pain that bore him—he feels he is floating above it, sprawled on the bed as on a cloud, stealing songs as they come into his head (*Across the hallway from the guidance room / Lives a French instructor called Mrs. Blum*), contemplating the view from the upstairs window (last summer's burdock stalks like the beginnings of an alphabet, an apple tree holding three rotten apples as if pondering why they failed to fall), yearning for Monday, for the ride to school with his father, for the bell that calls him to homeroom, for the excitements of class, for Broadway, for fame, for the cloud that will carry him away, out of this, out.

He returns from his paper-delivery route and finds a few Christmas presents for him on the kitchen table. I must guess at the year. 1913? Without opening them, he knocks them to the floor, puts his head on the table, and falls asleep. He must have been consciously dramatizing his plight: his father was sick, money was scarce, he had to work, to win food for the family when he was still a child. In his dismissal of Christmas, he touched a nerve: his love of anarchy, his distrust of the social contract. He treasured this moment of revolt; else why remember it, hoard a memory so bitter, and confide it to his son many Christmases later? He had a teaching instinct, though he claimed that life miscast him as a schoolteacher. I suffered in his classes, feeling the confusion as a persecution of him, but now wonder if his rebellious heart did not court confusion, not as Communists do, to intrude their own order, but, more radical still, as an end pleasurable in itself, as truth's very body. Yet his handwriting (an old pink permission slip recently fluttered from a book where it had been marking a page for twenty years) was always considerately legible, and he was sitting up doing arithmetic the morning of the day he died.

And letters survive from that yet prior son, written in brown ink, in a tidy tame hand, home to his mother from the Missouri seminary where he was preparing for his vocation. The dates are 1887, 1888, 1889. Nothing much happened: he missed New Jersey, and was teased at a church social for escorting a widow. He wanted to do the right thing, but the little sheets of faded penscript exhale a dispirited calm, as if his heart already knew he would not make a successful minister, or live to be old. His son, my father, when old, drove hundreds of miles out of his way to visit the Missouri town from which those letters had been sent. Strangely, the town had not changed; it looked just as he had imagined, from his father's descriptions: tall wooden houses, rain-soaked, stacked on a bluff. The town was a sepia postcard mailed homesick home and preserved in an attic. My father cursed: his father's old sorrow bore him down into depression, into hatred of life. My mother claims his decline in health began at that moment.

He is wonderful to watch, playing soccer. Smaller than the others, my son leaps, heads, dribbles, feints, passes. When a big boy knocks him down, he tumbles on the mud, in his green-and-black school uniform, in an ecstasy of falling. I am envious. Never for me the jaunty pride of the school uniform, the solemn ritual of the coach's pep talk, the camaraderie of shook hands and slapped back-sides, the shadow-striped hush of late afternoon and last quarter, the solemn vaulted universe of official combat, with its cheering mothers and referees exotic as zebras and the bespectacled timekeeper alert with his claxon. When the boy scores a goal, he runs into the arms of his teammates with upraised arms and his face alight as if blinded by triumph. They lift him from the earth in a union of muddy hugs. What spirit! What valor! What skill! His father, watching from the sidelines, inwardly registers only one complaint: he feels the boy, with his talent, should be more aggressive.

They drove across the Commonwealth of Pennsylvania to hear their son read in Pittsburgh. But when their presence was announced to the audience, they did not stand; the applause groped for them and died. My mother said afterwards she was afraid she might fall into the next row if she tried to stand in the dark. Next morning was sunny, and the three of us searched for the house where once they had lived. They had been happy there; I imagined, indeed, that I had been conceived there, just before the slope of the Depression steepened and fear gripped my family. We found the library where she used to read Turgenev, and the little park where the bums slept close as paving stones in the summer night; but their street kept eluding us, though we circled in the car. On foot, my mother found the tree. She claimed she recognized it, the sooty linden tree she would gaze into from their apartment windows. The branches, though thicker, had held their pattern. But the house itself, and the entire block, was gone. Stray bricks and rods of iron in the grass suggested that the demolition had been recent. We stood on the empty spot and laughed. They knew it was right, because the railroad tracks were the right distance away. In confirmation, a long freight train pulled itself east around the curve, its great weight gliding as if on a river current; then a silver passenger train came gliding as effortlessly in the other direction. The curve of the tracks tipped the cars slightly toward us. The Golden Triangle, gray and hazed, was off to our left, beyond a forest of bridges. We stood on the grassy rubble that morning, where something once had been, beside the tree still there, and were intensely happy. Why? We knew.

" 'No,' Dad said to me, 'the Christian ministry isn't a job you choose, it's a vocation for which you got to receive a call.' I could tell he wanted me to ask him. We never talked much, but we understood each other, we were both scared devils, not like you and the kid. I asked him, Had he ever received the call? He said No. He said No, he never had. Received the call. That was a terrible thing, for him to admit. And I was the one he told. As far as I knew he never admitted it to anybody, but he admitted it to me. He felt like hell about it, I could tell. That was all we ever said about it. That was enough."

He has made his younger brother cry, and justice must be done. A father enforces justice. I corner the rat in our bedroom; he is holding a cardboard mailing tube like a sword. The challenge flares white-hot; I roll my weight toward him like a rock down a mountain, and knock the weapon from his hand. He smiles. Smiles! Because my facial expression is silly? Because he is glad that he can still be overpowered, and hence is still protected? Why? I do not hit him. We stand a second, father and son, and then as nimbly as on the soccer field he steps around me and out the door. He slams the door. He shouts obscenities in the hall, slams all the doors he can find on the way to his room. Our moment of smilingly shared silence was the moment of compression; now the explosion. The whole house rocks with it. Downstairs, his siblings and mother come to me and offer advice and psychological analysis. I was too aggressive. He is spoiled. What they can never know, my grief alone to treasure, was that lucid many-sided second of his smiling and my relenting, before the world's wrathful pantomime of power resumed.

As we huddle whispering about him, my son takes his revenge. In his room, he plays his guitar. He has greatly improved this winter; his hands getting bigger is the least of it. He has found in the guitar an escape. He plays the Romanza wherein repeated notes, with a sliding like the heart's valves, let themselves fall along the scale:

The notes fall, so gently he bombs us, drops feathery notes down upon us, our visitor, our prisoner.

Daughter, Last Glimpses of

Just before she went away to live with the red-bearded harpsichord-maker, our daughter asked us how to jitterbug. She had found these old Glenn Miller records in the closet. Eileen and I were embarrassed to tell her we didn't know how; though the jitterbug had been of our era, it was an era of the survival of the fittest, and for every Jack and Jill triumphantly trucking and twirling on the gymnasium floor to the local version of the Big Band sound there was a clutch of Eileens and Geoffreys slumping enviously against the padded wall, or huddling in the bleachers, wondering how it was done, wondering if anyone who knew how would ever invite them to dance. How much kinder, we urged upon our daughter, of your own generation to invent dances that require no skill, that indeed cannot be done wrong, and that therefore do not create hurtful distinctions between the ins and the outs, the deft and the gauche, the beautiful and the un-.

Our daughter looked at us with wide eyes. Her face is mostly frontal, like a cat's. As she turned eighteen her eyes were exchanging that staring look of childhood for something softer and more inward, with a margin of distrust to it, to cushion amazement. But how, she seemed now to be asking, amazed, could two people unable even to jitterbug manage to get together and have *me?* She had been our first child. In our simplicity we had called her Joy.

There was dancing, in those last glimpses. My daughter had been taking ballet at school and would do backbends and cartwheels on the lawn, or slow, rolling splits and stretches in the front hall. For her birthday I had bought her an exercise bar, to use in her room, but she preferred the front hall, where the mailman sometimes showered letters in upon her. Her body, in black tights and leotard, was developing muscles and length; the front hall was too small, really, for these extensive exercises, which included resting her head—golden hair, platinum nape—between her knees, and then snapping it up, so that her eyes in her sudden round face looked surprised at something discovered in mine. On her body the black cloth paled wherever it stretched around a bulge.

Though we failed to teach her to jitterbug (the motions she improvised to go with "In the Mood" and "I've Got a Gal in Kalamazoo" owed more to the African Dance Troupe than to the crisp, tart Forties), she taught her younger brother how to hold a girl and sway to James Taylor and Carole King. They did this in the study, where years ago the record-player had been mistakenly installed. Looking up from trying to read, I would see his face on her shoulder, chin high because she was taller, the angel face of my second son half-lost in his sister's hair and engulfed by bliss, his eyelashes extensions of the sparkle of his slitted eyes as he and she swayed like seaweeds in the waves of amplified music—their feet, as far as I could see, doing no steps at all.

"Isn't Joy nice to Ethan?" I asked Eileen later, somewhat rhetorically.

"She's nice to all of us these days," she replied.

It was true. She set the dinner table for her mother and did the dishes. She read her little sister bedtime stories. I would see them, the two girls, framed by the doorway into Katharine's room, sitting on the bed beneath the tacked-up pictures of horses and dogs, Joy's face solemn as a Sunday-school teacher's. The two profiles bent toward each other symmetrically, for all the six years between them, but that the younger girl's forehead had an apprehensive outward curve whereas Joy's brow was—is—flat and determined and square. Katharine at twelve was going through a troubled time. Joy would be talking to her about grades, or diets, or their grandmother. My mother was dying, that same spring, of cancer. The last time she came to the house (she knew it was the last time but disdained to admit it, as she disdained to admit she was dying; she had been a lifelong understater; her last words, to the attending nurse and me, were "Well, much obliged"), Joy hugged her at parting. A shy sideways hug, for the old lady had grown frail as sticks, her walk a precarious shuffle. "Hope you soon feel better," Joy said, hesitating and coming to a blush over the "feel better," knowing it would take a miracle. How big my daughter looked!—freckled, with sloping dancer's shoulders, standing at the height of health beside the shrunken stoic wraith from whom she was descended. And for me it was as if, in one of those thrilling swift crossovers the good jitterbuggers could do, they had switched positions from the distant moment when my toddling infant daughter had fallen against a hot wood stove in Vermont and her grandmother, so calm the cigarette never left her mouth, applied ice and butter and soothing words to the scorched arm that must have felt, to the astonished, shrieking child, seized by Death itself.

At the funeral, in our ancestral Unitarian church, Joy and Katharine not only prayed, they got up on their knees on the kneeling stool in upright Episcopalian style. And, their faces covered by their hands, they looked like twins, in dresses Joy had made from the same dark, small-flowered cloth.

Her sewing worried me. "All she ever does is hang around the house and sit in her room and sew. She acts like some little spinster. Why doesn't she ever go out with boys? It isn't as if she's ugly. Is she?"

"Are you asking seriously?" my wife asked.

"I am. I can't tell. She's my daughter."

"You're shocking. She's gorgeous. Boys her own age just don't turn her on."

"The reason you're so complacent about it," I told Eileen, "is she does all your housework for you."

"She enjoys doing it. She's learning something."

"Yeah, how to be Cinderella."

"If that's your analogy, relax."

Left to rust in her room, the sewing machine is no trouble; but the rooster is. My daughter insisted, with all the determination in her solid brow (as a baby she used to beat it against the bars of the crib until we would lift her out), on getting chickens. Chickens? In our little yard? She said they would take up no room. They would turn our garbage into fresh eggs. They would in themselves constitute a natural cycle. Compared to an automobile, they consumed almost nothing. They would be aesthetic and amusing. Chickens.

Our bargain went that she would build the pen and little chicken house with me; but something about the hammering and sawing and the size of the nails and the roughness of my construction pained her, for she wandered away, and I built it alone. Mark, our older son, came out I thought to help, but he only intended to complain.

"God, Dad, it's homely."

"I'm making it the best I can."

"It's not you, it's the *idea*. Why should she have chickens? You won't even let me have a .22. Think of the noise pollution. Think of the feathers, Dad."

"I agree, I agree. Could you hold this two-by-four steady while I nail it down?"

"And another thing, I *hate* the way she drives the car. She's going to kill somebody, Dad, and you're going to have to pay for it."

Joy had consented to apply for her driver's license just that winter, after holding out, for ecology's sake, since the age of sixteen. It was true, when she drove the Ford the machine became loose-jointed and precarious in flight, like a flamingo. Beside her in the passenger's seat, I felt she was brushing things—mailboxes, hydrants—from the side of the road. Whereas when Mark, freshly sixteen and instantly equipped with a learner's permit, drives, the automobile crouches low to the ground and noses rapidly along the highway like a tracking beagle, with nervous, sniffing jerks. "Not to mention the fact," he continued, "she's gotten Ethan all stirred up about sex."

"We learn by living," I told him, and drove a nail to end the conversation. When the chicken house was done, Joy came out of hiding and admired it—the little sliding door, the roost hinged to swing upward so the poultry-keeper (ahem) could sweep and change the straw. In fact she did, at first, do a conscientious job, sweeping, scattering grain, gathering eggs in the morning dew like some thick-waisted lass out of Hardy. I remember how, as I sat down to breakfast, she would push open the back door with her shoulder, her eyes starry above the wonder of the eggs still warm in her hands. It was my paternal duty to eat one. The yolks were unpleasantly orange, thanks to the richness of our garbage. And my daughter danced around my eating, celebrating this miraculous completion, this cycle, this food for the breadwinner, this chicken and egg. She doted on those dowdy birds. She painted ivy on their house, watched them like a scientist, discovered that "pecking order" wasn't merely a phrase, papered the walls of her room with scratchy drawings of chickens, and even did poems; one line went, as I remember, *peck scrawk scrabble peck.* For all her mothering, the chickens gradually ceased to lay.

The idea of a rooster was hatched without consultation with me.

One Thursday after work I got out of the car and there he was, a little red-brown bird with absurdly long tail feathers and a dictatorial way of cocking his head. He was smaller than the hens, but already they followed him liquidly, bubbling in their throats and jostling for precedence, as he surveyed the pen and coop I had built, all unbeknownst for *him.* He had been brought in a psychedelic Volkswagen bus by a small bearded man with pink eyes and a mussed, unhappy air. Joy, Eileen, and Katharine were sitting with him at the kitchen table in the evening light. Strange thing, both Joy and Eileen had cigarettes in their hands. Eileen had quit when my mother's cancer was diagnosed, and as far as I knew Joy had never started. The rooster-bringer had heard of our need from a boyfriend of Joy's ecology instructor at school. Before I arrived, and though he mumbled, they had drawn a surprising mass of information from him: he was nearly thirty, his wife had left him a while ago, the "bunch of people" he was living with on this farm was breaking up, they were giving everything away—roosters, sheep, the Rototiller. Also, he had a cold, and couldn't find a satisfactory kind of industrial glue for his harpsichords. Soon after I arrived, he left.

"God, Dad, he was bogus," Mark said.

"I agree."

"I thought he was *cute*," Joy called from the other room. This was new; she never eavesdropped. What other people said or did, her stance had been these past years, did not touch her. She had lived in a world of her own making, with a serenity that floated dishes onto the table without a click.

Now, with a crash, her dependence on others, and ours on her, was declared. She begged or stole the Ford so often we had to buy a second car: just as the gas shortage overtakes the world. Eileen is back to doing the dishes and smoking a pack a day. Katharine says that if Joy could have chickens she doesn't see why she can't have some sheep in the back yard. They would keep the grass short for me. Their wool would be worth money. They would look pretty. Mark has offered to shoot the chickens with his new .22. Ethan, his first partner fled, now goes to dances at the junior high, one of my neckties knotted loose, his hair combed without our nagging; he is so dolled up and beautiful we all have to laugh at him before he goes. As to Joy's departure, it was hurried and at the time not very real to the rest of us. I retain no glimpses. What coat was she wearing? What suitcase did she take? Did she slam the door? She may have said "Much obliged," but I didn't hear it.

The house seems bigger. The record-player, after its spell of Ralph Kirkpatrick, is back to Carole King, or silent. The front hall is clear to traffic. We come and go. Sometimes days pass before one of us remembers to bring in the eggs. Irregularly fed, the flock has pecked a gap beneath the chicken wire, and gets into the neighbor's lettuce. During one such outing, another neighbor's Labrador carried off the white hen with a toe missing—the lowest in the pecking order, cannily. How did the dog know? He carried her in his mouth, white as fresh laundry in the dusk, up into the pines; the children heard her squawk and throbble until night fell.

If all is not well with his world, the rooster never admits it. Every morning, he gets up on those Ruberoid self-sealing Slate Green asphalt shingles I hammered down to make him a roof, a midair hop and skip from my bedroom window, and he crows. Lying awake, I can hear him practicing his crow in the small hours, inside his house: a rather gentle, even wheezy, half-unfurling of the magic scroll inside his chest. Maybe he is dreaming of the dawn, maybe the street light fools him. But there is no mistaking the real thing: as the windowpanes brighten from purple to mauve to white he flaps up on his roof with a slap like a newspaper hitting the porch and gives a crow as if to hoist with his own pure lungs that sleepy fat sun to the zenith of the sky. He never moderates his joy, though I am gradually growing deafer to it. That must be the difference between soulless creatures and human beings: creatures find every dawn as remarkable as all the ones previous, whereas the soul grows calluses.

Ethiopia

THE ADDIS ABABA HILTON has a lobby of cool and lustrous stone and a giant, heated, cruciform swimming pool.
The cross-shape is plain from the balconies of the eighth-
and ninth-floor rooms, from which also one can see the
long white façade of the Emperor's palace. In the other
direction, there are acres of tin shacks, and a church on a
hill like the nipple on a breast of dust. Emerging from the
pool, which feels like layers of rapidly tearing silk, one
shivers uncontrollably until dry, though the sun is brilliant, and the sky diamond-pure. The land is high, and
the air not humid. One dries quickly. The elevators are
swift and silent. From the high floors the white umbrellas
on the restaurant tables beside the pool make a rosary of
perfect circles. All this is true. What is not true is that
Prester John doubles as the desk clerk, and the Queen of
Sheba manages the glass-walled gift shop, wherein one
can buy tight-woven baskets of multicolored straw, metal
mirrors, and Coptic crosses of carved wood costing thou-

sands of Ethiopian dollars, which relate to the American dollar as seven to three.

The young American couple arrived at the hotel very tired, having been ten days in Kenya, where they had seen and photographed lions, leopards, cheetahs, hyraxes, oryxes, dik-diks, steinboks, klipspringers, oribis, topis, kudus, impalas, elands, Thomson's gazelles, Grant's gazelles, hartebeests, wildebeests, waterbucks, bushbucks, zebras, giraffes, flamingos, marabou storks, Masai warriors, baboons, elephants, warthogs, and rhinoceroses—everything hoped for, indeed, except hippos. There had been one asleep in a pool in the Ngorongoro Crater, but it had looked too much like a rock to photograph, and the young man of the American couple had passed it by, confident there would be more. There never were. It had been his only chance to get a hippopotamus on film. Prester John, cool behind his desk of lustrous green marble, divined this, and efficiently, gratuitously arranged that they spend the night away from Addis Ababa, in the Ethiopian countryside. The countryside was light brown. Distant figures swathed in white trod the tan landscape with the floating step of men trying to steady themselves on a trampoline. But these were women, all beautiful. The beauty of their black faces, glimpsed, lashed the windows of the car like fistfuls of thrown sand. Some carried yellow parasols. Some led white donkeys. A few rode in rubber-wheeled carts, rickety and polychrome, their mouths and nostrils veiled against the dust. He tried to photograph these women, but they turned their heads, and the results would be blurred.

The hotel was cushioned in bougainvillea and stuffed with Germans. At six o'clock a bus took all the Germans away and the young Americans became the only guests.

They walked the blossoming grounds, and looked from their balcony to the brown lake distilled from the tan landscape by a cement dam, and in their room read magazines taken from the hotel lobby—*Ce Soir, Il Tempo, Sturm und Drang,* the English edition of the official monthly publication of the Polish Chamber of Commerce, the annual handbook of Yugoslavian soccer, the quarterly journal of the Australian Dermatology Association (incorporating *Tasmanian Hides*). "God, I love this country," he announced aloud, letting his magazine sink beside him to the bed.

"Quiet," she said. "I'm reading." The Brazilian edition of *Newsweek.*

"If you ever get tired of reading," he began.

"It's too hot," she said.

"Really? Actually, as evening comes on, in these high, dry countries—"

"Have it your way, then," she said, noisily turning a tissue-thin page. "It's too cold."

There was a knock on the door. It was their driver, asking in his excellent English if they wanted to see the hippopotami before dinner. Their limousine wound through low, menacing foliage to a sluggish brown river. It seemed empty and scarcely flowing. They walked along a dim path beside the riverbank and met Prester John, barefoot, in rags, and carrying a staff. Though he seemed a shade darker than in his hotel uniform, he was recognizably the same man—small, clever, with beautiful feminine hands and a hurt, monkish, liverish look beneath his eyes. He looked, she thought, like Sammy Davis, Jr.; but then so many men in Ethiopia looked like Sammy Davis, Jr. Prester John led them to a shaggy point above the river and made a noise of sonorous chuckling deep in his throat

—deeper than his throat; his entire body and belly thrummed and resonated with the noise. And then in the dusk little snags appeared in the river current: hippopotamus eyes. And as the Americans grew accustomed to the dusk, and the dusk to them, to the eyes were added ears, and the tops of heads appeared above the water, and the bulbous immensity of a back arched upward into a dive. It was a family, a clan, with two babies among them, all calling to one another; their deep soft snorting continued underwater as an unheard, vibrating jubilance. The air became as full of it as the river, one brown world flooded with familial snorting, until the hippopotami had tugged themselves around the bend and into night. Prester John accepted his tip with a bow and the shadow of a genuflexion. The driver was relieved to find his car unharmed in the bushes. The young American couple were served dinner in solitary splendor. Unseen hands had prepared a banquet; for all its eerie isolation, the meal was delicious. He wondered how they turned a profit. Oh, if only he knew how to talk to her! The silence between them grated the plates and let the silver clash with the fury of swords. His thoughts moved on, to the hippos. If only there had been a notch or two more light! Oh, if only he had brought a longer lens!

Back in Addis, Prester John perceived that they were bored, and arranged to have a party thrown for them. He himself was the host; the Queen of Sheba was the hostess. Her hair was up in the halo of an Afro, and as she moved in her robe of all possible colors her body tapped now here, now there. The rings on her fingers formed a hoard and the little gold circles of her granny glasses gave her eyes a monkish humor. Her blackness was the shade in which God had designed Adam and Eve, a color from which the young American couple felt their own whiteness as a catastrophic falling-off, caused helter-skelter by the Northern clime, snow, wolves, camouflage, and the survival of the fittest. The Queen of Sheba introduced them to beautiful, static people formally designated as Ato, Woizero, and Woizerit. The Woizerits were unmarried. It seemed an elaborate way to say it. Also elaborate, the Emperor was never referred to but as His Imperial Majesty, which became HIM.

". . . until we are rid of HIM . . ."

". . . the latest story about HIM . . ."

"I understand," the young American said to a stately Woizerit who had studied three years at the University of Iowa, "you're in television."

Prester John gracefully interceded. "This lovely lady," he said, "*is* television." His magical female hand turned a dial, and there she was, giving news about the latest Palestinian hijacking.

"Hitler," a swarthy but handsome gentleman was telling the young American wife, "had the correct idea but was not permitted to complete it. A vivid proof of the lack of Providence."

"Suppose I told you," she said, "I was Jewish?"

He surveyed her face, and then her blond body, lovingly. "It would not lessen," he told her, "my reverence for Hitler." But reverence for her was what he expressed, for he clung pinchingly to her arm as if she had consented to join him in some superb indecency.

Her husband had found a fellow-American, a pale-tan Black woman from Detroit, in the pay of the American Embassy. They huddled close together, sharing remembrance of that remote exotic land of Lincoln Continentals and Drake's Cakes. "You happy here?" he asked at last.

"It'll do," she said, shrugging and, obliged to elaborate on the shrug, adding, "I can't get servants. They're very polite, and I offer top dollar, but the Ethiopians will not work for me."

"But why not?"

Seeing he didn't know, very graciously she made a little gesture as if parting curtains, disclosing—herself. Seeing he still didn't know, she elaborated, "They have this racial hang-up. They keep telling you how Semitic they are."

The Queen of Sheba clapped her hands imperiously. No Westerner could have produced that sound, as if with blocks of wood: worlds of body language are being lost. The guests sat to eat around great multicolored baskets lined with a delicious rubbery bread. One ate by tearing off pieces and seizing food as if picking up coals with a pot holder. The young Americans were delighted to be engaging in a custom. Prester John admired their pragmatism. His voice was high, reedy, and not accidentally unpleasant. "I would not want to say," he said, "the many negative things I could say about America. But you have done this one thing of genius. The credit card. Money without money. That is a thing truly revolutionary. The world is thus transformed, while the political philosophers amuse one another."

"Is that what you do? I mean, are you a political scientist? A teacher?" The American was not sure this was still Prester John—he seemed frailer, edgier.

"What do I do? I read Proust, over and over. And I write."

"Could I read your books?" the American wife chimed in, from across the basket, at whose rim the admirer of

: 82 :

Hitler was showing her how to eat raw meat, an Ethiopian delicacy.

"No," was the response, said caressingly. "In Ethiopia, there is no publishing."

"You understand," the television Woizerit murmured on the American's other side. "HIM."

"I write and I write," the frail clever host elaborated, "and then I read it all aloud to one special friend. And then I destroy it. All."

"How terrible. Is that friend here?"

"No," he smiled, forming a little prayer tent with his hands. He was certainly Prester John. A medieval face twitched in the midnight skin. "Do not eat raw meat. The uninitiated vomit for days." He relaxed, slumped in his gaudy robes. "Yes." His voice went high again, reedy, mockingly informative. "In this ancient kingdom, misplaced to Africa, we have been compelled to raise the art of living to the point of the tenuous."

Though the party was gathering strength, the young Americans were tired. The Queen of Sheba and Prester John insisted on accompanying them back to the hotel, since marauders roam the slums with impunity, the poverty is acute despite massive infusions of United States aid, corruption and reaction reign here as everywhere save China, not even one's driver of twenty years' service can be trusted, terrorists on behalf of Eritrean independence are ubiquitous. A curious optical effect: in the darkness within the car, the two legendary Ethiopians disappeared but for their clothes, which rustled with utmost courtesy, and but for their words, paraphrased above. Nevertheless, a disturbing and flattering possibility, indecent yet not impractical, communicated itself to the minds of their guests, as through layers of fluttering, tearing silk. In the cool lobby their shouted farewells echoed of disappointment. Oh, what *was* the custom?

In his twin bed on the ninth floor, the man of the young couple thought, The Queen of Sheba, black yet not Black, boyoboyoboy. Mine, she could be mine, as the darkness inside me is mine, as the spangled night sky is mine. God, I love this country. The jewels. The arid height. The Hilton corridors of greenish stone. The tiny dried-up Emperor. The bracing sense of never having been colonized by any European power. How long and lustrous her ebony limbs would feel in the darkness. But I might disappoint her. I might feel lost in her. She might mock me. My sickly pallor. My Free World hang-ups. Better simply snap her picture when she undresses. But the flash batteries died in the Serengeti, that night by the water hole. Darn it! Her breasts. Armpits. Belly. Down, down he is led from one dusky thought to the next. Would the granny glasses come off first, or last?

And beside him his fair wife on her twin bed thinks of airplanes. She dreads flying, especially in Ethiopia, with its high escarpments, small national budget, daredevil pilots trained by Alitalia. Perhaps if she slept with Prester John, by one of his miracles he could prevent her plane from crashing. Sleeping with men, especially black men, more fancy than fact, if they gave women decent educations they could think about something else. But still. . . . His wicked ascetic smile and look of monkish sorrow did cut into her. In the car, his touch, or a fold of his silken robe, accidentally? If he could guarantee on a stack of Bibles the plane wouldn't crash. . . . The dedicated hijackers with stockings over their faces, the sudden revolver shots from the security guards disguised as Lebanese businessmen, the rush of air, the lurch above the clouds, the inane patter of the brave stewardesses, the lurid burst of flame from the port engine, the long slow nightmare fall, the mile-wide splash of char on the earth, the scattered suitcases. . . . Oh God yes, I'll do anything you want, consider me your slave, your toy. For without life, how can there be virtue?

Because of security checks, one must appear at the airport two and a half hours before scheduled departure time. He is in the glass-walled hotel shop, dickering with the Queen of Sheba for a Coptic cross. He has reduced her price to fourteen hundred Ethiopian dollars, which is no longer divisible by seven in his head, because of the most recent American dollar devaluation. Fourteen hundred divided by two and one-third minus a little. . . . She is bored. The Queen of Sheba thrusts a retractable ball-point into her towering teased coiffure, and her ebony fingers drum with surprising percussive effect on a glass case. Her nose is straight, her nostrils narrow. She sighs. These Americans, rendered insubstantial by rising gold, like drops of water running from the back of an aroused crocodile. He asks, will she accept a credit card?

Prester John appears, in shabby livery, with the young American wife in tow. She is flushed, pink, sleepy. Though the lobby is cool, blond ringlets cling to her brow. Hurry, the clever little black man says, you must see the monastery, there is just time before the airplane, it has been arranged.

Trailing protests like dust, the young American is led through the lobby, away from his luggage. It is not the usual limousine this time but a little red Fiat. Prester John does not seem to understand the gears. As he grapples with them, he looks comically like Sammy Davis, Jr. They head out of the city, uphill; the paved road becomes dirt. Prester John gossips nervously about the Queen of Sheba. "She is a magnificent woman, but thoroughly Oriental. I enjoy her loyalty, but am vexed by, how shall I say, the lack of stereo in her sensibility. She cannot lift her thoughts above jewelry, lechery, and airbases. My intention was to irradiate her with Christian faith, fresh, even raw, from the desert Fathers—to make, here, upon this plateau, a dream to solace the tormented sleep of Europe. Instead, she has made of it something impossibly heavy, a mere fact, like the Catholicism of Ireland, or the Communism of Albania." He cannot move the gearshift above second gear, so thus roaring they proceed up a dirt road transected by ridges of rock like the backs of sleeping hippopotami. At first, clouds of people in white had rimmed the roadway; now they meet, and swerve to avoid, intermittent donkeys and women staggering beneath wide bundles of little trees. One of these women, bent double like a scorpion, in rags, her feet bare, with long dark heels and pale, cracked soles, looks familiar; the American turns in his seat. Dust obscures his view. He is certain only that she was not wearing her granny glasses.

Prester John sweats, embarrassed. The road is all rocks now, tan, with a white dusting. "I am growing worried," he confesses, "about your airplane. It is possible I underestimated the difficulty." He stops the car where the view falls away on one side. The Hilton pool twinkles like a dim star far below them. On the other side, stony sere pastures mount to a copse of viridian trees. Between the trees peep ruddy hints of a long wall. That is the monastery. "Perhaps," Prester John offers nervously, "a photograph?

I am profoundly sorry; the road, and these recalcitrant gears . . ."

What the young American sees through his finder looks exactly like the sepia illustrations in his Sunday-school Bible. He sets the lens at infinity and snaps the shutter. But his inward attention is upon his wife, for her calmness, as their next airplane flight draws nearer, puzzles him. Prester John grindingly backs the Fiat around and hurtles downward along the cruel road of rocks; she lightly smiles and with dusty fingertips brushes back the hair from her drying brow. She feels she is already on the airplane—all of Ethiopia is an airplane, thousands of feet above sea level; and it cannot crash. This is true.

Transaction

In December of the year 197–, in the city of N——, a man of forty was walking toward his hotel close to the hour of midnight. The conference that had kept him in town had dispersed; he was more than a touch drunk; in his arms he carried Christmas presents for his family. At the edge of the pavement, beneath his eyes, bloomed painted young women, standing against the darkened shop fronts in attitudes that mingled expectancy and insouciance, vulnerability and guardedness, solitude and solidarity. A scattered army, was his impression, mustering half-heartedly in retreat. Neon syllables glowed behind them; an unlit sign, MASSAGE PARLOR, hung at second-story level, and his face, uptilted, received an impression of steam, though the night was cold as the spaces between the stars.

A large Negress in a white fur coat drew abreast of him at a red light, humming. His eyes slid toward her; her humming increased in volume, was swelled from underneath, by a taunting suggestion of *la-di-da*, into almost a song. Fear fingered his heart. He shifted his paper Christmas bags to make a shield between him and this sudden, fur-coated, white-booted melodious body. The light broke; under the permission of green he crossed the avenue known as T—— and walked up the hard, faintly tugging slant of sidewalk that would lead him to the voluminous anonymity of his hotel, the rank of silver elevator doors, the expectant emptiness of his room.

A glass office building floated above his shoulder silent as an ice floe. Amid this deathly gray of winter and stone, a glistening confusion of contrary possibility was born in him, an incipient nest of color. In the unlit grated window of a corner drugstore, cardboard Magi were bringing their gifts. He turned left and circled the block, though his arms ached with his packages and his feet with the cold.

The routed but raffish army of females still occupied their corner and dim doorways beyond. Our non-passerby hesitated on the corner diagonally opposite, where in daytime a bank reigned amid a busy traffic of supplicants and emissaries only to become at nightfall its own sealed mausoleum. He saw the prettiest of the girls, her white face a luminous child's beneath its clownish dabs of rouge and green, approached by an evidently self-esteeming young man, a rising insurance agent or racketeer, whose flared trouser-legs protruded beneath a light-colored topcoat, correctly short. He talked to the girl earnestly; she listened; she looked diagonally upward as if to estimate something in the aspiring architecture above her; she shook her head; he repeated his importunity, bending forward engagingly; she backed away; he smartly turned and walked off.

Had it been a pack of schoolchildren, the others would have crowded around her, eager for details. But these others ignored her, maintaining their parallel vigil.

Yet seeing an approach having been made emboldened our onlooker to cross to their side of the avenue and to walk through the cloud of them again. His packages perhaps betrayed him, as a comet returning. He felt caught up, for all the good will in his heart, in a warfare of caution and invisibility. His breath held taut against some fantastic hazard, he passed through the prime concentration, centered upon the luminous face of the child beauty. Only when the cloud thinned did he dare glance sideways, at an apparition in a doorway, who, the glance told him, was far from pretty—bony, her narrow face schoolteacherishly beaked—but who, even as he reproached himself, did accept his signal.

"Hi," she said. The startling breadth of her smile—as if the doorway dimness had been suddenly slashed—offered him space in which to forgive himself. With triggered quickness she came forward from her niche and at the same mechanical speed inserted her hand in the crevice between his body and his arm, among the rustling bags decorated with bells, conifers, snowmen.

He answered, "Hi." He felt his voice dip deep into a treasure of composure, warmth, even power. Her touch was an immense relief.

"Thirty O.K.?" she asked in a rapid whisper.

"Sure." The back of his throat itched with silliness, that rose to counter the humorless slithering urgency of her question.

She posed another: "You got a place?"

He named the hotel, fearing it told too much about him —solid, square, past its prime.

Indeed, the name did seem to amuse her, for she repeated it, skipping with the same breath to put herself in step with him and tightening her grip on his arm. His clothes, layer upon layer, felt transparent. He plaintively accused, "You don't like my hotel."

"Why wouldn't I?" she asked, with that intimidating rapidity. He saw that the stratagems, the coaxing ironies useful and instinctive in his usual life, would have small application in this encounter. I produce, you produce. Provocation had zero value.

He wanted to do the right thing. Would she expect to be taken to a bar? He had already drunk, he estimated, more than enough. And wouldn't it be to her profit to go to his room promptly and be done? She was a treasure so clumsily wrapped as to be of indeterminate size. Experimentally, he turned left, as on his prior circuit; she did not resist; together they crossed the avenue and climbed the hard little slant of pavement he had climbed before. Her grip tightened on his arm; he felt a smile break the mask of cold on his face. He was her prize; she, his. She asked, "What's your name?"

Amid his sensations of cold and alcohol and pleasure at this body warm and strange and tugging against his, he imagined his real name would break the spell. He lied, "Ed."

She repeated it, as she had the name of the hotel, testing it in her mouth. Many names had passed through her mouth. Her voice, it seemed to him, had a Middle-Atlantic metallic flatness without being indigenous to N——. She volunteered, "Mine's Ann."

He was touched to sense that she was not lying. He said, "Hello, Ann."

"Hello." She squeezed his arm, so his mind's eye saw his bones. "What do you do, travel for some company?" Her question and answer were one.

"Sure," he said, and changed the subject. "Am I walking

too fast for you?" Something chalklike was coating his words. He mustn't, he told himself, be frightened of this woman; his fright would not serve either of them. Yet her presence nearly submerged his spirit in wonder. She loomed without perspective, like an abutment frozen in the headlights the moment after a car goes out of control. He glanced at her obliquely. City light had soaked into her face. Her long nose looked waxen. She was taller than the average woman, though still shorter than he.

She answered carefully. "No. You're walking fine. Who are the presents for?"

His own question, he felt, had been subtly mocked; he answered hers mockingly, "People."

They did not talk again for some minutes.

The little paved rise crested. His hotel filled the block before them. In its grid of windows some burned; most were dark. Midnight had passed. The great building blazed erratically, like a ship going down. He said, "There's a side entrance up this way." She may have known this, but didn't indicate so. Had she been here before? Often? He could have asked, but did not, as he did not ask so many questions she might have willingly answered. For women, it turns out, always in retrospect, were waiting to be asked.

The side entrance was locked. The revolving door was chained.

Against them? Not only was Ed a stranger to the etiquette of prostitution, but hotels puzzled him. Was a hotel merely a store that sells rooms, or is it our watchdog and judge, with private detectives eyeing every corridor through ostensible fire extinguishers and lawyers ready to spring from the linen closets barking definitions of legal occupancy? They had to walk, Ann and Ed, another half-block in the interstellar cold and to brave the front entrance. The maroon-capped doorman, blowing on his hands, let them pass as if by a deliberate oversight. Mounting the stairs to the lobby, Ed was aware of the brass rods, slimmer than jet trails, more polished than presentation pens, that held the red carpet to the marble. He was aware of the warmth flowing down from the lobby and of, visible beneath her black maxi-coat as she preceded him by a step, tall laced boots of purple suede. The lobby was calm. The cigar stand was shrouded for the night. Behind the main desk, men murmured into telephones and transposed coded numerals with the muffled authority of Houston manipulating a spacecraft. A few men in square gray suits, travelling men, rumpled but reluctant to be launched toward bed, stood about beneath the chandeliers. With his crackling packages and his bought woman packaged in black maxi and laced boots, Ed felt ridiculously encumbered. His eyes rigidly ahead, he crossed to the elevator doors of quilted colorless metal. He pushed the Up button. The wait built tall in his throat before an arriving car flung back a door. It was theirs. No one at the control desk looked up. At the last second, as the doors sighed to close, two men in gray pushed in with them, and stared at Ann, and smiled. One man began to hum.

Didn't she look like a wife? Didn't all young women dress like whores these days? She was plain, plainly dressed, severe, and pale. He could not quite look at her, or venture a remark, even as he inched closer to protect her from the strangers' gazing. The elevator grew suffocating with the exhalations of masculinity, masculinity inflated by booze. The humming grew louder, and plainly humorous. Perhaps an apparent age-difference had betrayed them; though Ed had always been told, by those who loved him, that he looked young for his years. One man shifted his weight. The other cleared his throat. Ed lifted his eyes to the indicator glow, as it progressed through the numbers 4, 5, and 6 and, after a yawning interval in which murder and rape might have been committed, halted at 7, his floor. As the two of them stepped out, she halted, not knowing whether to turn right or left. One of the men behind them called musically, "Goodnight."

Bastard. Buy your own whore.

"To the left," he told her, when the elevator door had sucked shut. In a mirror set diagonally where the corridor turned, he imagined a spectator, a paid moral agent of some sort, watching them approach the turning and then, after they turned, the agent—with his fat cigar and tinfoil badge—transposed in a magical knight's move to where they had been, now watching them recede, Ed's back eclipsing his packages, Ann's maxi swinging stiffly, a cloth bell tolling the corridor's guilty silence.

The key balked at fitting. He could not open the door to his room, which he had paid for. Struggling, blushing, he dropped a package, which the person with him stooped to retrieve. That was good of her. This service free of charge. The key turned. The door opened into a dark still space as tidy and kind as a servant waiting up.

He held open the door for Ann to precede him, and in this gesture discovered his mood: mock courtesy. The hotel corridor, with its walls of no nameable color and its carpet cut from an endless artificial tundra of maroon, came with her, past his nose, into the room; and the pallor of her face, momentarily huge, rebounded from the window, its rectangle of diffuse city light flayed by Venetian blinds. As his eyes adjusted, the walls glowed. The package she had retrieved she set down on the gleam of a glass bureau top; he set the other packages down; his arm ached in relief. He found the wall switch, but the overhead light, clicked on, was too bright. He could not look at her. He brushed the switch off and groped at the base of the large ceramic lamp standing on the bureau top. This light, softer, showed her a distance away, standing by the bed, her hand on the second button of her long dark coat, undoing it; by this gesture of undoing she transposed his sense of her as packaged from the coat to the room itself, to the opaque plaster walls that contained her, to the fussy ceiling fixture like the bow at the top of a box. She was his, something he had bought. Yet she was alive, a person, unpredictable, scarcely approachable indeed. For his impulse to kiss her was balked by unstated barriers, a prohibition she radiated even as she smiled again that unexpected slash of a good smile and, after hesitating, as she had when stepping from the elevator door, handed him her coat—heavy, chill, black—to hang in the closet, which he did happily, his courtesy not altogether mock.

He turned. Who are you? His apprehensions ricocheted confusedly, in the room's small space, off this other, who, standing in its center, simultaneously rendered it larger and many-sided and yet more shallow, as if she were a column faced with little mirrors. He stood motionless, perhaps also a column faced with mirrors—as in ballrooms, theatre lobbies, roller skating rinks. Absurd, of course, to place two such glittering pillars so close together in so modest a room: but then perhaps in just such disproportion does sex loom amid the standardized furniture of our lives.

She moved a step. Something half-spilled from one of the packages attracted her: a book. She pulled it forth; it was Blake's *Auguries of Innocence,* illustrated by Leonard Baskin—a present for his wife, who in the early years of their marriage used to carve a woodcut as their Christmas card. Ann opened the pages and the look of poetry on the page surprised her. "What's it about?" she asked.

"Oh," he said. "Social conditions in London." He heard a curious, invariable delay in the answers they made each other. Tennis with sponge rackets. It might have been his thicknesses of alcohol. The brandy had been the worst mistake.

She let a page turn itself under her fingers, idle. "I used to work in a library."

"Where?" Under cover of her apparent interest in the book, he moved two steps to be behind her, and touched the zipper at the back of her sweater. It was magenta, wool, a turtle-neck, somehow collegiate in quality, perhaps borrowing this quality from their bookish conversation. He thought of pulling the zipper and gingerly didn't dare; he thought of how, with any unbought woman, in such a sealed-off midnight room, hands and lips would have rushed into the vacuum of each other's flesh, sliding through clothes, cascading toward skin.

She answered his question reluctantly, not lifting her attention from the book. "In Rhode Island."

"What town?"

Her attention lifted. "You know Rhode Island?"

"A little. We used to have some friends we'd visit in Warwick."

"The library was in Pawtucket."

"What's Pawtucket like?"

She said, "Not bad. It's not all as ugly as what you see from Route One."

He pulled down her zipper, a little pink zipper at the back of the magenta throat, just enough to let her head slip through. Her cervical vertebrae and some down at her neck's nape were bared. "Did you like it," he asked, "working in the library?" Under his fingertips her nape down tingled; he felt her expecting him to ask how she had got from the library into this profession. He refused to ask, discovering a second mood, after mock courtesy, of refusal. For hadn't she, silently, by some barrier in her manner, refused him a kiss?

She moved away from his touch. "Yeah I did." She was young and lean, he saw, a brunette, her hair crimpy and careless and long. Not only her nose but her teeth were too big, so that her lips, in fitting over them, took on an earnest, purposeful expression; she appeared to him, again, as a schoolteacher, with a teacher's power of rebuke. He laughed, rebelling—laughed at her moving away from him so pensively. As the outdoor cold melted out of his body, the alcohol blossomed into silliness, foaming out of him like popcorn from a popper. Acting the bad boy, he pulled off his overcoat, suit coat, and tie; ashamed of his silliness and the fear it confessed, he went toward her as if for an embrace but instead tugged the hem of her sweater out of her skirt and pulled it upward. Understanding, surrendering, she shook her head to loosen her hair and raised her arms; the sweater came free. Lifting it from her hands, he saw she had long oval nails, painted with clear polish. Her bra was severely white, hospital-plain. This surprised him, in a world where even the squarest of suburban women wore coquettish, lace-trimmed underwear. And he was surprised that, though his whore's shoulders were bony and bore the same glazed pallor as her face, her breasts were a healthy size. Amid the interlock of these small revelations an element clicked apart and permitted him to place his arms around her hard shoulders and tighten them so that the winter chill and stony scent of her hair flowed from the top of her head into his nostrils. His voice leaping from the cliff of her tingling hair, he asked, "You want your thirty now or after?"

"Whichever," she said, then—a concession, her first, possibly squeezed from her by alarm, for his extreme reasonableness did, he perceived, resemble insanity—"after."

"So you're a librarian," he sighed.

His relief must have been too huge, too warm; she pushed his chest away with iron fingertips. "Why don't you go into the bathroom," she suggested, using a disciplinarian's deceptive softness of tone, "and"—she lightly tapped his fly with the back of her hand—"wash them up."

Them! The idea of designating his genitals a population, a little gabbling conclave of three, made his silliness soar and his complementary mood of refusal deepen, darken toward cruelty. With the deliberateness of an insult or of a routine of marriage he sat in the plastic hotel chair and took off his shoes and socks, tucking the socks in the shoes. Then he stood and, insolent but for the trembling of his fingers and the wave of alcohol tipping him forward, unbuttoned his shirt, pulled off his undershirt, managed the high-wire two-step of trouser removal. He was aware of her struck frozen by the bed, but could not look directly at her, to gauge the space she was reflecting, or to catch a glimmer of himself. She was a pillar of black facets. Then the wave of alcohol must have broken over him, for he lost her entirely, and found himself standing naked before the bathroom basin, on tiptoe, soaping his genitals above the lunar radiance of its porcelain and still smiling at the idea of calling them *them*.

As he washed, the concepts her directive had planted—dirt, germs, disease, spoilage—infiltrated the lathery pleasure, underminingly. His tumescence, he observed, was slight. He rinsed, splashing cold water with a cupped hand, dried himself with a towel, tucked the towel modestly about his waist, and walked out into the other room.

Ann was naked but for her boots. Purple suede, they were laced up to her knees. Were they too tedious to unlace? Was this a conventional turn-on? A put-down? An immense obscure etiquette whose principles hulked out of the city night to crowd them into this narrow space of possible behavior blocked him from asking why she had kept them on or whether she might take them off. As if another woman in undressing had revealed a constellation of moles or a long belly scar, he was silent, and accepted the boots along with the slim waxen whiteness of the rest of her, a milk snake with one black triangular marking.

He had worn the towel as provocation, hoping she might untuck it for him. His current mistress, most graciously, unlaced his shoes, and stayed on her knees. But Ann's sole move was to tuck back her hair as if to keep it clear of the impending spatter of dirty business. He let his towel drop and held her, with no more pressure than causes a stamp to adhere to an envelope, drying. He in bare feet, she still in boots, they came closer in height than on the street, and his prick touched her belly just above the pussy. She backed off sharply: "You're icy!"

"I washed like you told me to."

"You could have used warm water."

"I did, except to rinse."

She bent down, but to pick up the towel. She handed it to him. "Dry yourself, can't you?"

"Jesus, you're fussy." He must counterattack. "How about you?" he asked. "Don't you want to use the bathroom?"

"No."

"Don't you need to go wee-wee or anything, standing around on the street for hours?"

"No, thank you."

"It's a perfectly good bathroom."

Just when he had figured her as moronically one-track, she changed her mind. "O.K. I will." She went into the bathroom. She closed the door! So he couldn't watch. No free pleasures, he saw, was one of the rules. Naked, he sat on the bed, picked the Blake from the bureau top, and read,

> The Lamb misus'd breeds Public strife
> And yet forgives the Butcher's Knife.
> The Bat that flits at close of Eve
> Has left the Brain that won't Believe.

The toilet flushed; the faucets purred. She emerged still wearing those bothersome, unlovely boots, and gave his limp penis a glance he thought scornful. Only the alcohol helped him ask, "Want to lie down?"

Without voicing assent, she sat on the bed stiffly and let herself be pulled horizontal. Her skin felt too young, too firm and smooth. Passing his hands down the mathematically perfect curves of her sides and buttocks, he calculated that the journey of happiness from these hands into his head and from there down his spine to his prick was, rendered tenuous and errant by his drunkenness, too long. He stroked her breasts, so firmly and finely tipped as to feel conical. His sense of breasts had been shaped by his overflowing wife. Once when she was nursing one of their babies he had sucked a mouthful of milk from her and, not swallowing, filled her own mouth with it, so she too could know the taste. By comparison this kid's tits were so firm as to feel unkind. Her belly was flat, with the sheen of a tabletop beneath his fingers, and the hair of her pussy was thick, stiff, brushlike. The first time he had slept with a woman not his wife, she had been a mutual friend, a shy and guilty woman who had undressed out of sight and come back to him wearing her slip over nothing; touched, her pussy beneath the nylon had been so startlingly soft he had exclaimed, "Oh," and she with him—"Oh"—as if together on a walk they had simultaneously sighted a rare flower, or a vivid bed of moss.

Ann, stroked, took this as the signal to set her own hand, cool and unfeeling, on his prick. Too rapidly she twitched the loose skin back and forth; he huddled inside his drunkenness and giggled.

"What's so funny?" she asked.

"You're so nice," he lied.

She sat up to continue with better leverage her attack on his prick. It tickled, twittered, and stung; his consciousness drew back, higher, as a man climbs higher into the bleachers for a more analytical view of the game. Either this girl had no aptitude for her profession, or love cannot be aped. She flicked her head haughtily, stopped her futile agitation of his penis, put her mouth to his ear, and whispered with that slithering urgency she affected, "Do you like me?"

"Sure."

"Well *look* at it." She flipped it. He looked. It lay sideways, enviably asleep. She asked, "How long do you expect me to keep at it?"

"Not long," he said pleasantly; her fingers, inert, felt pleasant. "You can go now. I'll get you your thirty dollars. Sorry I'm such a flop."

Her face, soft in shadow, pondered. "Ed, look. I'll stay, but it'll take a little more."

"How much more, for how long?" The prompt specificity of his question took her aback. He helped her, though he was new at this and she wasn't. "How about one hour," he proposed, "for thirty more? In an hour the drinks should wear off enough so I can get it up. I'm sorry, I'd like to fuck you, I really would."

Displeasingly, her whisper hoarsened, becoming theatrical, seductive. "How about being Frenched? Like that? For twenty more I'll French you. Would you like that, Ed?"

Naked and lazy, he shifted position on the bed. Impotent or not, he was the boss. In daylight transactions he hated haggling; but this was different. She was so young she could be teased. Her youth furthermore made her an enemy. For this was the era of student revolts, of contempt for the old virtues, of energy-worship. "Twenty more!" he protested. "That makes eighty all told. You'll bankrupt me. Why would a nice girl like you want to come in off the street and bankrupt some poor bourgeois?"

She ignored his irony, asking with her closest approximation to true excitement, "How much cash you got?"

"Want me to count it?"

"Don't you *know*?"

"Like I said, I was Christmas shopping. Jesus. Hold on. Don't go away mad."

He hoisted himself from the bed, located his pants draped on the back of the plastic arm chair, found the wallet within them, and counted the bills. One hundred ten, one twenty, twenty-two, three. "O.K.," he told her. "Eighty-four dollars. I can just spare eighty and eat breakfast. That's for one hour, starting now, not when you came in, and including you Frenching me. Agreed?"

"O.K."

He considered asking that she remove her boots in the

bargain; but he feared she would put a new price on that, and, though he could inflict upon her the suspense of haggling, he would always end, he knew, by meeting her price. Also there was a mystery about the boots that made him squeamish. To watch him count his money, Ann had lifted herself on the bed, up on her knees like a little girl playing jacks. Ed touched her cold shoulder, silently bidding her to hold the position, and then fit himself into her pose so a nipple met his mouth. He lapped, sucked, rubbed. She said, "Ow."

He removed his mouth an inch. "What do you mean, 'Ow'?"

"Didn't you shave today?"

"Not since this morning. Can you notice?"

"*Feel* it," she said.

He rubbed his own chin and upper lip. "That can't hurt," he told her.

"It does."

He looked up, and her face and torso held in her stillness a shadow that for the first time, it seemed to his sheepish sense, admitted a glimmer of erotic heat into the frozen space between them. Since he could not impress her by anger, being a reasonable man, nor by being himself, since he had sold himself short by applying to her at all, he would employ compliance, extravagantly. He would overwhelm her with docility. "I'll go shave then."

She did not prevent him.

He asked, before moving, "Will the shaving time come out of my hour?"

She said, not even audibly bored, her voice was so flat, "If you're going to do it, do it."

Standing again above the basin's bright moon, he felt his genitals stir, sweeten, with the idea of it: the idea of shaving, so domestically, to oblige this ungrateful stringy whore in the next room, street-cold still clinging to her skin. When he returned, his cheeks gleaming, his loins bobbling, she observed his excitement and in an act of swift capture produced from somewhere (her boot?) a prophylactic and snapped it into place around his semi-erect prick and lay on her back with legs spread. Though he held stiff enough to enter her and momentarily think, *I'm fucking this woman,* the pinch of rubber, and an inelasticity within her, and something unready and resentful in himself—*she couldn't care less,* was the successor thought—combined to dwindle him. His few dud thrusts were like blank explosions by whose flash he exposed the full extent of their interlocked abasement. Apologetically, he withdrew, and tugged off the condom and, not knowing upon what hotel surface he could place it without offending her stern standards of hygiene, held the limp little second skin dangling in his hand as he stretched out sorrowfully beside her defeated female form.

What shall we do? Ann lay speechless, but he imagined a rift in the surface of her impatience, a ledge to which he might cling. With his free hand (the other arm tucked back under his head so the condom hung cleanly over the edge of the bed) he stroked the long cold curve of her side, illumined by the window. He told her, "You're gorgeous."

As if equivalently, she asked him, "You married?"

"Sure." She might have thought this was the door, at last, to the confident intimacy between them that he, she must now realize, needed. But it opened instead on a cul-de-sac, the marriage that had put them here; they lay inside his wife's sexual nature as in a padded, bolted dungeon. Ed could have attempted to share this vision with Ann, but attempted more simply to return the friendliness she seemed now willing, if only out of fear of being trapped with him forever, to concede. He asked her, "How old are you?"

"Twenty-two." A new tone, bitter. Did she feel her life so soon destroyed? Her beakish colorless profile lifted above him, into the square cloud of light leaking from the circumambient city. "You?"

"Fortyish."

"The prime of life."

"Depends." He rubbed his mouth across her nipples, then his cheek, asking, "That smooth enough?"

"It's better."

"You like it? I mean, normally, does it leave you cold, turn you off, or what?"

She didn't answer; he had trespassed, he realized, into another dark clause of their contract: her pleasure was not at issue. Able to do no right, and therefore no wrong, he slid his face from her breast to her belly and, as she lay back, past her pubic brush to her thigh. He rested his head there. He laid the condom on the sheet beside her waist and with his hands parted her thighs; she complied guardedly. An edge of one boot scraped his ear as he moved his head back, as when reading a telephone book, to see better. Between her legs lay darkness. He stroked her mons Veneris, and the tendoned furred hollows on either side; he ran his thumb the length of her labia, parted them, softly sank his thumb in the cleft in which, against all tides of propriety and reasonableness, a little moisture was welling. He withdrew his thumb and inserted his middle finger, his thumb finding socket on her anus.

The diffuse light was gathering to his eyes now, and

he saw the silver plane of the inner thigh turned to the window, and the same light sliding on his tapering fore-arm and moving wrist, and the two bright round corners of her buttocks beneath, and the pale meadow of her fore-shortened belly, the small hills of her breasts, the far un-derside of her chin. From the angle of her chin she was gazing out the window, at the strange night sky of N——, like the sky of no other city, brown and golden, starless, permeated with the aureole of its own swampfire static. Through the warp and blur of alcohol the inner configura-tions of her cunt, the granular and budded walls, the elu-sive slippery central hardness, began to cut an image in his mind, and to give him a jeweller's intent steady joy.

She spoke. Her voice floated hoarse across the silver ter-rain of her body, cool and twenty-two. Her words were most surprising. "Do you ever," she asked, hesitating be-fore finishing, "use your tongue?"

"Sure," he said.

Bending his face to her aperture, he felt blow through his skull the wind of all those who had passed this way be-fore him. Yet, though no doubt men had flooded this space with their spunk and not vomit nor shit had been spared her body by strangers struggling to feel alive, her cunt did not taste of any of this; it was firmer than a housewife's and clean of any scent, even that of perfume, and its sur-round of faintly brushlike hair had the prickly innocence of a child's haircut or of the pelt of a young nocturnal omnivore such as a raccoon. He regretted that in the poli-tics of their positioning his mouth did not come at it up-side down but more awkwardly, frontally, with his body trailing between and beyond her legs like an unusably heavy kite tail, and with his neck bent back to the point of aching. Seeking to penetrate, his tongue tensed behind it the entire length of his spine. Opening his eyes, he saw a confused wealth of light-struck filaments that might be vegetation on Mars, or mildew under the microscope.

A miracle, she seemed to be moving. In response. She was. She was heaving her hips to help his tongue go deeper. He suspected a put-on. He was willing to believe that he could arouse his demure mathematical mistress: he was an astronomer, she his statistician, and when she would swing her ass around to his face its spread wet halves would swamp his consciousness like a star map of both hemispheres, not only the stars one saw but the southern constellations—Lupus, Phoenix, Fornax. But this waxen street lily surely was beyond him, another galaxy. Yet the girl lifted her pelvis and rotated it and forcefully sighed. She had been so unemphatic and forbidding in all else, he doubted she would fake this. The thought that he was giving her pleasure invited cruelty, as a clean sheet invites mussing. His prick was becoming a weapon; in the air beyond the foot of the bed he felt it enlarging, presenting more surface to the air. Ed pulled himself up, still drunker than he should be, his chin wet with her, and asked, "Didn't you say you'd French me?"

As if abruptly awakened, Ann seemed to find her body heavy. She pushed her weight up onto her arms as he relaxed his length into the trough of warmth she had left on the narrow, single bed. She tucked back her hair from her temples. She straightened his stiffened prick with her fingers and bent her lips to the glans. Her lips made a silent O as he pushed up. Her head bobbed in and out of the cloud of light. She moved her mouth up and down as rapidly and ruthlessly as she had her hand; he watched with drowsy amazement, wondering what book of instructions she had read. This fanciful impression, that she had learned to perform this service from a manual and was performing it mechanically, an application of purely exterior knowledge, with none of the empathy for the other sex that Eros in blindness bestows, excited him, so he did not lose his erection to his schoolmarm's rote blowing. How many times a night did she do this? He saw, dismally but indulgently, his prick as a product, mass-produced and mass-consumed in a few monotonous ways. Poor dear child. With a distant affection he let his fingertips drift to one nipple and followed its sympathetic rise and fall; so Copernicus followed the rhythmic radiance of Jupiter's revolving satellites. Hard and small and perfect and glossy and cool, her nipple. Hers. He was growing accustomed to her, her temperature, texture, manner, pulse, and saliva. His prick glittered when her profile did not eclipse it.

Time slipped by for him, but a meter in her head told her she had Frenched twenty dollars' worth. Swiftly, as a fisherman transfers the kicking fish to the net, she lifted the circle of her lips from his phallus, retrieved the condom from the bedsheet, rerolled it, slipped it down upon him, and set herself astride, handsome and voracious in silhouette. She told him, with a trace of her old slithering, too-practiced urgency—modified in tone, however, by something unpracticed, young, experimental, and actually interested—"We'll try it with me on top." She lowered herself carefully, and he was inside her. Magnetically his fingertips had never left her nipple.

"That's a good way," he told her, just to say something, so she wouldn't feel utterly alone.

She moved her cunt and her body with it up and down with the same unfeeling presto that must be, he deduced, the tempo most men like; how had he been misled into languorous full pulls and voyeuristic lingering? Too many prefatory years, he supposed, of fantasy and masturbation.

Though her fucking felt like an attack, his prick held its own, and his hypnotic touch on her nipple also held. They were a strange serene boat, its engine pumping, gliding it could be forever through the glowing tan fog of the city night. With his other hand, again to let her know she was not wholly alone with the mechanical problem she was being paid to solve, he patted, then pushed, her bottom. He thought, *I haven't fucked a woman so young for years,* and knew he was home. The canal lock had lifted, scenic point in the mountain pass had been attained, it was all downhill, he would have to come. The girl was virtually jumping now, out of a squat and back into it. Her boots were rough on his sides, her hair swung like a mop, her skin felt cool as a snake's: never mind, he would come, he would give it to her, the gift we are made to give, the scum the universe exists to float.

She squatted deep. His sleepy prick released a little shivery dream. Not a thumping come, but distinct, and for such a drunk, triumphant. Her shoulders and face were above him, dark, as the madonna in the icon is dark in that Russian movie where the damned hero attempts to pray.

But her darkness held a smile. She had made him come. She was above him like a mother nursing, darkness satisfied and proud, having been challenged and found not wanting.

"Oh thank you," he said. "*Thank* you. Sorry to have made you work so hard. *Sorry* to be so much trouble. Usually I come like a flash."

She did not bother to doubt this. There was no way he could win promotion from her classroom of the sexually defective. Indeed, had he not shown that only the most patient manipulation could enroll him among even the weakest of comers? Ann lifted her loins from his, with a delicate shrug of disentanglement—a giantess wading through muck on her knees. A novel sensation told him that she was not carrying his seed away with her, as a wife would; rather, she had sealed it in upon him, sticky consequences. He disdained to remove the condom. She had enlisted him in a certain hostility toward the third member of their party, the pivotal presence in the room, though silent—his willful, sulky prick. Stew in your own juice.

Ann, too, acted lazy. Instead of wading on, out of his narrow bed, she lay down beside him in her boots. He felt why: it was warm here, and enclosed, and now she knew him, and was not frightened of him. He asked her, "Aren't you anxious to get back out on the street?" He giggled, as if the joke were still on himself. "And get away," he continued, "from these awful out-of-town husbands who are too drunk to fuck decently?"

She mistook him, still viewing him as a conquest. Absurd in her booted nakedness, she cuddled against him and said in the slithering breathy voice of her propositions, "If you paid me enough I could stay all night. I bet you don't have enough money for me to stay all night."

"I bet too I don't," he told her soberly.

"For another thirty you might talk me into it." Had she seen into his wallet?

He calculated: if the alcohol wore off, and he got a few hours' sleep, he could manage one more fuck; but then getting her out of here in the morning light, through the bustle of breakfast trays and suitcases, loomed as a perilous campaign. He knew from the men in the elevator that she looked like a whore. With her in this narrow bed with him he'd sleep badly and drag through the rest of the day. Not worth it. He told her, "Honest, I don't have thirty more. I don't have *any* more."

He stared down into her face for the seconds it took her to realize she was being spurned. His fear now was that she would offer to stay free. She sat up. He sat up on the edge of the bed with her. She waved her hand, as if to touch (but she did not touch) his penis, shrunken, wearing the trailing white prophylactic like an old-fashioned nightcap. *And Ma in her kerchief, and I in my cap* . . .

She asked, "You gonna keep that as a souvenir?"

He asked, "You want it back?"

"No, Ed. You can keep it."

"Thanks. I keep saying 'Thanks' to you, you notice?"

"I hadn't noticed." She stood, her buttocks fair as Parian marble. "Mind if I use your john before I go?"

"No, please do. Please."

"Don't want to keep you from your beauty sleep." But even this mild revelation of injury must have tasted unprofessional, passing her lips, for she relented and, gesturing again at the sheath on his prick, offered, "Want me to flush that for you?"

"No. It's mine. I want it."

She gathered some clothes and he regretted afterwards that he had not pressed into his memory these last poses of her naked body. But a wave of blankness was emitted by the still-operant alcohol and ended by the soft slam of the bathroom door. Delicately he pulled off the condom and held it, pendulous, while debating where to set it. At home he was hyperconscious of wine-glass and water stains on furniture; but here, looking for a coaster, he saw only an ashtray. Removing the matches, he laid the sheath in it. She was taking her time in the bathroom. He picked up the

Blake and tried to resume where he had left off. He couldn't find the place; instead his eye was taken by the typographical clasps of

Every Morn & every Night
Some are Born to sweet delight.
Some are Born to sweet delight,
Some are Born to Endless Night.

What was she doing in the bathroom? Did he hear her gargle and spit? He read on, more lines that also seemed too simple:

We are led to Believe a Lie
When we see not Thro' the Eye
Which was Born in a Night to perish in a Night
When the Soul Slept in Beams of Light.

He didn't understand this, nor why Blake hadn't bothered to make the lines scan.

She emerged from the bathroom wearing the purple boots, her antiseptically white bra, and the maxi-skirt whose color he had not observed before (charcoal). She glanced around for her sweater; he spotted its magenta spilled at the foot of the bed and held it out to her with a courtesy mocked by his total nakedness. She took it without a smile and pulled it over her head. She needed more fun in her life; in a better world his function might have been to brighten her gray classroom with a joke or two. She awkwardly reached behind her; he darted to her back and pulled up the zipper, covering her three cervical vertebrae and the faint translucent down. In a gentle voice he asked, "Want me to get dressed and escort you out of the hotel?"

"No, Ed. I can find my way. I'll be all right."

"All alone?"

She did not accept his invitation to say that she was always alone.

"I hate to think of you going back to stand around on that cold corner where it says Massage Parlor."

To this, too, any reply would have been playing his game.

He chose to understand that she was eager to return, to the street of others grosser and more potent than he. You whore. You poor homely whore. You don't love me, I don't love you. "What do you do in the day?" he asked.

That she answered was startling, as was the answer. "Take care of my kid."

"You have a kid?" His sense of her underwent a revolution. Those small hard nipples had given milk; that brisk cunt had lent passage to a baby's head.

She nodded. The climate around her was exactly that as when she had answered, "Twenty-two." A central fact had been taken from her. Of the many possible questions, the one he asked, with stupid solicitude, was, "Who's taking care of it now?"

"A babysitter," Ann said.

What color was the babysitter? What color was the child? What about its future schooling? When are you going back to the library? How do you get out of this? How do I? He said, "Your money. We got to get you your money."

He went to his pants and picked the wallet from them too swiftly; the thin wedge of a hangover headache was inserted with the motion. "Thirty," he said, counting off tens to steady himself, "and then thirty more for staying the hour, and twenty for the Frenching. Right? And then let's add ten for the babysitter. Ninety. O.K.?" Handing her the bills, he inspected her smile; it was not as wide as the smile she had brought forward from the doorway. An extra ten might have widened it, but he held it back, and instead said, to win her denial, "Sorry I was such a difficult customer."

She considered her answer deliberately; she was not an easy grader. "You weren't a difficult customer, Ed. I've had lots worse, believe me. Lots worse." Her lingering on this thought felt irritatingly like a request for pity.

"Pass with push, huh?" he said.

The joke didn't seem to register; perhaps by the time she had gone to high school the phrase had disappeared. She lifted her skirt and tucked the folded bills into one of her boots. Her boots were her bank, no wonder she wouldn't remove them. Still, by keeping them on, she had held a potential beauty in him—in him and her together, naked—prisoner. "I hate thinking," he said, "of you walking down that long corridor all by yourself."

"I'll be all right, Ed." Her saying his false name had become a nagging. As she put on her heavy all-concealing coat, her movements seemed slowed by the clinging belief that he would relent and ask her to spend the night.

Naked, he dodged by her to the door. Her coat as he passed breathed the chill of outdoors onto his skin. "O.K., Ann. Here we go. Thank you very much. You're great."

She said nothing, merely tensed—her long nose wax-white, her eyelids the color of crème de menthe—in expectation of his opening the door. As he reached for the knob, his hand appeared to him a miracle, an intricate marvel of bone and muscle and animating spirit. An abyss of loss seemed disclosed in the wonder of such anatomy. Her body, breathless and proximate, participated in the wonder; yet he could not think, anxious to sleep and seal himself in, of anything further to do but dismiss this body, this person.

The turn and click of the knob came like the snap of a bone breaking. He opened the door enough to test the emptiness of the corridor, but while he was still testing she pushed past him and into the hall. "Hey," he said. "Good-bye." Forgive me, help me, worship me, shelter me, forget me, carry me with you into the street.

Ann turned in surprise, recalled to duty. She whispered, from afar, " 'Bye," and gave him half of her slash of a smile, the half not turned to the future. With that triggered quickness of hers she turned the corner and was gone. Her steps made no retreating sound on the hotel carpet.

Ed closed the door. He put across the safety chain. He took the prophylactic from the ashtray into the bathroom, where he filled it full of water, to see if it leaked. The rubber held, though it swelled to a vanilla balloon in which water wobbled like life eager within a placenta. Good girl. A fair dealer. She had not given him venereal disease.

What she had given him, delicately, was death. She had made sex finite. Always, until now, it had been too much, bigger than all system, an empyrean as absolute as those first boyish orgasms, when his hand would make his soul pass through a bliss dense as an ingot of gold. Now at last, at forty, he saw through it, into the spaces between the stars. He emptied the condom of water and brought it with him out of the bathroom and in the morning found it, dry as a husk, where he had set it, on the bureau top among the other Christmas presents.

Separating

THE DAY was fair. Brilliant. All that June the weather had
mocked the Maples' internal misery with solid sunlight—
golden shafts and cascades of green in which their conversations had wormed unseeing, their sad murmuring selves
the only stain in Nature. Usually by this time of the year
they had acquired tans; but when they met their elder
daughter's plane on her return from a year in England
they were almost as pale as she, though Judith was too
dazzled by the sunny opulent jumble of her native land
to notice. They did not spoil her homecoming by telling
her immediately. Wait a few days, let her recover from
jet lag, had been one of their formulations, in that string
of gray dialogues—over coffee, over cocktails, over Coin-
treau—that had shaped the strategy of their dissolution,
while the earth performed its annual stunt of renewal
unnoticed beyond their closed windows. Richard had
thought to leave at Easter; Joan had insisted they wait until the four children were at last assembled, with all exams
passed and ceremonies attended, and the bauble of sum-

mer to console them. So he had drudged away, in love, in dread, repairing screens, getting the mowers sharpened, rolling and patching their new tennis court.

The court, clay, had come through its first winter pitted and windswept bare of redcoat. Years ago the Maples had observed how often, among their friends, divorce followed a dramatic home improvement, as if the marriage were making one last effort to live; their own worst crisis had come amid the plaster dust and exposed plumbing of a kitchen renovation. Yet, a summer ago, as canary-yellow bulldozers gaily churned a grassy, daisy-dotted knoll into a muddy plateau, and a crew of pigtailed young men raked and tamped clay into a plane, this transformation did not strike them as ominous, but festive in its impudence; their marriage could rend the earth for fun. The next spring, waking each day at dawn to a sliding sensation as if the bed were being tipped, Richard found the barren tennis court —its net and tapes still rolled in the barn—an environment congruous with his mood of purposeful desolation, and the crumbling of handfuls of clay into cracks and holes (dogs had frolicked on the court in a thaw; rivulets had eroded trenches) an activity suitably elemental and interminable. In his sealed heart he hoped the day would never come.

Now it was here. A Friday. Judith was re-acclimated; all four children were assembled, before jobs and camps and visits again scattered them. Joan thought they should be told one by one. Richard was for making an announcement at the table. She said, "I think just making an announcement is a cop-out. They'll start quarrelling and playing to each other instead of focusing. They're each individuals, you know, not just some corporate obstacle to your freedom."

"O.K., O.K. I agree." Joan's plan was exact. That evening, they were giving Judith a belated welcome-home dinner, of lobster and champagne. Then, the party over, they, the two of them, who nineteen years before would push her in a baby carriage along Fifth Avenue to Washington Square, were to walk her out of the house, to the bridge across the salt creek, and tell her, swearing her to secrecy. Then Richard Jr., who was going directly from work to a rock concert in Boston, would be told, either late when he returned on the train or early Saturday morning before he went off to his job; he was seventeen and employed as one of a golf-course maintenance crew. Then the two younger children, John and Margaret, could, as the morning wore on, be informed.

"Mopped up, as it were," Richard said.

"Do you have any better plan? That leaves you the rest of Saturday to answer any questions, pack, and make your wonderful departure."

"No," he said, meaning he had no better plan, and agreed to hers, though to him it showed an edge of false order, a hidden plea for control, like Joan's long chore lists and financial accountings and, in the days when he first knew her, her too-copious lecture notes. Her plan turned one hurdle for him into four—four knife-sharp walls, each with a sheer blind drop on the other side.

All spring he had moved through a world of insides and outsides, of barriers and partitions. He and Joan stood as a thin barrier between the children and the truth. Each moment was a partition, with the past on one side and the future on the other, a future containing this unthinkable *now*. Beyond four knifelike walls a new life for him waited vaguely. His skull cupped a secret, a white face, a face both frightened and soothing, both strange and known, that he wanted to shield from tears, which he felt all about him, solid as the sunlight. So haunted, he had become obsessed with battening down the house against his absence, replacing screens and sash cords, hinges and latches—a Houdini making things snug before his escape.

The lock. He had still to replace a lock on one of the doors of the screened porch. The task, like most such, proved more difficult than he had imagined. The old lock, aluminum frozen by corrosion, had been deliberately rendered obsolete by manufacturers. Three hardware stores had nothing that even approximately matched the mortised hole its removal (surprisingly easy) left. Another hole had to be gouged, with bits too small and saws too big, and the old hole fitted with a block of wood— the chisels dull, the saw rusty, his fingers thick with lack of sleep. The sun poured down, beyond the porch, on a world of neglect. The bushes already needed pruning, the windward side of the house was shedding flakes of paint, rain would get in when he was gone, insects, rot, death. His family, all those he would lose, filtered through the edges of his awareness as he struggled with screw holes, splinters, opaque instructions, minutiae of metal.

Judith sat on the porch, a princess returned from exile. She regaled them with stories of fuel shortages, of bomb scares in the Underground, of Pakistani workmen loudly lusting after her as she walked past on her way to dance school. Joan came and went, in and out of the house, calmer than she should have been, praising his struggles with the lock as if this were one more and not the last of their long succession of shared chores. The younger of his sons for a few minutes held the rickety screen door while his father clumsily hammered and chiseled, each blow a kind of sob in Richard's ears. His younger daughter, having been at a slumber party, slept on the porch hammock through all the noise—heavy and pink, trusting and forsaken. Time, like the sunlight, continued relentlessly; the sunlight slowly slanted. Today was one of the longest days. The lock clicked, worked. He was through. He had a drink; he drank it on the porch, listening to his daughter. "It was so sweet," she was saying, "during the worst of it, how all the butchers and bakery shops kept open by candlelight. They're all so plucky and cute. From the papers, things sounded so much worse here—people shooting people in gas lines, and everybody freezing."

Richard asked her, "Do you still want to live in England forever?" *Forever*: the concept, now a reality upon him, pressed and scratched at the back of his throat.

"No," Judith confessed, turning her oval face to him, its eyes still childishly far apart, but the lips set as over something succulent and satisfactory. "I was anxious to come home. I'm an American." She was a woman. They had raised her; he and Joan had endured together to raise her, alone of the four. The others had still some raising left in them. Yet it was the thought of telling Judith—the image of her, their first baby, walking between them arm in arm to the bridge—that broke him. The partition between his face and the tears broke. Richard sat down to the celebratory meal with the back of his throat aching; the champagne, the lobster seemed phases of sunshine; he saw them and tasted them through tears. He blinked, swallowed, croakily joked about hay fever. The tears would not stop leaking through; they came not through a hole that could be plugged but through a permeable spot in a membrane, steadily, purely, endlessly, fruitfully. They became, his tears, a shield for himself against these others—their faces, the fact of their assembly, a last time as innocents, at a table where he sat the last time as head. Tears dropped from his nose as he broke the lobster's back; salt flavored his champagne as he sipped it; the raw clench at the back of his throat was delicious. He could not help himself.

His children tried to ignore his tears. Judith, on his right, lit a cigarette, gazed upward in the direction of her too energetic, too sophisticated exhalation; on her other side, John earnestly bent his face to the extraction of the last morsels—legs, tail segments—from the scarlet corpse. Joan, at the opposite end of the table, glanced at him surprised, her reproach displaced by a quick grimace, of forgiveness, or of salute to his superior gift of strategy. Between them, Margaret, no longer called Bean, thirteen and large for her age, gazed from the other side of his pane of tears as if into a shopwindow at something she coveted—at her father, a crystalline heap of splinters and memories. It was not she, however, but John who, in the kitchen, as they cleared the plates and carapaces away, asked Joan the question: *"Why is Daddy crying?"*

Richard heard the question but not the murmured answer. Then he heard Bean cry, "Oh, no-oh!"—the faintly dramatized exclamation of one who had long expected it.

John returned to the table carrying a bowl of salad. He nodded tersely at his father and his lips shaped the conspiratorial words "She told."

"Told what?" Richard asked aloud, insanely.

The boy sat down as if to rebuke his father's distraction with the example of his own good manners. He said quietly, "The separation."

Joan and Margaret returned; the child, in Richard's twisted vision, seemed diminished in size, and relieved,

relieved to have had the bogieman at last proved real. He called out to her—the distances at the table had grown immense—"You knew, you always knew," but the clenching at the back of his throat prevented him from making sense of it. From afar he heard Joan talking, levelly, sensibly, reciting what they had prepared: it was a separation for the summer, an experiment. She and Daddy both agreed it would be good for them; they needed space and time to think; they liked each other but did not make each other happy enough, somehow.

Judith, imitating her mother's factual tone, but in her youth off-key, too cool, said, "I think it's silly. You should either live together or get divorced."

Richard's crying, like a wave that has crested and crashed, had become tumultuous; but it was overtopped by another tumult, for John, who had been so reserved, now grew larger and larger at the table. Perhaps his younger sister's being credited with knowing set him off. "Why didn't you *tell* us?" he asked, in a large round voice quite unlike his own. "You should have *told* us you weren't getting along."

Richard was startled into attempting to force words through his tears. "We *do* get along, that's the trouble, so it doesn't show even to us—" *That we do not love each other* was the rest of the sentence; he couldn't finish it.

Joan finished for him, in her style. "And we've always, *especially*, loved our children."

John was not mollified. "What do you care about *us*?" he boomed. "We're just little things you *had*." His sisters' laughing forced a laugh from him, which he turned hard and parodistic: "Ha ha *ha*." Richard and Joan realized simultaneously that the child was drunk, on Judith's homecoming champagne. Feeling bound to keep the center of the stage, John took a cigarette from Judith's pack, poked it into his mouth, let it hang from his lower lip, and squinted like a gangster.

"You're not little things we had," Richard called to him. "You're the whole point. But you're grown. Or almost."

The boy was lighting matches. Instead of holding them to his cigarette (for they had never seen him smoke; being "good" had been his way of setting himself apart), he held them to his mother's face, closer and closer, for her to blow out. Then he lit the whole folder—a hiss and then a torch, held against his mother's face. Prismed by tears, the flame filled Richard's vision; he didn't know how it was extinguished. He heard Margaret say, "Oh stop showing off," and saw John, in response, break the cigarette in two and put the halves entirely into his mouth and chew, sticking out his tongue to display the shreds to his sister.

Joan talked to him, reasoning—a fountain of reason, unintelligible. "Talked about it for years . . . our children must help us . . . Daddy and I both want . . ." As the boy listened, he carefully wadded a paper napkin into the leaves of his salad, fashioned a ball of paper and lettuce, and popped it into his mouth, looking around the table for the expected laughter. None came. Judith said, "Be mature," and dismissed a plume of smoke.

Richard got up from this stifling table and led the boy outside. Though the house was in twilight, the outdoors still brimmed with light, the lovely waste light of high summer. Both laughing, he supervised John's spitting out the lettuce and paper and tobacco into the pachysandra. He took him by the hand—a square gritty hand, but for its softness a man's. Yet, it held on. They ran together up into the field, past the tennis court. The raw banking left by the bulldozers was dotted with daisies. Past the court and a flat stretch where they used to play family baseball stood a soft green rise glorious in the sun, each weed and species of grass distinct as illumination on parchment. "I'm sorry, so sorry," Richard cried. "You were the only one who ever tried to help me with all the goddam jobs around this place."

Sobbing, safe within his tears and the champagne, John explained, "It's not just the separation, it's the whole crummy year, I *hate* that school, you can't make any friends, the history teacher's a scud."

They sat on the crest of the rise, shaking and warm from their tears but easier in their voices, and Richard tried to focus on the child's sad year—the weekdays long with homework, the weekends spent in his room with model airplanes, while his parents murmured down below, nursing their separation. How selfish, how blind, Richard thought; his eyes felt scoured. He told his son, "We'll think about getting you transferred. Life's too short to be miserable."

They had said what they could, but did not want the moment to heal, and talked on, about the school, about the tennis court, whether it would ever again be as good as it had been that first summer. They walked to inspect it and pressed a few more tapes more firmly down. A little stiltedly, perhaps trying now to make too much of the moment, Richard led the boy to the spot in the field where the view was best, of the metallic blue river, the emerald marsh, the scattered islands velvety with shadow in the low light, the white bits of beach far away. "See," he said. "It goes on being beautiful. It'll be here tomorrow."

"I know," John answered, impatiently. The moment had closed.

Back in the house, the others had opened some white wine, the champagne being drunk, and still sat at the table, the three females, gossiping. Where Joan sat had become the head. She turned, showing him a tearless face, and asked, "All right?"

"We're fine," he said, resenting it, though relieved, that the party went on without him.

In bed she explained, "I couldn't cry I guess because I cried so much all spring. It really wasn't fair. It's your idea, and you made it look as though I was kicking you out."

"I'm sorry," he said. "I couldn't stop. I wanted to but couldn't."

"You *didn't* want to. You loved it. You were having your way, making a general announcement."

"I love having it over," he admitted. "God, those kids were great. So brave and funny." John, returned to the house, had settled to a model airplane in his room, and kept shouting down to them, "I'm O.K. No sweat." "And the way," Richard went on, cozy in his relief, "they never questioned the reasons we gave. No thought of a third person. Not even Judith."

"That *was* touching," Joan said.

He gave her a hug. "You were great too. Very reassuring to everybody. Thank you." Guiltily, he realized he did not feel separated.

"You still have Dickie to do," she told him. These words set before him a black mountain in the darkness; its cold breath, its near weight affected his chest. Of the four children, his elder son was most nearly his conscience.

: 125 :

Joan did not need to add, "That's one piece of your dirty work I won't do for you."

"I know. I'll do it. You go to sleep."

Within minutes, her breathing slowed, became oblivious and deep. It was quarter to midnight. Dickie's train from the concert would come in at one-fourteen. Richard set the alarm for one. He had slept atrociously for weeks. But whenever he closed his lids some glimpse of the last hours scorched them—Judith exhaling toward the ceiling in a kind of aversion, Bean's mute staring, the sunstruck growth in the field where he and John had rested. The mountain before him moved closer, moved within him; he was huge, momentous. The ache at the back of his throat felt stale. His wife slept as if slain beside him. When, exasperated by his hot lids, his crowded heart, he rose from bed and dressed, she awoke enough to turn over. He told her then, "Joan, if I could undo it all, I would."

"Where would you begin?" she asked. There was no place. Giving him courage, she was always giving him courage. He put on shoes without socks in the dark. The children were breathing in their rooms, the downstairs was hollow. In their confusion they had left lights burning. He turned off all but one, the kitchen overhead. The car started. He had hoped it wouldn't. He met only moonlight on the road; it seemed a diaphanous companion, flickering in the leaves along the roadside, haunting his rearview mirror like a pursuer, melting under his headlights. The center of town, not quite deserted, was eerie at this hour. A young cop in uniform kept company with a gang of T-shirted kids on the steps of the bank. Across from the railroad station, several bars kept open. Customers, mostly young, passed in and out of the warm night, savoring summer's novelty. Voices shouted from cars as they passed; an immense conversation seemed in progress. Richard parked and in his weariness put his head on the passenger seat, out of the commotion and wheeling lights. It was as when, in the movies, an assassin grimly carries his mission through the jostle of a carnival—except the movies cannot show the precipitous, palpable slope you cling to within. You cannot climb back down; you can only fall. The synthetic fabric of the car seat, warmed by his cheek, confided to him an ancient, distant scent of vanilla.

A train whistle caused him to lift his head. It was on time; he had hoped it would be late. The slender draw-gates descended. The bell of approach tingled happily. The great metal body, horizontally fluted, rocked to a stop, and sleepy teen-agers disembarked, his son among them. Dickie did not show surprise that his father was meeting him at this terrible hour. He sauntered to the car with two friends, both taller than he. He said "Hi" to his father and took the passenger's seat with an exhausted promptness that expressed gratitude. The friends got in the back, and Richard was grateful; a few more minutes' postponement would be won by driving them home.

He asked, "How was the concert?"

"Groovy," one boy said from the back seat.

"It bit," the other said.

"It was O.K.," Dickie said, moderate by nature, so reasonable that in his childhood the unreason of the world had given him headaches, stomach aches, nausea. When the second friend had been dropped off at his dark house, the boy blurted, "Dad, my eyes are killing me with hay fever! I'm out there cutting that mothering grass all day!"

"Do we still have those drops?"

"They didn't do any good last summer."

"They might this." Richard swung a U-turn on the empty street. The drive home took a few minutes. The mountain was here, in his throat. "Richard," he said, and felt the boy, slumped and rubbing his eyes, go tense at his tone, "I didn't come to meet you just to make your life easier. I came because your mother and I have some news for you, and you're a hard man to get ahold of these days. It's sad news."

"That's O.K." The reassurance came out soft, but quick, as if released from the tip of a spring.

Richard had feared that his tears would return and choke him, but the boy's manliness set an example, and his voice issued forth steady and dry. "It's sad news, but it needn't be tragic news, at least for you. It should have no practical effect on your life, though it's bound to have an emotional effect. You'll work at your job, and go back to school in September. Your mother and I are really proud of what you're making of your life; we don't want that to change at all."

"Yeah," the boy said lightly, on the intake of his breath, holding himself up. They turned the corner; the church they went to loomed like a gutted fort. The home of the woman Richard hoped to marry stood across the green. Her bedroom light burned.

"Your mother and I," he said, "have decided to separate. For the summer. Nothing legal, no divorce yet. We want to see how it feels. For some years now, we haven't been doing enough for each other, making each other as happy as we should be. Have you sensed that?"

"No," the boy said. It was an honest, unemotional answer: true or false in a quiz.

Glad for the factual basis, Richard pursued, even garrulously, the details. His apartment across town, his utter accessibility, the split vacation arrangements, the advantages to the children, the added mobility and variety of the summer. Dickie listened, absorbing. "Do the others know?"

"Yes."

"How did they take it?"

"The girls pretty calmly. John flipped out; he shouted and ate a cigarette and made a salad out of his napkin and told us how much he hated school."

His brother chuckled. "He did?"

"Yeah. The school issue was more upsetting for him than Mom and me. He seemed to feel better for having exploded."

"He did?" The repetition was the first sign that he was stunned.

"Yes. Dickie, I want to tell you something. This last hour, waiting for your train to get in, has been about the worst of my life. I hate this. *Hate* it. My father would have died before doing it to me." He felt immensely lighter, saying this. He had dumped the mountain on the boy. They were home. Moving swiftly as a shadow, Dickie was out of the car, through the bright kitchen. Richard called after him, "Want a glass of milk or anything?"

"No thanks."

"Want us to call the course tomorrow and say you're too sick to work?"

"No, that's all right." The answer was faint, delivered at the door to his room; Richard listened for the slam that went with a tantrum. The door closed normally, gently. The sound was sickening.

Joan had sunk into that first deep trough of sleep and was slow to awake. Richard had to repeat, "I told him."

"What did he say?"

"Nothing much. Could you go say goodnight to him? Please."

She left their room, without putting on a bathrobe. He sluggishly changed back into his pajamas and walked down the hall. Dickie was already in bed, Joan was sitting beside him, and the boy's bedside clock radio was murmuring music. When she stood, an inexplicable light—the moon? —outlined her body through the nightie. Richard sat on the warm place she had indented on the child's narrow mattress. He asked him, "Do you want the radio on like that?"

"It always is."

"Doesn't it keep you awake? It would me."

"No."

"Are you sleepy?"

"Yeah."

"Good. Sure you want to get up and go to work? You've had a big night."

"I want to."

Away at school this winter he had learned for the first time that you can go short of sleep and live. As an infant he had slept with an immobile, sweating intensity that had alarmed his babysitters. In adolescence he had often been the first of the four children to go to bed. Even now, he would go slack in the middle of a television show, his sprawled legs hairy and brown. "O.K. Good boy. Dickie, listen. I love you so much, I never knew how much until now. No matter how this works out, I'll always be with you. Really."

Richard bent to kiss an averted face but his son, sinewy, turned and with wet cheeks embraced him and gave him a kiss, on the lips, passionate as a woman's. In his father's ear he moaned one word, the crucial, intelligent word: "Why?"

Why. It was a whistle of wind in a crack, a knife thrust, a window thrown open on emptiness. The white face was gone, the darkness was featureless. Richard had forgotten why.

Augustine's Concubine

To CARTHAGE I *came, where there sang all around me in my ears a cauldron of unholy loves. I loved not yet, yet I loved to love, and out of a deep-seated want, I hated myself for wanting not. I sought that I might love, in love with loving, and safety I hated, and a way without snares.*

She was, in that cauldron of the dark and slim, fair enough to mock, with a Scythian roundness to her face, and in her curious stiff stolidity vulnerable, as the deaf and blind are vulnerable, standing expectant in an agitated room. "Why do you hate me, Aurelius?" she asked him at a party preceding a circus.

"I don't," he answered, through the smoke, through the noise, through the numbness that her presence even then worked upon his heart. "Rather the contrary, as a matter of fact." He was certain she heard this last; she frowned, but it may have been an elbow in her side, a guffaw too close to her ear. She was dressed compactly, in black, intensifying her husband's suit of dark gray, suiting her female smallness, which was not yet slimness, her waist and arms and throat being, though not heavy, rounded, of substance, firm, pale, frontal. She had, he felt, no profile; she seemed always to face him, or to have her back turned, both positions expressive of not hostility (he felt) but of a resolution priorly taken, either to ignore him, or to confront him, he was baffled which. She was, he sensed, *new*, new, that is, to life, in a way not true of himself, youth though he was (*aet.* eighteen), or true of the Carthaginians boiling about them.

"Love your dress," he said, seeing she would make no reply to his confession of the contrary of hatred.

"It's just a dress," she said, with that strange dismissive manner she had, yet staring at him as if a commitment, a dangerous declaration, had been made. They were to proceed by contradiction. Her eyes were of a blue pale to the whiteness of marble, compared with the dark Mediterranean glances that upheld them like the net of a conspiracy, beneath the smoke and laughter and giddying expectation of a circus.

"Absolute black," he said. "Very austere." Again meeting silence from her, he asked, a touch bored and *ergo* reckless, "*Are* you austere?"

She appeared to give the question unnecessarily hard thought, the hand accustomed to holding the cigarette (she had recently given up smoking) jerking impatiently. Her manner, contravening her calm body, was all stabs, discontinuous. "Not austere," she said. "Selective."

"Like me," he said, instantly, with too little thought, automatically teasing his precocious reputation as a rake, her manner having somehow saddened him, sharpened within him his hollow of famine, his hunger for God.

"No," she replied, seeming for the first time pleased to be talking with him, complacent as an infant who has seized, out of the blur of the world, a solid toy, "not like you. The opposite, in fact."

For this space of nine years (from my nineteenth year to my eight-and-twentieth) we lived seduced and seducing, deceived and deceiving, in divers lusts; openly, by sciences which they call liberal; secretly, with a false-named religion; here proud, there superstitious, every where vain!

At their first trysts, the pressure of time, which with his other conquests had excited him to demonstrations of virile dispatch, unaccountably defeated him; her calm pale body, cool and not supple compared to the dark warm bodies he had known, felt to exist in a slower time, and to drag him into it, as a playful swimmer immerses another. What was this numbness? Her simplicity, it crossed his mind, missed some point. She remained complacent through his failures, her infant's smile of seizure undimmed. Her waist was less voluptuously indented than he had expected, her breasts smaller than they appeared when dressed. She offered herself unembarrassed. There was some nuance, of shame perhaps, of sin, that he missed and that afflicted him, in the smiling face of her willingness, with what amounted to loss of leverage. Yet her faith proved justified. She led him to love her with a fury that scourged his young body, that terrified the empty spaces within him.

Strangely, he did not frighten her. She met his lust frontally, amused and aroused, yet also holding within her, companion to her wanton delight, the calm and distance of the condemned.

In those years I had one,—not in that which is called lawful marriage, but whom I had found out in a wayward passion, void of understanding; yet but one, remaining faithful even to her; in whom I in my own case experienced what difference there is betwixt the self-restraint of the marriage-covenant, for the sake of issue, and the bargain of a lustful love, where children are born against their parents' will, although, once born, they constrain love.

Her husband, dark gray shadow, she did not forsake; nor did she, under questioning, reveal that love between them had been abandoned. Rather, she clave to this man, in her placid and factual manner, and gave him what a man might ask; that her lover found this monstrous, she accepted as another incursion, more amusing than not, into this her existence, which she so unambiguously perceived as having been created for love.

"You love him?" However often posed, the question carried its accents of astonishment.

Her hand, small and rounded as a child's, though cleaner, made its impatient stab in air, and an unintended circlet of smoke spun away. She had resumed the habit, her one concession to the stresses of her harlot's life. "We make love."

"And how is it?"

She thought. "Nice."

"Perhaps you were right. I do hate you."

"But he's my husband!"

The word, religious and gray, frightened him. "Is it as it is," he asked, "with me?"

"No. Not at all." Her white eyes stared. Was she sincere?

How often do you do it? In what positions? Are you silent, or do the two of you speak throughout? What do you say? The litany, attempting to banish the mystery of her rounded limbs so simply laid open for another, won from her more tears than answers; it appeared, to this amorous youth whose precocious and epochal intuition it already was to seek truth and truth's Lord not in mathematics nor the consensus of the *polis* but in reverent examination of one's own unique and uniquely configured self, that the details eluded her, she had forgotten, they didn't matter. Incredible! His jealousy would not rest, kept gnawing at this substantial shadow, her husband. He permitted the scandal to become open, and her husband faded a little, out of pride. The man's attentions, sensed through the veil of her, became indifferent, ironical; still her husband lived with her, shared her nights, could touch her at whim, shared the rearing of their children, a sacred sharing. This could not be borne. Aurelius made her pregnant.

And the husband did vanish, with their common goods. The lover and his concubine traveled to Rome, and then to Milan. Their child they called Adeodatus. The name, surprisingly, came from her; it subtly displeased him, that she fancied herself religious.

. . . *time passed on, but I delayed to turn to the Lord; and from day to day deferred to live in Thee, and deferred not daily to die in myself. Loving a happy life, I feared it in its own abode, and sought it, by fleeing from it. I thought I should be too miserable, unless folded in female arms . . .*

Her compliance disturbed him. Her love seemed unreasoning, demonic in its exemption from fatigue. Years after she should have wearied of his body, he would wake and find that in their sleep she had crowded him to the edge of the bed, her indistinct profile at rest in the curve of his armpit. The city's night traffic gleamed and glittered below; travelling torchlight shuddered on the walls. A cry arose, close to them. She would rise and smother the child with her breasts, that the father might sleep. Lying nevertheless awake, he felt her merge with the darkened room, in which there was this unseen horizon, of smallness and limit, of the coolness with which she assumed any position, placated any need, however sordid. Her spirit was too bare, like her face when, each morning, for coolness in the humid Italian heat, she pulled back her hair with both hands to knot it; her face gleamed taut and broad, perspiring, a Scythian moon of a face. She had grown plump in her years of happiness. He remembered her smoking, and wished she would begin again. He wished she would die. The blanched eyes, the blunt nose, the busy plump selfforgetful hands. Her lips, pouting in concentration, were startled to a smile by sudden awareness of his studying her; she would come forward and smother him as if he, too, had been crying. *Concupiscentia.* Its innocence disturbed him, the simplicity of her invitation to descend with her into her nature, into Nature, and to be immersed. Surely such wallowing within Creation was a deflection of higher purposes. Like bubbles, his empty spaces wanted to rise, break into air, and vanish. Their bodies would become one, but his soul was pulled back taut, like the hair at the back of her skull.

Meanwhile my sins were being multiplied, and my concubine being torn from my side as a hindrance to my marriage, my heart which clave unto her was torn and wounded and bleeding. And she returned to Afric, vowing unto Thee never to know any other man, leaving with me my son by her.

She had been, the mother of Adeodatus, strangely calm

in receiving the news, anxious foremost to understand, to avoid misunderstanding; her quest for clarity, which had made her appear rigid, frontal, iconic, brusque at the party more than a decade ago, had tunneled through all their intervening ecstasies. She was in his arms, her face tear-blurred but held back from his, contemplating his naked shoulder as if the truth might rest upon it like a butterfly. "Monica has found you a wife?"

"My mother deems it crucial to my salvation that I marry."

"And the betrothed—?"

"Is two years under the fit age."

"Not fit, but beautiful?" she asked. *De pulchro et apto* had been the title of his first dissertation, composed in Carthage and read aloud to her there. She was illiterate. Since, he had ceased to share his compositions, *De vita beata, De immortalitate animae.* He had felt these subjects as betrayals of her, prefatory to this great betrayal.

"Not beautiful, but sufficiently pleasing," he factually answered, unprepared for the sirocco of her grief. "But not you, not like you," were all the words he could call into her weeping, repeating, "Not like you at all," recognizing, at last, her firmness and smallness so close yet remote in his arms as that of a child, an unformed person. The recognition hardened his heart. His cruelty as he held her heightened him. He saw over her head, where gray hairs had come, scarcely distinguishable, to mingle with the fair, back to the fact that she had had a husband and had accepted that husband and her lover as if they were kindred manifestations of the same force, as if he himself were not incomparable, unique, with truth's Lord within him. For this she was rightly punished. Punished, nay, obliterated, as a heresy is obliterated, while love for the heretic burns in the heart of the condemner. Aurelius grew immortally tall against her grieving; he felt in her, who had so often sobbed in love's convulsion against his body, the benign enemy he was later to find in Pelagius, who held that Adam's sin touched only Adam, that men were born incorrupt, that unbaptized infants did not go to Hell. Such liberal plausibilities poisoned the water of life as it sprang from the stricken rock. So with her softness, her stolid waist and child's small eager hands, the austerity of her dress, the brazen circlets she wore as earrings, the halo of fine white hairs her skin bore everywhere; the sum was ease, and ease was deception, and deception evil. So with her perfect love for him. There was more. There must be more.

Nor was that my wound cured, which had been made by the cutting away of the former, but after inflammation and most acute pain, it mortified, and my pains became less acute, but more desperate.

To Thee be praise, glory to Thee, Fountain of Mercies. I was becoming more miserable, and Thou nearer.

In Africa, the sky never shows a cloud. The heat the desert bestows upon its green shore is severe but not oppressive, unlike that heavy Milanese heat wherein she had pulled back her hair from damp temples. She, too, could taste the dry joy of lightness, of renunciation. She cut off her hair. She forgot her son. Nor would she ever make love again; there was no moderation in what mattered.

Among the women of the cenobium she entered, she moved not as one with a great grief behind her but as one who, like a child, had yet to live. Blue was the color of the order, her color, between Hellenic white and medieval black. *The beautiful and the fitting*: this, the first of Augustine's dissertations, and the only one of which she was the substance, stayed in her memory and conspired, among these whispering gowned women and these sun-dazed walls of clay, to refine that aesthetic of rite and symbol with which half-formed Christianity, amid its renunciations, was to enrich the vocabulary of beauty. Though illiterate, she drew to herself, from these her sisters—the maimed and fanatic and shy—authority. Her limbs, veiled in blue, became emblems. Her complacence, that had never doubted the body's prerogatives, seemed here, in these corridors cloistered from the sun, to manifest Grace. Her shamelessness became serenity. Her placid carriage suggested joy. It was as if her dynamic and egocentric lover, whom she had never failed to satisfy, in his rejection of her had himself failed, and been himself rejected, even as his verbal storms swept the Mediterranean and transformed the world.

She was a saint, whose name we do not know. For a thousand years, men would endeavor to hate the flesh, because of her.

The Man Who Loved
Extinct Mammals

Sapers lived rather shapelessly in a city that shall be nameless. It was at a juncture of his life when he had many ties, none of them binding. Accordingly, he had much loose time, and nothing, somehow, better filled it than the perusal of extinct mammals. Living species gave him asthma, and the dinosaurs had been overdone; but in between lay a marvellous middle world of lumpy, clumping, hairy, milk-giving creatures passed from the face of the earth. They tended to be large: "During these early periods," writes Harvey C. Markman in his pamphlet "Fossil Mammals" (published by the Denver Museum of Natural History), "many of the mammals went in for large size and absurdity." For example, *Barylambda*. It was nearly eight feet long and half as high. It had a short face, broad feet, muscular legs, and a very stout tail. "It combined"—to quote Markman again—"many anatomical peculiarities which together had little survival value. One might say of this race, and other aberrant groups, that they tried to specialize in too many ways and made very little progress in the more essential directions." It was extinct by the end of the Paleocene. "Who could not love such a creature?" Sapers asked himself.

And who is to say what is an "essential direction"?

Barylambda was an amblypod, meaning "blunt foot." This order (or suborder) of ungulates had, Webster's Dictionary told Sapers, "very small smooth brains." The "small" was to be expected, the "smooth" was surprising. It was nice. The man who loved extinct mammals resented the way Markman kept chaffing the amblypods; nothing about them, especially their feet and their teeth, was specialized enough to suit him. One could hear Markman sigh, like the sardonic instructor of a class of dullards, as he wrote, "At least one more family of amblypods must be mentioned: the uintatheres. By late Eocene time some of these grotesque creatures had attained the size of circus elephants. Arranged along the face and forehead they had three pairs of bony protuberances resembling horns. . . ." In the accompanying photograph of a *Uintacolotherium* skull, the bony protuberances looked artful, Arplike. Sapers didn't think them necessarily grotesque, if you tried to view them from the standpoint of the Life Force instead of from ours, the standpoint of Man, with his huge, rough brain. Sapers shut his eyes and tried to imagine the selective process whereby a little bud of a bony protuberance achieved a tiny advantage, an edge, in battle, food-gathering, or mating, that would favor an exaggeration from generation to generation. He almost had it in focus—some kind of Platonic ideal pressing upon the uintathere fetuses, tincturing uintathere milk—when the telephone shrilled near his ear.

It was Mrs. Sapers. Her voice—alive, vulnerable, plaintive, his—arose from some deep past. She told him, not uninterestingly, of her day, her depressions, her difficulties. Their daughter had flunked a math exam. The furnace was acting funny. Men were asking her to go out on dates. One man had held her hand in a movie and her stomach had flipped over. What should she do?

"Be yourself," he advised. "Do what feels natural. Call the furnace man. Tell Dorothy I'll help her with her math when I visit Saturday."

"If I had a gun, some nights I'd shoot myself."

"That's why they have firearms-control laws," he said reassuringly, wondering then why she wasn't reassured.

For she began to cry into the telephone. He tried to follow her reasoning but gathered only the shadowy impression that she loved him, which he felt to be a false impression, from previous field work as her husband. Anyway, what could he do about it now? "Nothing," Mrs. Sapers snapped, adding, "You're grotesque." Then, with that stoic elegance she still possessed, and he still admired, she hung up.

Mammae, he read, are specialized sweat glands. A hair is a specialized scale. When a mammal's body gets too hot, each hair lifts up so the air can reach the skin. The bizarre *Arsinoitherium*, superficially like a rhinoceros but anatomically in a class by itself, may be distantly related to the tiny, furry hyrax found in nooks of Asia and Africa. The sabre-toothed tiger was probably less intelligent than a house cat. Its "knife tooth" (*smilodon*) was developed to prey on other oversize mammals, and couldn't have pinned a rabbit. Rabbits have been around a long time—though nothing as long, of course, as the crocodile and the horseshoe crab. Sapers thought of those sabre teeth, and of the mastodon's low-crowned molars, with the enamel in a single layer on top, that were superseded by the mammoth's high-crowned molars, that never wore out, the enamel distributed in vertical plates, and he tried to picture the halfway tooth, or the evolutionary steps to baleen, and his thoughts wandered pleasantly to the truth that the whale and the bear and Man are late, late models, *arrivistes* in the fossil record. What is there about a bear, that we love him? His flat, archaic feet. The amblypods are coming back. Joy! There was a delicate message Sapers could almost make out, a graffito scratched on the crumbling wall of time. His mistress called, shattering the wall.

She loved him. She told him so. He told her *vice versa,* picturing her young anatomy, her elongate thighs, her small smooth head, its mane, her spine, her swaying walk, and wondering, mightn't his middle-aged body break, attempting to cater to such a miracle? She told him of her day, her boredom, her boring job, her fear that he would go back to his wife.

"Why would I do that?" he asked.

"You think I'm too crass. I get so frightened."

"You're not especially crass," he reassured her. "But you *are* young. I'm old, relatively. In fact, I'm dying. Wouldn't you like to get a nice youngish lover, with a single gristly horn, like a modern-day rhinoceros, one of the few surviving perissodactyls?"

He was offering to divert her, but she kept insisting on her love, his bones crunching at every declaration. Rhinoceroses, he learned when at last she had feasted enough and hung up, had been backed with unguarded enthusiasm by the investment councils of the Life Force. Some species had attained the bulk of several elephants.

There had been running rhinoceroses—"long legged, rather slender bodied"—and amphibious rhinoceroses, neither of them the ancestor of the "true" rhinoceros; that honor belonged to hornless *Trigonias,* with his moderate size, "stocky body," fourteen toes, and "very conservative" (Sapers could hear Markman impatiently sighing) dentition.

What *is* this prejudice in favor of progress? The trouble with his mistress, Saper decided, was that she had too successfully specialized, was too purely a mistress, perfect but fragile, like a horse's leg, which is really half foot, extended and whittled and tipped with one amazing toenail. The little *Eohippus,* in its forest of juicy soft leaves, scuttled like a raccoon; and even *Mesohippus,* though big as a collie, kept three toes of each foot on the ground. *Eohippus,* it seemed to Sapers, was like a furtive little desire that evolves from the shadows of the heart into a great, clattering, unmanageable actuality.

His wife called back. Over the aeons of their living together she had evolved psychic protuberances that penetrated and embraced his mind. "I'm sorry to keep spoiling your wonderful privacy," she said, in such a way that he believed in her solicitude for his privacy even as she sarcastically invaded it, "but I'm at my wit's end." And he believed this too, though also knowing that she could induce desperation in herself as a weapon, a hooked claw, a tusk. Perhaps she shouldn't have added, "I tried to call twice before but the line was busy"; yet this hectoring, too, he took into himself as pathos, her jealousy legitimate and part of her helplessness, all organs evolving in synchrony. She explained that their old pet dog was dying; it couldn't eat and kept tottering off into the woods, and she and their daughter spent hours calling and searching and luring the poor creature back to the house. Should they put the dog into the car and take her to the vet's, to be "put to sleep"?

Sapers asked his wife what their daughter thought.

"I don't know. I'll put her on."

The child was fourteen.

"Hi, Daddy."

"Hi, sweet. Is Josie in much pain?"

"No, she's just like drunk. She stands in the puddle in the driveway and looks at the sky."

"She sounds happy, in a way. Whose idea is it to take her to the vet's?"

"Mommy's."

"And what's your idea?"

"To let Josie do what she wants to do."

"That sounds like my idea too. Why don't you let her just stay in the woods?"

"It's beginning to rain here and she'll get all wet." And the child's voice, so sensible and simple up to this point, generated a catch, tears, premonitions of eternal loss; the gaudy parade of eternal loss was about to turn the corner, cymbals clanging, trombones triumphant, and enter her mind. Keep calm, Sapers told himself. One thing at a time.

He said, "Then put her in the back room with some newspapers and a bowl of water. Talk to her so she doesn't feel lonely. Don't take her to the vet's unless she seems to be in pain. She always gets scared at the vet's."

"O.K. You want to talk any more to Mom?"

"No. Sweetie? I'm sorry I'm not there to help you all."

"That's O.K." Her voice grew indifferent, small and smooth. She was about to hang up.

"Oh, and baby?" Sapers called across the distance.
"Yeah?"
"Don't flub up any more math exams. It drives Mommy wild."

Giant and bizarre mammalian forms persisted well after the advent of Man. The splendid skeleton of an imperial mammoth, *Archidiskodon imperator,* exhibited in the Denver Museum of Natural History, was found associated with a spear point. Neanderthal men neatly stacked, with an obscure religious purpose, skulls of *Ursus spelaeus,* the great cave bear. Even the incredible *Glyptodon,* a hard-shelled mammal the size and shape of a Volkswagen, chugged about the South American pampas a mere ten thousand years ago, plenty late enough to be seen by the wary, brown-faced forebears of the effete Inca kings. Who knows who witnessed the fleeting life of *Stockoceros,* the four-pronged antelope? Of *Syndyoceras,* the deerlike ruminant with two pairs of horns, one pair arising from the middle of its face? Of *Oxydactylus,* the giraffe-camel? Of *Daphoenodon,* the bear-dog? Of *Diceratherium,* the small rhinoceros, or *Dinohyus,* the enormous pig? Again and again, in the annals of these creatures, Sapers found mysterious disappearances, unexplained departures. "By the end of the Pliocene period all American rhinos had become extinct or wandered away to other parts of the world." "After the horse family had been so successful in North America . . . its disappearance from this hemisphere has no ready explanation."

Sapers looked about his apartment. He observed with satisfaction that there was no other living thing in it. No pets, no plants. Such cockroaches as he saw he killed. But for himself, the place had a Proterozoic purity. He breathed easy.

The telephone rang. It was his mother. He asked, "How are you?" and received a detailed answer—chest pains, neuralgia, shortness of breath, numbness in the extremities. "What can I do about it?" he asked.

"You can stop being a mental burden to me," she answered swiftly, with a spryness unseemly, he thought, in one so dilapidated. "You can go back to your loved ones. You can be a good boy."

"I *am* a good boy," he argued. "All I do is sit in my room and read." Such behavior had pleased her once; it failed to do so now. She sighed, like Markman over a uintathere, and slightly changed the subject.

"If I go suddenly," she said, "you must get right down here and guard the antiques. Terrible things happen in the neighborhood now. When Mrs. Peterson went, they backed a truck right up to the door, so the daughter flew in from Omaha to find an empty house. All that Spode, and the corner cupboard with it."

"You won't go suddenly," he heard himself telling her; it sounded like a rebuke, though he had meant it reassuringly.

After a pause, she asked, "Do you ever go to church?"

"Not as often as I should." . . . *no ready explanation.*

"Everybody down here is praying for you," she said.

"Everybody?" *The herds had just wandered away.*

"I slept scarcely an hour last night," his mother said, "thinking about you."

"Please stop," Sapers begged. When the conversation ended, he sat still, thinking, We are all, all of us living, contemporary with the vanishing whale, the Florida manatee, the Bengal tiger, the whooping crane.

The Man Who Loved Extinct Mammals

He felt asthmatic. The pages about extinct mammals suffocated him with their myriad irrelevant, deplorable facts. *Amebelodon,* a "shovel-tusker" found in Nebraska, had a lower jaw six feet long, with two flat teeth sticking straight out. Whereas *Stenomylus* was a dainty little camel. Why is a horse's face long? Because its eyes are making room for the roots of its high-crowned upper grinders. But even *Eohippus,* interestingly, had a diastema. Creodonts, the most primitive of mammalian carnivores, moved on flat, wide-spreading feet; indeed, the whole animal, Sapers had to admit, looked indifferently engineered, compared to cats and dogs. "The insectivores, however, have made very little progress in any direction"—with a sudden light surge of cathexis that shifted his weight in the chair, Sapers loved insectivores; he hugged their shapeless, shameless, fearful archetype to his heart. "Feet and teeth provide us with most of our information about an extinct mammal's mode of existence. . . ." Of course, Sapers thought. They are what hurt.

Problems

1. During the night, *A*, though sleeping with *B*, dreams of *C*. *C* stands at the furthest extremity or (if the image is considered two-dimensionally) the apogee of a curved driveway, perhaps a dream-refraction of the driveway of the house that had once been their shared home. Her figure, though small in the perspective, is vivid, clad in a tomato-red summer dress; her head is thrown back, her hands are on her hips, and her legs have taken a wide, confident stance. She is flaunting herself, perhaps laughing; his impression is of intense female vitality, his emotion is of longing. He awakes troubled. The sleep of *B* beside him is not disturbed; she rests in the certainty that *A* loves her. Indeed, he has left *C* for her, to prove it.

PROBLEM: Which has he more profoundly betrayed, *B* or *C*?

2. *A* lives seven blocks from the Laundromat he favors. He lives 3.8 miles from his psychiatrist, the average time of transit to whom, in thick afternoon traffic, is 22 minutes. The normal session, with allowances for pre- and post-therapy small talk, lasts 55 minutes. The normal wash cycle in the type of top-loader the Laundromat favors runs for 33 minutes. The psychiatrist and the Laundromat are in the same outbound direction.

PROBLEM: Can *A* put his laundry in a washer on the way to his psychiatrist and return without finding his wet clothes stolen?

PROBLEMS FOR EXTRA CREDIT: If the time of the psychiatric appointment is 3 P.M., and a city block is considered to be one-eighth (⅛) of a mile, and if *A* arranges the two purgative operations serially, placing the laundry second, and if, further, the drying cycle purchasable for a quarter (25¢) lasts a quarter of an hour (15 minutes) and the average load requires two such cycles or else is too damp to be carried home without osmotically moistening the chest of the carrier, at what time will *A* be able to pour himself a drink? Round to the nearest minute.

Calculate the time for two drinks.

Calculate the time for three, with a wet chest.

3.   *A* has four children. Two are in college, two attend private school. Annual college expenses amount to $6,300 each, those of private school to $4,700. *A*'s annual income is *n*. Three-sevenths (³⁄₇) of *n* are taken by taxes, federal and state. One-third (⅓) goes to *C*, who is having the driveway improved. Total educational expenses are equivalent to five twenty-firsts (⁵⁄₂₁) of *n*. The cost each week of a psychiatric session is $45, of a Laundromat session $1.10. For purposes of computation, consider these *A*'s only expenses.

PROBLEM: How long can *A* go on like this? Round to the nearest week.

4.   The price of peastone is $13 a cubic yard. A truckload consists of 3¼ cubic yards. *C*'s driveway is 8′ 6″

wide and describes an ellipse of which the foci are two old croquet stakes 31 yards apart. A line perpendicular to a line drawn between the stakes and intersecting this line at midpoint strikes the edge of the driveway in just nine paces, as paced off by the driveway contractor. He is a big man and wears size 12 shoes. The average desirable depth, he says, of peastone in a suburban driveway is one and one-half inches (1½″). Any more, you get troughing; any less, you don't get that delicious crunching sound, like marbles being swished in a coffee can.

In addition to the ellipse there is a straight spur connecting it to Pleasant Avenue. The length of the spur is to the radius of the ellipse as $\sqrt{2}$ is to π.

In addition to the base cost per truckload there is $10.50 an hour for the driver, plus an occasional gratuitous, graciously offered beer, @ $1.80 per six-pack.

PROBLEM: Why is C doing all this?

5. A's psychiatrist thinks he is experiencing growth, measurable in psychic distance attained from C. However, by Tristan's Law appealingness is inversely proportional to attainability. Attainability is somewhat proportional to psychic distance. As a psychic mass M is reduced in apparent size by the perspectives of recession, its gravitational attraction proportionally increases. There exists a curve whereby gravitational attraction overpowers reason, though the apparent source of attraction may be, like the apparent position of all but the nearest stars, an illusion.

PROBLEM: Plot this curve. Find the starlike point where A's brain begins to bend.

HELPFUL HINTS: The "somewhat" above translates to ¾.

Midas's Law: Possession diminishes perception of value, immediately.

6. *B* is beautiful. Clear blue eyes, blue denim miniskirt, dear little blue veins behind her silken knees. *C* is receding rapidly, a tomato-red speck in an untroubled azure. *A*'s four children have all been awarded scholarships. His psychiatrist has moved his couch to walnut-panelled, shag-carpeted quarters above the Laundromat, up just one quick flight of 22 steps. The price of peastone has dropped dramatically, because of the recession. It is a beautiful day, a bright blue Monday.

PROBLEM: Something feels wrong. What is it?

Domestic Life in America

THE WIVES get the houses. It is easier for the lawyers this way, and Fraser's had talked him around on Friday. So Saturday morning, walking down through the field for his weekend visit (Greta, for fear of meeting Jean, let him off at the field's far corner), he saw the place for the first time as one he had no legal part of. A lovely place.

The air was warm for mid-December, and the ground bare, with a glisten of mud at the edges of the road. The white of what had been his house made a brilliant contrast with the green of the pines massed behind it and the blue of the tidal creek beyond. It was a serene and impressive structure from the outside, but the inside was cut up rather awkwardly, and hard to heat, and hard to find a peaceful corner in. The one detail of life there that he would miss was not interior but exterior—the plunge, on a hot summer day, naked, from a boardwalk and float he had built into the only piece of salt water he would ever own. Even at low tide a flat dive would carry him into water over his head, in the center of the channel; from here the surrounding world, of dark clay bank and green marsh grass, would be subtly, marvellously transformed by the low perspective, the world as early life saw it, looming, unpeopled, delicate, strange. Though cars and bicyclists passed on the bridge not far away, Fraser would choose his moment and shuck his city clothes and dive boldly in—his householder's prerogative.

The dogs barked, then at his scolding voice came running to greet him. They thought he still owned them. They had torn up, for the hundredth time, the patch of pachysandra Jean had tried to start under the lilacs by the kitchen door; Fraser bent to replace several of the stones of the little retaining wall he had built here in the hopes of giving an amorphous area order. The dogs, incorrigibly, had chosen this very spot as their favorite for digging and lying and gnawing on the savory cardboard and tin they obtained by spilling the trash cans. Domestic life funnels through certain centers of congestion; the back door was one, where the dogs, the lilacs, and the trash can converged, all but blocking the steps to the back porch, which was cluttered with skis and snow shovels and last summer's flowerpots and rusted garden tools. The door opened between the washer and the dryer, in a side portion of the kitchen. A previous owner had built an unhandy set of shelves over the radiator; on the lowest shelf a cat napped on a nest of drying mittens and gloves. Jean was at the sink, the other cat rubbing around her ankles. She looked over in mock astonishment. "Well, look who's here!"

"Where's everybody?" Fraser asked, keeping his distance. It had been relatively easy to wean himself from kissing her in greeting. Living together, they had seldom kissed; the kissing had come along as part of the separation, when they were still unused to saying hello and goodbye.

"Get *away*," Jean said, to the cat, and with a flip of her foot sent the animal skidding across the linoleum. "Nancy's spent the night with the Harrisons after a dance, and Kenny's out testing his new driver's license. The other two are at college—but you know that, don't you?"

"I pay their bills," Fraser said. "Kenny passed? That's great. Isn't it?"

"It is if he doesn't kill himself. All he talks about is 'cruisin'.' He wants to drive you back into Boston tonight. I told him certainly not."

"Why do you think I'm going back to Boston?"

"My God, haven't you had *enough* of her? Why don't you just move *in*?"

"We thought you couldn't stand it."

"That's right. I couldn't. How smart of you both."

He must work out a different visitation pattern. Less might be more. But some need, in him or them, kept him coming, over and over. The scene of his crime. Fraser hung up his coat, looking a long time for an unburdened hook. Clothes from every stage of his children's growing-up seemed to be still here—ski parkas, peacoats, denim jackets, yellow slickers. He had outfitted an army. "What's the point of my visiting the children if they're never here?" he asked Jean. "The only person I wind up visiting is *you*."

"Pathetic, isn't it? Want a cup of coffee?"

"Love some," he said, though Greta had already given him two cups of her own strong brew. "Any house problems?"

"They fixed the TV for ninety-two dollars. They came and looked at the furnace but it still makes that rattly noise when the thermostat tries to switch it on."

"But the house is warm enough?"

"I suppose," Jean said grudgingly, setting the coffee before him at the kitchen table. For weeks after he left, she had once told him, she had kept pouring two demitasses after dinner, out of habit. Then one night when he was here she had brought in only one cup, out of new habit.

"I'll look at it," Fraser said. "Does Kenny ever work in the basement?" The child had been a budding workman; he had helped build the boardwalk. It had been a happy experience, the boy and he hammering together in the mud and sun, the flat marsh echoing.

"Not often," Jean said. Seeing that this saddened him, she changed the subject. "How are things, uh, *chez elle?*"

"Melancholy," he told her. "Her furnace isn't working very well either. Billy keeps trying to get his father on the phone. He's learned to dial. It's driving her crazy. It makes her feel guilty."

"Well, she should feel guilty," Jean stated; but her voice failed to supply the emphasis the assertion needed. It was an intonation of hers he knew well—her moralistic reflex blunted by his predictable mockery.

"Why?" he said listlessly. "Don't you find even guilt gets boring?" The effort of getting here, of closing Greta's car door and walking down through the field and opening Jean's kitchen door, had left him tired. He pushed up from the table. "I'll check out the cellar. Also I was going to do something about the storm windows in our bedroom—in your bedroom. You put them in all wrong. The damn things are numbered, you know."

"I put them in the best I could." She added defiantly, "I like a cold bedroom."

"So I remember." He regretted saying it; they should be beyond such carping. Placatingly, he asked, "How do you like owning the whole house? Your lawyer tell you?"

"He called, yes. He seemed delighted, I couldn't see why. I didn't mind co-owning it. I trust you."

"Don't. You have a lawyer to trust." Her blithe passivity angered him. "You're a hard woman to please," he told her. "Give you a whole big house with this glorious field and creek, you don't even say thank you."

Jean shrugged. "As you say, I can't put in the storm windows."

While Fraser was struggling with these windows, Kenny returned in the car, making the driveway stones crunch and the dogs scatter. Fraser went downstairs. His son, at sixteen, had become disconcertingly beautiful; beauty was associated in Fraser's mind with fragility and decay, with precarious balance. The boy's face was broad and smooth and his smile was broad, and his hair, grown long, waved out in two wings from a central parting. His eyes, once innocently candid when he looked at his father, had become clever and twinkling and shy. Fraser felt shy with him, too. "How was it?" he asked him.

"Groovy. I made it skid. It's starting to snow."

"Jesus, don't do that. You'll kill yourself."

"Ah, I can handle it." The boy put a bag of groceries on the sink counter; he had become the man of the house.

"Congratulations on passing the test," Fraser told him. "I flunked, the first time."

"The cop was pretty nice. I tried to start with the hand brake on and he didn't write it down. When do we get our Christmas tree?" He asked this more of his mother than of his father.

"He wants to cut one out of the woods," Jean explained to Fraser.

"Sure, why not?" Fraser said. His head was still full of storm-window numbers, of edges that didn't quite fit.

Jean's brow wore its vexed crease. "If he does it this early, it'll be all dried out. I don't want a house full of needles."

"Screw you," Kenny said to her, with the sudden anger that lay close now under his smooth skin. He blushed, and took a more pleading tone. "It's only a week away."

"A week and a half," Fraser interceded. "Why not wait till *next* Saturday? I'll help you then. The others will be back from college."

"I don't need any help."

"He's picked out the tree already," Jean said.

"Well, then let the kid cut it. You can sweep up needles once a year."

"You can both go to hell," Kenny said, and stalked heavily from the room.

Fraser imagined he had seen tears in the boy's eyes. "Why did he say that?" he asked Jean.

"He hates to hear us fight."

"But we *weren't* fighting." He followed Kenny into the living room, expecting a scene in which he would do poorly; he had forfeited his right to moral indignation, and the boy knew it. The unspoken ground note of all his conversations with his children was Fraser's request for forgiveness.

Kenny was stretched out in the blue armchair, smiling and humming and gazing at his driver's license. The license was encased in a rectangle of plastic, and contained a Polaroid mug shot of his face along with his statistics. "It was neat," he told his father, "the way they did it; it was still warm when they handed it to me." He handed the precious rectangle to his father; Fraser was startled by how old the face on it looked, how pugnacious and determined—thuggish, even. "Have you started shaving?" he asked.

The snow continued fitfully all afternoon, scarcely accumulating. Nancy called to say she would be home from the Harrisons' after lunch. Jean served Kenny and Fraser clam chowder and announced she had a date to play indoor tennis. "You're not going to abandon us?" Fraser protested, but off she went in the snow, in her tennis sneakers, with two of his old golf partners and one of their wives. Kenny sideslipped the suggestion that he help with the storm windows and went off again in the car. Fraser visited the furnace, stroked the cats, walked the dogs to the bridge and back. In the house, he examined the books, wondering how he and Jean could ever divide them, except in those instances where they had taken the same courses in college and owned duplicates. There were two identical volumes of collected Yeats side by side; he carried one of them to the sofa. The bigger of the two dogs (until recently there had been three) came and laid his muzzle on Fraser's chest; Fraser found this emotional demand—the warm moist nostril-breath, the golden-brown eyes anxiously alert—so exhausting that he fell asleep. The kitchen door banged and Nancy was home. Still plump at fourteen, but now tall, she had been fasting.

"Dad, I've only had one dish of coleslaw since Thursday."

"Baby, you must eat."

"Why? I think it's a disgusting habit."

"Actually," he confessed sleepily, "you look terrific." Her face, a shade thinner, was shaped like a heart, and red with the cold.

"It's going to storm out," she told him. "Want to carry Penny's stone into the woods before we can't?" Penny had been their first dog, a sweet-tempered golden retriever. She became very old and stiff, and her back arched with pain, yet she didn't know how to die. On one of his visits Fraser had dug her grave, in case she died before the next one, and the dog had come with him into the woods and lain down beside the hole as it enlarged, enjoying the smell of fresh earth, the stir of human activity. At one point he had measured her with the shovel handle, and she had wagged her tail, amused. Still she wouldn't die. The following weekend, they called the vet to the place. Penny had liked the vet, but dreaded his kennels. She held up her foreleg, and he injected a violet fluid. For a second or two she gazed upward for approval, then swooned to the lawn with an astonishing relaxation. As they watched in a ring (Kenny had stayed in the house, listening to records, refusing to watch), her breathing grew more and more shallow. Then she was dead, in the November sun's long shadows. When Fraser lifted the dog, her skin had become a sack for her bones; as he laid her floppy body in the hole he had dug, it appeared to him through his absurd, excessive tears that he was burying a dozen golden summers, his children's childhood and his own blameless prime.

Nancy had found a rock flat on one side and painted it with green touchup paint: "PENNY 1963–1975." Fraser carried it for her. The stone looked momentous and dignified in place, on the snow-dusted earth in the leafless twilit woods, but in summer, he foresaw, it would be overgrown with poison ivy and lost amid sumac. "Want to say a prayer or anything?" he asked Nancy.

The child looked over, to see how much it meant to him, and said, "I guess not."

"We'll put some daffodils there in the spring," he offered.

"You'll still be coming here then?"

"Well, of course."

Jean came home just in time to make supper, having had drinks with her tennis friends. She offered Fraser their gossip, but it was like reading the comic strips in the newspapers around the house; he had lost the continuity. At the table Kenny brought up the Christmas tree again, and they countered with questions about his homework. He swore and left the table. Nancy said to her father, "What a spoiled bastard he's turning out to be. Dad, you ought to hear how he talks to Mom."

Jean said, "All children talk that way now. They say things we never even thought."

" 'The center cannot hold,' " Fraser quoted. " 'Mere'—ten points."

" 'Mere anarchy is loosed upon the world,' " she completed.

Nancy looked from one to the other of them, and the hope in her eyes was like the dog's warm moist muzzle, a weight laid on Fraser's chest.

Jean remembered to bring two cups of coffee. With her he went over the budget she had prepared for her lawyer. Food, clothing, heat, electricity—it all seemed so impoverishing, set down in a list. "What's this thousand dollars for entertainment?" he asked.

"It was his idea. He told me to put something in."

"Don't be so defensive. I don't mind. I just wondered what you envisioned."

"I envision nothing. A big black hole. A trip. Just the snow today made me homesick for the Caribbean. We'll never go to Sint Maarten again together, will we?"

"I don't see how."

"If I agreed to a Haiti divorce, would you go with me?"

"I can't, Jean. Let's talk about this clothing figure. It seems low."

"Who do I need to dress for?"

"I really must go pretty soon."

"When does she expect you?"

"She knows I have dinner with the kids."

"Well, dinner's not over. Want some Chartreuse?"

"Where does the money for Chartreuse come in?"

"Under 'household necessities.' "

Nancy wanted to go back to the Harrisons' for the night, and Kenny offered to take her in the car. "When will you be back?" Fraser asked him.

"Eventually."

"How will I get back to Boston?"

"Mom says you're not going back to Boston."

"Drive very carefully," he said.

"Sure thing," Kenny said. Perhaps, Fraser thought, it was the boy's heavy eyebrows and girlish lashes that gave his eyes that murky, accusatory look.

When the children were gone, and the Chartreuse was drunk, he pleaded, "I must go. Please."

"Who's stopping you?" Jean asked.

Not her, he realized, surprised. The obstacle to leaving was within himself. "I hate leaving you to an empty house."

She shrugged. "I'm used to it. Kenny will be back eventually." This reminded her: "How will you get there, without a car?"

"Walk," he said, rising. He had rediscovered the pleasures of walking; he liked the sensation of being upright, unencumbered, an irreducible unit visiting one or another of the pieces of his life scattered like the treasure of a miser outsmarting thieves.

"I'll go with you part way up the road," Jean said.

Snow kissed their faces in the dark. The dogs came along, thrashing in circles around them. Since the road was slippery, she took his arm. Near the spot at the corner of the field where he had been let off that morning, she halted, under a street light; in the globe of its illumination, flakes of snow fell as in a glass ball that has been inverted. "Here's where the dogs start getting into fights," she said.

"How do we keep them from following?"

"I'll go back. You stand still until I call them." She embraced him, clinging, her lips confused with snowflakes, her body bulky and padded in one of the children's parkas. "Why are you so nice suddenly?" she asked.

"I'm not," Fraser said. When she had put a safe distance between them, he called, "Thanks for a lovely visit. Phone me if Kenny cracks up the car or anything."

She called the dogs, and when they came to her she frisked with them, slapping her thighs with her mittens, skipping as they leaped at her face, receding from the periphery of light, disappearing back to her empty house on the edge of town. Fraser walked on, past smaller and smaller front yards, to the town's center.

Greta was picking mealybugs off her house plants in the kitchen. Fraser stood a minute in the back yard watching her; she had lined the plants up on the counter and was moving along the row, systematically pinching the little invisible pests to death. A cigarette smoldered on the counter, and she picked it up and dragged when each plant was done. He pushed open the door without knocking; her face, startled, then softening in recognition of him, shed the furious abstracted concentration he had spied. He took her into his arms, and the sensation, so soon after holding Jean's padded bulk, of this thinner, younger, discontented body made him so tired that he begged, "Let's go to bed."

"Want a beer first?"

"I'll split one."

"How was your day?" she asked.

"Exhausting. The kids came and went. Mostly went."

"Jean yammer at you?"

"No, she seemed oddly cheery. Frisky, even."

"Oh. You look so hurt. She doesn't mean it."

"How was your day?"

"Lousy, as usual."

"The kids asleep?"

"Of course. Do you know how late it is?"

"What'd you have for dinner?" She expressed her anger with her husband, as they seesawed toward a financial settlement, by cutting dramatic corners in the household budget.

"Oh, cat food as usual."

"Seriously. Don't joke about it. It makes my stomach hurt."

"We had a very nice meal," Greta said, "of hot dogs and bananas."

"Ow." He drank the whole beer while she finished off the mealybugs. In rhythm with her pinching, she said, "That makes me *mad,* the way your children *treat* you. They should stay home, when their father's *good* enough to visit. I'd be so *grate*ful, if Ray would give us any time; but oh, *no*—"

"Different situation," Fraser interrupted. Mention of her husband made him uncomfortable, she spoke with too much heat. He could not imagine himself ever drawing from her the intensity of attention that Ray—his very name burned—even in retreat generated. Fraser stood behind her as she concentrated on the plants. He unpinned her hair. Together they turned off the lights and went to bed; it was as when, tired and dirty from work, Fraser had stripped and given himself to that sustaining element, the water in the center of the channel, which answered every movement of his with a silken resistance and buoyed him above its own black depth.

He awoke, once, to the sound of a match scratching; its flare filled the bedroom to the corners. The digital-clock face said 2:22. "What're you doing?" he asked, irritated.

"Oh, stewing," she said. The cigarette glowed as she dragged.

"What about?"

She named her husband, and Fraser went back to sleep, awaking again to the sound of her sons getting ready for church. Her youngest, Billy, came and sat on the bed and had Fraser tie his Ski-Doo boots. The child, five, in honor of the snowfall had put boots on over his pajamas; when Fraser attempted to point out the incongruity, Billy dimpled and laughed, as if this naked man in his mother's bed were pretending that life isn't made of incongruities.

Billy's twin brothers clattered breakfast together downstairs, having activated the television set in passing, and then upstairs, with many outcries of loss and theft, assembled, piece by piece, their church outfits; Greta also dodged back and forth, gleamingly naked, then in plum-colored bikini underpants, and finally decent in jeans and a ribbed rust jersey retrieved from the scattered laundry and oddly placed closets of this house. Fraser seized a moment when none of them was passing through the bedroom to get back into the clothes he had dropped by the bed. At night he did not feel he was trespassing, the house seemed his to use along with the woman in it; but by day it seemed to belong to others—to the children, to the sunshine, to the neighborhood, to the stream of guilt-free life that encountered, in his presence here, an obstacle it must flow around. At breakfast the twins regarded Fraser politely, without curiosity, like a section of the Sunday paper that was neither funnies nor sports. Greta asked them, with that sharp motherly brightness of hers, "How would you boys like, when you come back from church, to go buy our Christmas tree? Mr. Fraser will help us put it up."

The identical faces greeted the idea with a flush of unthinking enthusiasm, then, considering, faded. In the year past, their world had soured, the idea of Christmas had cooled. "Naw," the slightly blonder of them said. "Why don't you and Billy and Mr. Fraser get it?"

The slightly less blond one said, "I bet Daddy would help put it up if you asked."

Fraser glanced over at Greta; she lit a cigarette and betrayed that she felt rejected only by waving out her match with a single effective snap of her wrist. She and Billy and Fraser did venture out and buy a tree; it was fat and full and symmetrical. Greta's trees always were. The trees he and Jean had acquired, usually at night, at the last minute, had always looked scrawny, with gaps that had to be turned to the wall, only to reveal more gaps.

The twins returned from church and were sent into the attic to bring down the decorations. These heirlooms were elaborate and fragile: oblong balls with ribbed concavities, blown-glass turnip-shapes, linked chains of enamelled tin, a crèche carved small enough to dangle from a twig, four angels of artfully folded and tinted papier mâché. As he handled this precious heritage, Fraser's hands, so clumsily intruding into a web of property and tradition, began to tremble. He felt hopelessly misplaced. And his mood spread to the youngest child; Billy, still in Ski-Doo boots, stood back staring at the tree as if a fragrant ogre, armored in tinsel, had invaded his living room. Fraser stepped back, and tried to face the sudden stranger with him. "What do you think, Billy?" he asked the child conspiratorially.

A twin squirmed under the tree to a socket and the lights winked on. Billy whimpered and fled the room. Greta, chasing him, was unable to dig out the reason for his sulk, and put it down to tiredness. She herself was exhausted, she announced as she fed them all lunch. Billy announced, "I hate the food in this house," and slipped from his chair. As the four others sipped their chicken soup, they could hear him furtively dialling the telephone in the living room. His little voice sounded clear as chimes.

"Hi . . . this is Billy . . . my father there? . . . Daddy? Can you come get me? . . . I don't want to . . . I know . . . O.K." Before Greta could react, the child had hung up. Billy brought a proud, radiant face into the kitchen. "Daddy's going to come over and take me away."

Greta's mouth, hardening to speak, looked parched. "But you were going to visit Donald at *his* house this afternoon!"

Only a little radiance deserted the child's upward gaze. "Couldn't you call him?" he asked, with a lilting slyness that made one of his brothers laugh.

"I suppose," Greta said weakly, and Fraser felt compelled to step in.

"Billy," he said, "you *must* talk to your mother before you call your father like that. Your father may have had other plans, and now Donald's feelings will be hurt. You saw your father yesterday. You can't see your father every day."

Billy didn't take his eyes from his mother's face. "His feelings won't be hurt," he said, in his soft hopeful singsong.

Fraser said to Greta, "Why don't you call Ray and cancel? Talk to him."

"I can't."

"Why not?"

"I'm frightened."

"Come *on*. He'd be relieved. He doesn't want to come all the way over here. You can't let a five-year-old push you around like this."

The cloudiness in her face became a pale, self-absorbed wrath. "Because of me," she said stonily, "Billy has no father."

Fearful of goading her into widening the indictment, Fraser shrugged. "Do what you want. This isn't my house."

Greta lit a cigarette, went to the phone, and talked to Donald's mother. Her manner regained efficiency; Fraser thought she should have apologized more. "I'm so sorry, Billy's been fussy all morning, and . . . I know . . . I don't feel it's up to me to come between him and his father. . . . *Do* give us a rain check. . . . Thank you so much. Good-by-yie." Fraser heard in her signing-off the same chiming, faintly mocking lilt her youngest son had used. While she had been talking, Fraser had put on his coat and gloves.

"I'm sorry," he said. "I thought I'd stay the afternoon, but I can't. I feel too strange. It's not you, it's not us, we're fine, it's just—it." He added as an afterthought, "I don't want to run into Ray."

She rested her face on his overcoat shoulder. "I don't know what else to *do*," she said. "I know I should be firmer, but Billy has such a rotten life now. He goes around asking everybody, 'Are you divorced yet?' "

Fraser laughed obligingly.

"Don't be mad at me," she begged. "I'll get better at it."

"I'm not mad," he said. "I love you. But you and Ray should work out some communications on this, you'll be raising a tyrant otherwise."

She lifted her face; its wrath had become pink in color.

"How can we communicate," she asked, "when the bastard and his lawyer are making me feed his own children cat food!"

"You don't have to feed them cat food," Fraser told her impatiently. "That's neurotic. I'll call you tonight."

"Let me drive you to the station."

"Let me walk. I need the exercise. You have to be here when Ray comes. Talk to him."

"I hide," she said. "I hide in the bathroom." Greta offered this detail knowing it would please him.

Fraser did not walk to the station; he walked back down the road to his old house. It was on his mind that Kenny had wanted to cut a tree from the woods and had received no encouragement, and next year would be too old to care. In his mind's eye he saw the ax slip; the boy's blood gushed onto the fresh snow. Plows had scraped the road not quite clean. A car that seemed Fraser's own appeared around the bend by the field and bore down upon him; perhaps he was hard to see against the pines here. The car, Jean's orange Saab, swerved and skidded to a diagonal halt beyond him, up the hill. Her face was framed in the driver's window, furious. "What are you doing on this road?" she shouted. "Why don't you stay put someplace? You nearly made me wreck the car."

"I thought I might be of some use to the kids before I go back to town," he said, drawing nearer.

"If you want to be so useful why don't you live with us?"

"I can't," Fraser told her. "Has anything happened to Kenny?"

"How did you know? He couldn't do some geometry just now and I couldn't help him and he swore at me and

I told him to call you up at Greta's, I'd be damned if I would."

"Why not? Little Billy calls his father all the time."

"Oh, *screw* little Billy, I don't want to hear about this darling second family of yours."

"They're just people," Fraser said, wondering if he should make a snowball and throw it at her.

She must have read the thought, for her cross expression almost let a smile through. "You're making me late for tennis," she said.

He came up to the car and rested his hand on the ledge of her open window. "How much tennis can you play with those creeps?"

"None of your business," she said. "Go talk to the children." As Jean pulled away, he made a snowball and threw it at the back of her car. By a predictable geometrical curve, it fell short.

Opening the door of the house, he sensed a change, an unfamiliar-familiar, sacred-secular smell. Christmas. In the living room Kenny was lying on the sofa studying his driver's license and a spindly, gappy pine was standing in a bucket of bricks by the piano. "You did it," Fraser accused him. "Without me."

The boy continued smiling at his own image.

"It looks great," Fraser told him. The tree was so sparse and feathery he could look through it to the snowy yard, the monkey swing on the dying elm, and the tidal creek beyond. Only on second look did he see that some ornaments were already attached. Nancy brought in another box of decorations from the attic. "They're mostly broken, Dad," she said cheerfully. They were cheap, fragile balls, bought in five-and-tens here and there over the years, many of them missing the little silver cap that held the hook.

"We'll buy some more," he promised. The box of ornaments contained an ancient cotton clown, in a little jacket of red felt and a conical hat with a cotton tassel; he had made it for his parents' tree long ago. Nancy let him hang it, higher up than she could reach.

Then Fraser settled with the geometry. "Look, Kenny," he said. "If you have two angles of a triangle, you have the third, because you know what they all add up to. To prove similarity, all you need is two angles each. To prove congruity, you need two angles and a side, that gives you the size, or two sides and an angle, if the angle's between them, because, you see"—and here he began to have to draw, and both he and his son began to frown above the book.

Nancy looked from one to the other of them with delight, and said, "You both have the same eyebrows."

Jean eventually returned, and they fed him again, and again there was the Chartreuse, and Jean's head tilted in candlelight with a flirtatious tension he had not seen for twenty years. He excited her, Fraser saw sadly. "Don't make me miss the train," he said.

"Don't be so uptight," she said. "Stay. It's pathetic, to see you so married to that little—poodle."

"I wish," he told her, "you'd been this seductive when I could have used it."

She had trouble finding her boots, and then her gloves, and, sure enough, as the station came in sight the golden train windows were starting to move, like the windows of a house being nudged by an earthquake. "I knew it," he said, "I *knew* it," and could have cried.

"Oh, shut up, what a baby," Jean said. She skidded the car up to the platform with a thud. The Buddliner had failed to accelerate, and Jean, looking in her padded parka like a kind of baggage handler, leaped around and waved the train to a halt. The engineer, a young man with a twirled mustache, leaned down from his window and they exchanged excited courtesies as Fraser slunk to the steps. "So describe this to Greta when she says I'm clingy," Jean said, rejecting his kiss.

As the tracks multiplied near Boston, there were fires burning to keep the switch-points from freezing—struggling flames scattered through the fields of parallel iron as if an army had encamped here, then vanished. The sight consoled him, each fire burning alone, apparently untended yet part of a design of care, of perpetuation. Fraser's face, reflected in the window, eclipsed the glittering rails as the train eased into the station. In the air, his face became a mask. The cold had become bitter. He walked the drab uphill blocks from the station. In his life alone, he welcomed discomfort, as somehow justifying him. The trees in the Common had been festooned with their Christmas strands, but they were unlit. There seemed no life afoot but his, no spark of life but the image cupped in his head of his apartment, his room-and-a-half, its askew rug and unmade bed, its dirty windows and beckoning warmth. Proceeding toward this domestic vision numbly, he crossed the lagoon bridge in the Public Garden, dividing a lunar perfection down the middle. On either side of him, his walking rolled smears of light across the icy whiteness. Above Beacon Hill, in the general direction of his lawyer's, an electric sign announced in alternation, remarkably, 10:01 and 10°. Fraser regretted there was no one with him to help witness this miracle.

Love Song,
for a Moog Synthesizer

SHE WAS GOOD IN BED. She went to church. Her I.Q. was 145. She repeated herself. Nothing fit; it frightened him. Yet Tod wanted to hang on, to hang on to the bits and pieces, which perhaps were not truly pieces but islands, which a little lowering of sea level would reveal to be rises on a sunken continent, peaks of a subaqueous range, secretly one, a world.

He called her Pumpkin, or Princess. She had been a parody of a respectable housewife—active in all causes, tireless in all aspects of housekeeping from fumigation to floor-waxing, an ardent practitioner of the minor arts of the Halloween costumer and the Cub Scout den mother, a beaming, posing, conveniently shaped ornament to her husband at cocktail parties, beach parties, dinner parties, fund-raising parties. Always prim, groomed, proper, perfect.

But there was a clue, which he picked up: she never

listened. Her eyebrows arched politely, her upper lip lifted alertly; nevertheless she brushed her gaze past the faces of her conversational partners in a terrible icy hurry, and repeated herself so much that he wondered if she were sane.

Her heart wasn't in this.

She took to jabbing him at parties, jabbing so hard it hurt. This piece of herself, transferred to his ribs, his kidneys, as pain, lingered there, asked to be recognized as love.

His brain—that impatient organ, which deals, with the speed of light, in essences and abstractions—opted to love her perhaps too early, before his heart—that plodder, that problem-learner—had had time to collect quirks and spiritual snapshots, to survey those faults and ledges of the not-quite-expected where affection can silt and accumulate. He needed a body. Instead there was something skeletal, spacy.

But then the shivering. That was lovable. As they left a fine restaurant in an elegant, shadowy district of the city, Princess complained (her talk was unexpectedly direct) that her underpants kept riding up. Drunk, his drunkenness glazing the bricks of the recently restored pavement beneath them, the marquee of the cunningly renovated restaurant behind them, the other pedestrians scattered around them as sketchily as figures in an architectural drawing, and the artificially antique street lamp above them, its wan light laced by the twigs of a newly planted tree that had also something of an architect's stylization about it, Tod knelt down and reached up into her skirt with both hands and pulled down her underpants, so adroitly she shivered. She shivered, involuntarily, expressing—what? Something that came upon her like a breeze.

Then, recovering poise, with an adroitness the equal of his, she stepped out of her underpants. Her black high heels, shiny as Shirley Temple dancing pumps, stepped from the two silken circles on the bricks—one, two, primly, quickly, as she glanced over her shoulder, to see if they had been seen. She was wearing a black dress, severe, with long sleeves, that he had last seen her wear to a mutual friend's funeral. Tod stood and crumpled his handful of gossamer into his coat pocket. They walked on, her arm in his. He seemed taller, she softer. The stagy light webbed them, made her appear all circles. She said she could feel the wind on her cunt.

He had loved that shiver, that spasm she could not control; for love must attach to what we cannot help—the involuntary, the telltale, the fatal. Otherwise, the reasonableness and the mercy that would make our lives decent and orderly would overpower love, crush it, root it out, tumble it away like a striped tent pegged in sand.

Time passed. By sunlight, by a window, he suddenly saw a web, a radiating system, of wrinkles spread out from the corners of her eyes when she smiled. From her lips another set of creases, so delicate only the sun could trace them, spread upward; the two systems commingled on her cheeks. Time was interconnecting her features, which had been isolated in the spaces of her face by a certain absent-minded perfection. She was growing old within their love, within their suffering. He examined a snapshot he had taken a year ago. A smooth, staring, unlistening face. Baby fat.

Tod liked her ageing, felt warmed by it, for it too was involuntary. It had happened to her with him, yet was not his fault. He wanted nothing to be his fault. This made her load double.

As mistress, she adapted well to the harrowing hours, the phone conversations that never end, the posing for indecent photographs, the heavy restaurant meals. She mainly missed of her former, decent, orderly life the minor blessings, such as shopping in the A. & P. without fear of being snubbed by a fellow-parishioner, or of encountering Tod's outraged wife across a pyramid of dog food.

Their spouses' fixed fury seemed rooted in a kind of professional incredulity; it was as if they had each been specialists (a repairer of Cyrillic typewriters, or a gerbil currier) whose specialty was so narrow there had been no need to do it very well.

But how he loved dancing with Pumpkin! She was so solid on her feet, her weight never on him, however close he held her. She tried to teach him to waltz; her husband having been a dashing, long-legged waltzer. But Tod could not learn: the wrong foot, the foot that had just received his weight, would dart out again, as if permanently appointed Chief Foot, at the start of the new trio of steps; he was a binary computer trying to learn left-handedness from a mirror.

So Tod too had his gaps, his spaces. He could not learn to repeat himself. He could do everything only once.

On a hotel bed, for variety, he sat astride her chest and masturbated her, idly at first, then urgingly, the four fingers of his right hand vying in massage of her electric fur, until her hips began to rock and she came, shivering. He understood that shivering better now. He was the conduit, the open window, by which, on rare occasions, she felt the *ventus Dei*. In the center of her sensuality, she was God's plaything.

And then, in another sort of wind, she would rage, lifted above reason; she would rage in spirals of indignation and frenzy fed from within, her voice high, a hurled stone frozen at the zenith of its arc, a mask of petulance clamped so hard upon her face that the skin around the lips went quite white. Strange little obstructions set her off, details in her arrangements with her husband; it was a fault, a failure, Tod felt, in himself, not to afford her an excuse for such passion. She would stare beyond him, exhausted in the end as if biologically, by the satisfaction of a cycle. It fairly frightened him, such a whirlwind; it blew, and blew itself out, in a region of her where he had never lived. An island, but in a desert. Her lips and eye-whites would look parched afterwards.

Sometimes it occurred to him that not everyone could love this woman. This did not frighten him. It made him feel like a child still young enough to be proud that he has been given a special assignment.

And yet he felt great rest with her. Her body beside his, he would fall in the spaces of her, sink, relax, one of her cool hands held at his chest, and the other, by a physical miracle he never troubled to analyze, lightly clasped above his head, by the hand of his of which the arm was crooked beneath his head as a pillow. How her arm put her hand there, he never could see, for his back was turned, his buttocks nestled in her lap. Sleep would sweep them away simultaneously, like mingled heaps of detritus.

Though in college a Soc. Sci. major, and in adult life a do-gooder, she ceased to read a newspaper. When her husband left, the subscription lapsed. Whereas Tod, sleeping with her, his consciousness diffused among the vast sacred spaces of her oblivion, dreamt of statesmen, of Gerald Ford and Giscard d'Estaing, of the great: John Lennon had a comradely arm about him, and Richard Burton, murmuring with his resonant actor's accent, was seeking marital advice.

Sometimes her storms of anger and her repetitions threatened to drive him away, as the blows in his ribs had offered to do. (Was that why he held her hands, sleeping— a protective clinch?) And he thought of organizing a re- treat from sexuality, a concession of indefensible territory: Kutuzov after Borodino, Thieu before Danang. A mag- nificent simplification.

But then, a hideous emptiness. "O Pumpkin," he would moan in the dark, "never leave me. Never: promise." And the child within him would cringe with a terror for which, when daylight dawned bleak on the scattered realities of their situation, he would silently blame her, and hope to make her pay.

They became superb at being tired with one another. They competed in exhaustion. "Oh, God, Princess, how long can this go on?" Their conversations were so boring. Them. Us. Us and them others. The neighbors, the chil- dren, the children's teachers, the lawyers' wives' invest- ment brokers' children's piano teachers. "It's killing me," she cheerfully admitted. Away from her, he would phone when she was asleep. She would phone in turn when he was napping. Together at last, they would run to the bed, hardened invalids fighting for the fat pillow, for the side by the window, with its light and air. They lay on their rumpled white plinth, surrounded by ashtrays and books, subjects of a cosmic quarantine.

First thing in the morning, Pumpkin would light a cigarette. Next thing, Tod would scold. She wanted to kill herself, to die. He took this as a personal insult. She was killing herself to make him look bad. She told him not to be silly, and inhaled. She had her habits, her limits. She had her abilities and her disabilities. She could not pronounce the word "realtor." She could spread her toes to make a tense little monkey's foot, a foot trying to become a star. He would ask her to do this. Grimacing pridefully, she would oblige, first the right foot, then the left, holding them high off the sheets, the toe tendons white with the effort, her toenails round and bridal as confetti bits. He would laugh, and love, and laugh again. He would ask her to say the word "realtor."

She would refuse. This tiny refusal stunned him. A blow to the heart. They must be perfect, must. He would beg. He had wagered his whole life, his happiness and the happiness of the world around him, on this, this little monkey's stunt she would not do. Just one word. "Realtor."

Still she refused, primly, princesslike; her eyes brushed by his in a terrible icy hurry. He could pronounce "realtor" if he wanted, she chose not to.

She had her severe limitations.

And yet, and yet. One forenoon, unforeseen, he felt her beside him and she was of a piece, his. They were standing somewhere, in a run-down section of the city, themselves tired, looking at nothing, and her presence beside him was like the earth's beneath his feet, continuous, extensive and dry, there by its own rights, unthinkingly assumed to be there. She had become his wife.

From the Journal
of a Leper

Oct. 31. I have long been a potter, a bachelor, and a leper. Leprosy is not exactly what I have, but what in the Bible is called leprosy (see Leviticus 13, Exodus 4:6, Luke 5:12–13) was probably this thing, which has a twisty Greek name it pains me to write. The form of the disease is as follows: spots, plaques, and avalanches of excess skin, manufactured by the dermis through some trifling but persistent error in its metabolic instructions, expand and slowly migrate across the body like lichen on a tombstone. I am silvery, scaly. Puddles of flakes form wherever I rest my flesh. Each morning, I vacuum my bed. My torture is skin deep: there is no pain, not even itching; we lepers live a long time, and are ironically healthy in other respects. Lusty, though we are loathsome to love. Keen-sighted, though we hate to look upon ourselves. The name of the disease, spiritually speaking, is Humiliation.

I have come back from Copley Square, to this basement where I pot. Himmelfahrer was here this morning, and praised my work, touching the glazes and rims in a bliss erotic and financial both. He is my retailer, my link with the world, my nurturing umbilicus. Thanks to him I can crouch unseen in clayey, kiln-lit dimness. His shop is on Newbury Street. Everything there is beautiful, expensive, blemishless; but nothing more so than my ceramics. If the merest pimple of a captured dust mote reveal itself to my caress, I smash the bowl. The vaguest wobble in the banding, and damnation and destruction ensue. He calls me a genius. I call myself a leper. I should have been smashed at birth.

Tomorrow begins my cure. I ventured out for lunch to celebrate this, and to deposit Himmelfahrer's mammoth check. Boston was impeccable in the cold October sunlight, glazed and hardened by summer. The blue skin of the proud new Hancock folly rose sheer and unfractured into a sky of the same blue, mirrored. For a time, the building had shed windows as I shed scales, and with more legal reverberation, but it has been cured, they say. I look toward it still, hoping to see some panes missing, its perfection still vulnerable. The strange yellow insect that cleans its windows is at work. In its lower surfaces Trinity Church, a Venetian fantasy composed of two tones of tawny stones, admires itself, undulating. The Square itself, a cruel slab laid upon Back Bay's heart, is speckled with survivors—the season's last bongo drummer, the last shell-necklace seller, the last saffron frond of Hare Krishna chanters. They glance at me and glance away, pained. My hands and my face mark me. In a month I can wear gloves, but even then my face will shout of disgrace: the livid spots beside my nose, the crumbs in my eyelashes, the scurvy patch skipping along my left cheek, the silver cupped in my ears. A bleary rummy in a flapping overcoat comes up to me and halts his beggar's snarl, gazing at my visage amazed. I give him a handful of coin nonetheless. Light beats on my face mercilessly.

In the shadows of Ken's, I order matzo-ball soup and find it tepid. Still, it is delicious to be out. The waitress is glorious, her arms pure kaolin, her chiselled pout as she scribbles my order a masterpiece of Sèvres *biscuit*. When she bends over, setting my pastrami sandwich before me, I want to hide forever between her cool, perfect, yet flexible breasts. She glances at me and does not know I am a leper. If I bared my arms and chest she would run screaming. A few integuments of wool and synthetic fibre save me from her horror; my enrollment in humanity is so perilous. No wonder I despise and adore my fellow-men —adore them for their normal human plainness, despise them for not detecting and destroying me. My hands would act as betrayers, but while eating I move them constantly, to blur them. Picking the sandwich up, my right hand freezes; I had forgotten how hideous it was. Usually, when I look down, it is covered with clay. It has two garish spots, one large and one small, and in the same relation to one another as Australia and Tasmania. The woman next to me at the counter, a hag in pancake makeup and mink, glances down with me. Involuntarily, she starts. Her fork clatters to the floor. Deftly I pick it up and place it on the Formica between us, so she does not have to touch me. Even so, she asks for another.

Nov. 1.   The doctor whistles when I take off my clothes. "Quite a case." But he is sure I will respond. "We have this type of light now." He is from Australia, oddly, but does not linger over the spots on my hand. "First, a few photographs." The floor of his office, I notice, is sprinkled with flakes. There are other lepers. At last, I am not alone. He squints and squats and clicks and clucks. "Good seventy per cent I would say." He has me turn around, and whistles again, more softly. "Then some blood tests, *pro forma*." He explains the treatment. Internal medication straight from the ancient Egyptians will open me like a flower to lengthening doses of artificial light. His own skin bears the dusty-rose ebb of a summer's tan. His scalp is flawlessly bald and dreamily smooth. I wonder what perversity drove him into dermatology. "When you clear," he says casually, toward the end. When I clear! The concept is staggering. I want to swoon, I want to embrace him, as one embraces, in primitive societies, a madman. On his desk there is a tawdry flesh-pink mug with a tea bag in it, and I inwardly vow to make him a perfect teacup if he makes good his promise. "Nasty turn in the weather today," he offers, buttoning up his camera; but it is a lame and somehow bestial business, polite conversation between two men of whom one is dressed and the other is naked. As I drag my clothes on, a shower of silver falls to the floor. He calls it, professionally, "scale." I call it, inwardly, filth.

I told Carlotta tonight of his casual promise to make me "clear." She says she loves me the way I am. "How *can* you!" I blurt. She shrugs. She was late this evening, having been hours at devotions. It is All Saints' Day. We make love. Stroking her buttocks, I think of the doctor's skull.

Nov. 8. First treatment. The "light box" has six sides lined with vertical tubes. A hexagonal prism, as the Hancock Tower is a rhomboidal prism and a Toblerone chocolate bar is a triangular one. A roaring when it switches on, so one has astronautical sensations; also sensations of absurdity, standing nude as in a "daring" play where the stage lights have consumed the audience. The attendant, a tremulous young man with a diabolically pointed beard, gave me goggles to protect my retinas; I look down. I am on fire! In this kiln my feet, my legs, my arms, wherever there are scales, glow with a violet-white intensity like nothing but certain moments of film as it develops in a darkroom pan. To make sure the legs are mine, I do a little dance. The Dance of Shiva, his body smeared with ashes, his hair matted and foul. My legs, chalky as logs about to fall into embers, vibrate and swing in the cleansing fire. The dance is short-lived; the first dose is but a minute. The box has a nasty, rebuking snort when it shuts off.

Dressed, stepping out from behind the curtain, I make future arrangements with the attendant and wonder what has led him into work of this sort. Dealing with people like me is a foul business, I am certain.

Nov. 12. No perceptible change. Carlotta tells me to relax. Dr. Aus (his real name keeps escaping me) says two weeks pass before the first noticeable effects. Himmelfahrer tells me Christmas is coming. I work past midnight on an epic course of vases, rimmed and banded with a very thin slip tinctured with cobalt oxide. The decoration should not strike the appraiser at first glance; he should think first "vase," and then "blue," and then "blue and not-blue." The Chinese knew how to imbue this mystery, this blush in the glaze, this plenitude of nothingness. I scorn incision, sgraffito, wax resist, relief. Smoothness is the essence, the fingers must not be perturbed. The wheel turns. My hand vanishes up past the wrist into the orifice of whistling, whispering clay, confiding the slither of its womb-wall to me, while the previous vase dries.

My dose was two minutes today.

The disease is frightened. Its surface feigns indifference, but deeper it itches with subtle rage, so that I cannot sleep. It has spread across my shoulders, to the insides of my arms, to my fingernails, whitening and warping them with ridges that grow out from beneath the cuticle like buried terrors coming to light.

Nov. 13.   I have been taken off the treatment!

A leper among lepers, doubly untouchable.

Aus says my antibody count is sinisterly high. "A few more tests, to be on the safe side." Tells me stories of other lepers—cardiac patients, claustrophobes, arthritics—who had to be excluded. "Don't want to cure the disease and kill the patient." Please do, I beg him. He tut-tuts, his Commonwealth sanity recoiling from our dark American streak. Tells me that like all lepers I have very naturally "fallen in love with the lights."

I cannot work, I cannot smile.

I know now the box *exists*, that is the torture. It is there, out there, a magical prism in this city of dungeons and coffins and telephone booths. Boston, that honeycomb of hospitals, has a single hexagon of divine nectar, a decompression chamber admitting me to Paradise, and it is locked. I marvel at, in the long history of trapped mankind, the inability of our thoughts to transport bodies, to remove them cell by cell from the burning attic, the sunk submarine. Mine is the ancient prayer, *Deliver me*. Carlotta says that all her prayers are that I be granted the strength and grace to bear my disappointments. A vapid petition, I narrowly refrain from telling her. Confessionals, lavatories, one-room apartments, tellers' booths —they rattle through my mind like dud machine-gun cartridges. I want to be in my light box.

Nov. 15. Blood tests all morning. The nurse drawing the samples from my veins looms comely as the dawn, solid-muscled as a young puma. She handles my horrible arm without comment. I glance down and imagine that the leprosy on its underside shines less brightly. She chatters over my head to a sister nurse of childish things, of downtown movies and horny interns and TV talk shows, her slender jaw ruminating on a wad of chewing gum. In her forgetfulness of me, as I fill vial after vial, her breasts drift in their starched carapace inches from my nose. I want to suck them, to counteract the outward flow of my blood. Yin and Yang, mutually feeding.

Carlotta, coming tonight to console me, finds me almost excessively manly.

Nov. 18. Last night's dreams. I am skiing on a white slope, beneath a white sky. I look down at my feet and they are also white, and my skis are engulfed by the powder. I am exhilarated. Then the dream transfers me to an interior, a ski hut where the white walls merge into the domed ceiling indistinguishably. There is an Eskimo maiden, muscular, brown, naked. I am dressed like a doctor, but more stiffly, in large white cards. I awaken, immensely ashamed.

In the negative print of this dream, I am sitting on a white bowl and my excrement overflows, unstoppably, unwipably, engulfing my feet, my thighs in patches I try to scrape. I awaken and am relieved to be in bed, between clean sheets. Then I look at my arms in the half-light of dawn and an ineluctable horror sweeps over me. This is real. This skin is me, I can't get out.

Himmelfahrer adores my new vases. He fairly danced with anticipation of his profit, stroked their surface—matte white and finely crackled à la early T'ang ware—as if touching something holy. I feel his visits indignantly, as invasions of my cave of dimness. I wear gloves at all times now, save when molding the clay. If I could only wear a mask—ski, African, Halloween—my costume would be impregnable.

3 *a.m.* I was in a dark room. A narrow crack of light marked a doorway. I tiptoed near, seeking escape, and there is no door to open; the light is a long fluorescent tube. I grip it and it is my own phallus.

Nov. 22.   Miracle!

Aus called before nine and said the tests appear normal; the first must have been a lab error. It showed, he confessed, that I was fatally ill with lupus, and that ultraviolet light was pure poison to me. I am reinstated. Come Thursday and *resume.*

Carlotta brings champagne this evening to celebrate, and I am secretly offended. She does *not* love me the way I am, apparently. She shyly asks if I want to give thanks and I coldly reply, "To whom?"

Nov. 25.   The attendant welcomed me back without enthusiasm or acknowledgment of my hiatus. His face pale as candle tallow above the wispy inverted flame of his beard. I scan the remnant of his face left beardless and detect no trace of leprosy. Also, my fellow-lepers, piled like so many overcoats in the tiny anteroom, waiting for their minutes of light, have perfect skin to my eyes. Most are men: squat, swarthy, ostentatiously dapper types—rug or insurance salesmen, their out-of-season tans bespeaking connections in Florida. There is a youngish woman, too. Her skin is so deeply brown her lips look pale by contrast. She sits primly, as before confession. Her plump throat, her tapered fingers, and round wrists betray a sumptuous body—the brown vision of my Eskimo maiden, adipose to withstand the embrace of ice. I follow her in with my eyes, see her feet step out of their shoes beneath the white curtain, and then be disengaged by a naked hand from the silken tangle of fallen tights. Desire fills me. I take my own turn, in an adjacent box, with some impatience, as something my due, like breathing, like walking on unbroken legs. My time is two minutes—where I left off. It seems longer. I fall to counting the tubes, and notice that one is burnt out. I discover, touching it to effect a repair, that all the tubes are touchable, they are not the skin of the sun. I tell the attendant of the malfunctioning tube, and he nods bleakly.

And walking home, through the twilight that comes earlier and earlier, I look up and see that a pane has fallen from my beloved, vexed Hancock Tower. It wasn't in the newspapers.

And Himmelfahrer, his rather abrasive voice close to tears, calls to cry that two of the vases have turned up cracked in his storeroom. In the mood of benevolence that the renewal of my treatment has imbued me with, I volunteer that the flaw may have been in my firing, and we agree to share the loss. He is grateful.

Dec. 7. I am up to eight minutes. Carlotta says that my skin feels different. She confesses that my bumps had become a pattern in her mind, that my shoulders had felt as dry and ragged to her fingers as unplaned lumber, that she had had to steel herself to touch me ardently, fearful that I would hurt. It had startled her, she says, to wake up in the morning and find herself dusted with my flakes. She confides all this lightly, uncomplainingly, but her tone of relaxation implies that a trial for her is past. I had dared dream that I was beautiful, if not in her eyes and to her touch, then in her heart, in the glowing heart of her love. But even there, I see now, I was a leper, loved in one of those acts of inner surmounting that are the pride and the insufferable vanity of the female race. Drunk on wine, I had an urge to pollute her, and I glazed her breasts with an *englobe* of honey, peanut butter, and California Chablis.

In the mirror I see little visible change—just a grudging sort of darkening in those isthmuses of normal skin between the continental daubs of silver and scarlet. The cure is quackery. I am a slave of quackery and crockery. And lechery. I long to see again the lovely female leper, whose ankles, as I remember my glimpse beneath the curtain, bore a feathery hint of scaliness. Papagena. We are all dreadful, but how worse to be a woman, when men have so little capacity for inner surmounting. Yet how correspondingly grateful and ardent to be touched. Yet Papagena is never at the clinic. If there is any pattern in their appointments, it is that no leper sees another more than once.

In the corridors, though, we see cripples and comatose post-operatics being wheeled from the elevator, the dwarfed and the maimed, the drugged and the baffled, the sick and the relatives of the sick, bearing flowers and complaints. The visitors bring into the halls chill whiffs of the city, and a snuffly air of having been wronged; they merge indistinguishably with the sick, and altogether these crowds, lifted by the random hand of misfortune from the streets, make in these overburdened halls a metropolis of their own. A strange, medieval effect of *thronging*. Of Judgment Day and of humanity posing for the panoramic camera disaster carries. Monstrous moving clumps of faces—granular, asymmetrical, earthen.

Dec. 12. Small bowls on the little wheel all week, and some commissioned eggshell cups and saucers. The handles no thicker than a grape tendril. Stacking the kiln a tricky, teetery business. The bisque firing on Tuesday, and then the glaze: feldspar and kaolin for body, frits and colemanite for flux, seven-per-cent zircopax for semiopacity, a touch of nickel oxide for the aloof, timeless gray I visualize. Kiln up to 2250°; Cone No. 6 doffed its tip in the peephole, Cone 5 melted on its side, Cone 7 upright, an impervious soldier at attention in Hell. Turned kiln off at midnight. Eyes smarting, dots dancing. Nicest time to sleep, while kiln cools, the stoneware tucked safe into its fixed extremity of hardness.

In the morning, the gray a touch more urgent, less aloof than I had hoped. Two rims crystallized. Smashed these, then five more of the twenty, favoring the palest. Held the eighth in my mind, remembering my impulse to give a teacup to Dr. Aus. He has kept his promise. The mirror notices a difference, so does Carlotta. I find something crass lately in her needs, her bestowals, her observations. She says my tan is exciting, on my bottom as well, like a man in a blue movie. We used to go to blue movies, the darkest theatres, to hide me; I would marvel at all the unleprous skin.

A strange recurring fantasy: when we spend the night together her skin and mine will melt together, like the glazes of two pots set too close together in the kiln.

Dec. 13. St. Lucy's Day. The saint of dim-sightedness, of the winter dark, Carlotta tells me. My stomach feels queasy—perhaps the mystical Pharaonic pills that compel my skin to interact with the light. Couldn't get going all day. My brain feels soft.

Dec. 16. Aus whistles when I take off my clothes. "Quite an improvement." Yet he scarcely examines me, smiles dismissively when I try to show him the recalcitrant spots, the uneven topography of the healing. "You've forgotten the shape you were in, my friend." It is true. My life up to now has been unreal, a nightmare. He offers to show me the "snaps" he took. I say no. He takes new photographs. I elaborate my sensation that the leprosy, chased from my skin, is fleeing to deeper tissue, and will wait there to be reborn, in more loathsome and devilish form. He scorns this notion. "All you lepers get greedy." A clinical stage, evidently, like anger in the dying. I am *good enough,* his manner states. He accepts the teacup indifferently, with a grazing glance. "My wife'll adore it." My stomach turns. I should have saved out two. It never occurred to me he was married. Did he choose her, I wonder, for her pelt? One of the wonders of our world: the love life of gynecologists, etc.

Dec. 17. When I asked Himmelfahrer how our Beacon Hill patroness liked the cups, he replies she was rapturous. But his manner of relating this is not rapturous. He seems dull, I feel dull. Instead of working the afternoon through, I leave a few pieces to air-dry and walk in the city, parading my passable face, my fair hands. I tend to underdress these days. I have caught cold. I never catch colds.

Dec. 21. The nadir of the year. The faces in Copley Square are winter-thinned and opaque. I miss the thronging, gaudy effect of the hospital halls. Here, on the pavements, the faces drift like newspapers of two days ago, printed in a language we will never take the trouble to learn. Their death masks settle upon their features, the curve toward disintegration implicit in the present fit. I used to love people; they seemed lordly, in permitting me to walk among them, a spy from the scabrous surface of another planet. Now I am aware of loving only the Hancock Tower, which has had its missing pane restored and is again perfect, unoccupied, changeably blue, taking upon itself the insubstantial shapes of clouds, their porcelain gauze, their adamant dreaming. I reflect that all art, all beauty, is reflection. The faces on Boylston Street appear to me sodden, spongy, drenched with time, self-absorbed. The waitress at Ken's, whom I once thought exquisite, seems sullen and doughy. The matzo-ball soup is so tepid I push it away, into the arm of the man next to me at the counter. I wait for him to apologize, and he does. Afterwards, picking the pastrami from between my teeth, I cross Copley Square and look at myself in the Hancock panes. There I am, distorted so that parts of me seem a yard broad and others as narrow as the waist of an hourglass. I look up and the foreshortened height of the structure, along its acute angle, looms like the lifted prow of a ship. I wait for it to topple, and it doesn't.

Carlotta tells me I am less passionate. It is morning. She has just left, leaving behind her a musky afterscent of dissatisfaction.

Dec. 25.   I am beautiful. I keep unwrapping myself to be sure. Even on my shins leprosy has vanished, leaving a fine crackle of dry skin, à la T'ang ware, that bath oil will ease. On my thighs, a faint pink shadow such as a whiff of copper oxide produces in a reduction atmosphere. The skin looks babyish, startled, disarmed: the well-known blankness of health. I feel between my self and my epiderm a gap, a thin space where a wedge of spiritual dissociation could be set. I have a thin headache, from last eve's boozy spat with Carlotta. And a tooth that is shrinking away from its porcelain filling seems to be dying; at least there is a neuralgic soft spot under my cheekbone. Perhaps, too, it hurts me to be alone. The light box is closed for the holiday. Carlotta is spending Christmas in religious retreat with an order of Episcopalian nuns on Louisburg Square.

Notes for a new line of stoneware: bigger, rougher, rude, with granulations and leonine stains of iron oxide.

Dec. 29.   Caressing Carlotta, my fingertips discovered a pimple at the nape of her neck. Taking her to the window, I saw that the skin of her upper chest, stretched taut across the clavicles, was marred by a hundred imperfections—freckles, inflamed follicles, a mole with a hair like a clot of earth supporting the stem of a single dead flower, the red indentations left by the chain of her crucifix, the whitish trace of an old wound or boil, indescribably fine curdlings and mottlings. My hand in contrast bore nothing of the kind; even the ghostly shadow of my Australia-shaped lesion had been smoothed away. We discovered, Carlotta and I, that while examining her shoulders I had lost my readiness for love; nothing we did could will it back. I had wilted like a No. 5 cone. An incident unprecedented in our relationship. She seized the opportunity to exercise her womanly capacity for forgiveness, but I was not gulled, knowing who, at bottom, was to blame. Her spots danced on the insides of my lids.

Jan. 6. Dr. Aus has pronounced me "clear." He, by the way, is going home for a month, during which time I am to be given, like a new car, "maintenance checks." He takes my photographs for his collection, and looks forward to being away. It will be high summer Down Under. "We live on the beaches." I picture him suspended upside down in a parallelepiped of intense white sun, and feel abandoned.

Jan. 11. Carlotta says we should cool it. She has been seeing another man, a lay priest. I have been impotent with her twice since the initial fiasco, but she says that is not it. She will always love me, it is just that a woman needs to be needed, if I can understand. I pretend that I do. A worse blow falls when Himmelfahrer visits. He surveys my new work, pyramids of it, some of it still warm from the kiln, which I have enlarged. He appears disconsolate. He agrees to take only half, and that on consignment. He says it is the slow season. He touches a gargoylish pitcher (the spout a snout, the handle a tail) and observes there has been a change. I say the design is a joke, a fancy. He says he is speaking not of intent but of texture. He says these are good pots but not fanatic, that in today's highly competitive world you got to be fanatic to be even good. He is a heavy gray man, who moves with many leaden sighs. I feel a pang of guilt, knowing that I spend fewer hours than formerly in my studio, preferring to walk out into the city, clad as lightly as the cold allows, immersing myself in mankind and in the snow, which has been falling abundantly. There is a contagion of bliss in a city, in its miasma of digested disaster— the sirens wailing from the rooftops, the unexplained volume of smoke down the block, the blotchy-faced drunk shrieking at phantoms and hawking into the war-memorial urn.

Himmelfahrer apologizes for his own disappointment, and relents. He offers to take this new batch on our former terms if I will revert to my former small scale and muted tone and exquisite finish. I spurn him, of course. I see the plot. He and Carlotta are trying to make me again their own, their toy within the gilded cage of my disease. No more. I am free, as other men. I am whole.

Here Come the Maples

THEY HAD ALWAYS BEEN a lucky couple, and it was just their luck that, as they at last decided to part, the Puritan Commonwealth in which they lived passed a no-fault amendment to its creaking, overworked body of divorce law. By its provisions a joint affidavit had to be filed. It went, "Now come Richard F. and Joan R. Maple and swear under the penalties of perjury that an irretrievable breakdown of the marriage exists." For Richard, reading a copy of the document in his Boston apartment, the wording conjured up a vision of himself and Joan breezing into a party hand in hand while a liveried doorman trumpeted their names and a snow of confetti and champagne bubbles exploded in the room. In the two decades of their marriage, they had gone together to a lot of parties, and always with a touch of excitement, a little hope, a little expectation of something lucky happening.

With the affidavit were enclosed various frightening financial forms and a request for a copy of their marriage license. Though they had lived in New York and London, on islands and farms and for one summer even in a log cabin, they had been married a few subway stops from where Richard now stood, reading his mail. He had not been in the Cambridge City Hall since the morning he had been granted the license, the morning of their wedding. His parents had driven him up from the Connecticut motel where they had all spent the night, on their way from West Virginia; they had risen at six, to get there on time, and for much of the journey he had had his coat over his head, hoping to get back to sleep. He seemed in memory now a sea creature, boneless beneath the jellyfish bell of his own coat, rising helplessly along the coast as the air grew hotter and hotter. It was June, and steamy. When, toward noon, they got to Cambridge, and dragged their bodies and boxes of wedding clothes up the four flights to Joan's apartment, on Avon Street, the bride was taking a bath. Who else was in the apartment Richard could not remember; his recollection of the day was spotty —legible patches on a damp gray blotter. The day had no sky and no clouds, just a fog of shadowless sunlight enveloping the bricks on Brattle Street, and the white spires of Harvard, and the fat cars baking in the tarry streets. He was twenty-one, and Eisenhower was President, and the bride was behind the door, shouting that he mustn't come in, it would be bad luck for him to see her. Someone was in there with her, giggling and splashing. Who? Her sister? Her mother? Richard leaned against the bathroom door, and heard his parents heaving themselves up the stairs behind him, panting but still chattering, and pictured Joan as she was when in the bath, her toes pink, her neck tendrils flattened, her breasts floating and soapy and slick. Then the memory dried up, and the next blot showed her and him side by side, driving together into the shimmering noontime traffic jam of Central Square. She wore a summer dress of sun-faded cotton; he kept his eyes on the traffic, to minimize the bad luck of seeing her before the ceremony. Other couples, he thought at the time, must have arranged to have their papers in order more than two hours before the wedding. But then, no doubt, other grooms didn't travel to the ceremony with their coats over their heads like children hiding from a thunderstorm. Hand in hand, smaller than Hänsel and Gretel in his mind's eye, they ran up the long flight of stairs into a gingerbread-brown archway and disappeared.

Cambridge City Hall, in a changed world, was unchanged. The rounded Richardsonian castle, red sandstone and pink granite, loomed as a gentle giant in its crass neighborhood. Its interior was varnished oak, pale and gleaming. Richard seemed to remember receiving the license downstairs at a grated window with a brass plate, but an arrow on cardboard directed him upward. His knees trembled and his stomach churned at the enormity of what he was doing. He turned a corner. A grandmotherly woman reigned within a spacious, idle territory of green-topped desks and great ledgers in steel racks. "Could I get a c-copy of a marriage license?" he asked her.

"Year?"

"Beg pardon?"

"What is the year of the marriage license, sir?"

"Nineteen fifty-four." Enunciated, the year seemed distant as a star, yet here he was again, feeling not a minute older, and sweating in the same summer heat. Nevertheless, the lady, having taken down the names and the date, had to leave him and go to another chamber of the archives, so far away in truth was the event he wished to undo.

She returned with a limp he hadn't noticed before. The ledger she carried was three feet wide when opened, a sorcerer's tome. She turned the vast pages carefully, as if the chasm of lost life and forsaken time they represented might at a slip leap up and swallow them both. She must once have been a flaming redhead, but her hair had dulled to apricot and had stiffened to permanent curls, lifeless as dried paper. She smiled, a crimpy little smile. "Yes," she said. "Here we are."

And Richard could read, upside down, on a single long red line, Joan's maiden name and his own. Her profession was listed as "Teacher" (she had been an apprentice art teacher; he had forgotten her spattered blue smock, the clayey smell of her fingers, the way she would bicycle to work on even the coldest days) and his own, inferiorly, as "Student." And their given addresses surprised him, in being different—the foyer on Avon Street, the entryway in Winthrop House, forgotten doors opening on the corridor of joint addresses that stretched from then to now. Their signatures— He could not bear to study their signatures, even upside down. At a glance, Joan's seemed firmer, and bluer. "You want one or more copies?"

"One should be enough."

As fussily as if she had not done this thousands of times before, the former redhead, smoothing the paper and repeatedly dipping her antique pen, copied the information onto a standard form.

What else survived of that wedding day? There were a few slides, Richard remembered. A cousin of Joan's had posed the main members of the wedding on the sidewalk outside the church, all gathered around a parking meter. The meter, a slim silvery representative of the municipality, occupies the place of honor in the grouping, with his narrow head and scarlet tongue. Like the meter, the groom is very thin. He blinked simultaneously with the shutter, so the suggestion of a death mask hovers about his face. The dimpled bride's pose, tense and graceful both, has something dancerlike about it, the feet pointed outward on the hot bricks; she might be about to pick up the organdie skirts of her bridal gown and vault herself into a *tour jeté.* The four parents, not yet transmogrified into grandparents, seem dim in the slide, half lost in the fog of light, benevolent and lumpy like the stones of the building in which Richard was shelling out the three-dollar fee for his copy, his anti-license.

Another image was captured by Richard's college roommate, who drove them to their honeymoon cottage in a seaside town an hour south of Cambridge. A croquet set had been left on the porch, and Richard, in one of those stunts he had developed to mask unease, picked up three of the balls and began to juggle. The roommate, perhaps also uneasy, snapped the moment up; the red ball hangs there forever, blurred, in the amber slant of the dying light, while the yellow and green glint in Richard's hands and his face concentrates upward in a slack-jawed ecstasy.

"I have another problem," he told the clerk as she shut the vast ledger and prepared to shoulder it.

"What would that be?" she asked.

"I have an affidavit that should be notarized."

"That wouldn't be my department, sir. First floor, to the left when you get off the elevator, to the right if you use the stairs. The stairs are quicker, if you ask me."

He followed her directions and found a young black

woman at a steel desk that bristled with gold-framed images of fidelity and solidarity and stability, of children and parents, of a somber brown boy in a brown military uniform, of a family laughing by a lakeside; there was even a photograph of a house—an ordinary little ranch house somewhere, with a green lawn. She read Richard's affidavit without comment. He suppressed his urge to beg her pardon. She asked to see his driver's license and compared its face with his. She handed him a pen and set a seal of irrevocability beside his signature. The red ball still hung in the air, somewhere in a box of slides he would never see again, and the luminous hush of the cottage when they were left alone in it still travelled, a capsule of silence, outward to the stars; but what grieved Richard more, wincing as he stepped from the brown archway into the summer glare, was a suspended detail of the wedding. In his daze, his sleepiness, in his wonder at the white creature trembling beside him at the altar, on the edge of his awareness like a rainbow in a fog, he had forgotten to seal the vows with a kiss. Joan had glanced over at him, smiling, expectant; he had smiled back, not remembering. The moment passed, and they hurried down the aisle much as now he hurried, ashamed, down the City Hall stairs to the street and the shelter of the subway.

As the subway racketed through darkness, he read about the forces of nature. A scholarly extract had come in the mail, in the same mail as the affidavit. Before he lived alone, he would have thrown it away without a second look, but now, as he slowly took on the careful habits of a Boston codger, he read every scrap he was sent, and even stooped in the alleys to pick up a muddy fragment of newspaper and scan it for a message. *Thus,* he read, *it was already known in 1935 that the natural world was governed by four kinds of force: in order of increasing strength, they are the gravitational, the weak, the electromagnetic, and the strong.* Reading, he found himself rooting for the weak forces; he identified with them. *Gravitation, though negligible at the microscopic level, begins to predominate with objects on the order of magnitude of a hundred kilometers, like large asteroids; it holds together the moon, the earth, the solar system, the stars, clusters of stars within galaxies, and the galaxies themselves.* To Richard it was as if a faint-hearted team overpowered at the start of the game was surging to triumph in the last, macrocosmic quarter; he inwardly cheered. The subway lurched to a stop at Kendall, and he remembered how, a few days after their wedding, he and Joan took a train north through New Hampshire to summer jobs they had contracted for, as a couple. The train, long since discontinued, had wound its way north along the busy rivers sullied by sawmills and into evergreen mountains where ski lifts stood rusting. The seats had been purple plush, and the train incessantly, gently swayed. Her arms, pale against the plush, showed a pink shadowing of sunburn. Uncertain of how to have a honeymoon, yet certain that they must create memories to last till death did them part, they had played croquet naked, in the little yard that, amid the trees, seemed an eye of grass gazing upward at the sky. She beat him, every game. *The weak force, Richard read, does not appreciably affect the structure of the nucleus before the decay occurs; it is like a flaw in a bell of cast metal which has no effect on the ringing of the bell until it finally causes the bell to fall into pieces.*

The subway car climbed into light, to cross the Charles.

Sailboats tilted on the glitter below. Across the river, Boston's smoke-colored skyscrapers hung like paralyzed fountains. The train had leaned around a bay of a lake and halted at The Weirs, a gritty summer place of ice cream dripped on asphalt, of a candy-apple scent wafted from a shore of childhood. After a wait of hours, they caught the mail boat to the island where they would work. The island was on the far side of Lake Winnipesaukee, with many other islands intervening, and many mail drops necessary. Before each docking, the boat blew its whistle—an immense noise. The Maples had sat on the prow, for the sun and scenery; once there, directly under the whistle, they felt they had to stay. The islands, the water, the mountains beyond the shore did an adagio of shifting perspectives around them and then—each time, astoundingly —the blast of the whistle would flatten their hearts and crush the landscape into a wad of noise; these blows assaulted their young marriage. He both blamed her and wished to beg her forgiveness for what neither of them could control. After each blast, the engine would be cut, the boat would sidle to a rickety dock, and from the dappled soft paths of this or that evergreen island tan children and counsellors in bathing trunks and moccasins would spill forth to receive their mail, their shouts ringing strangely in the deafened ears of the newlyweds. By the time they reached their own island, the Maples were exhausted.

Quantum mechanics and relativity, taken together, are extraordinarily restrictive and they, therefore, provide us with a great logical engine. Richard returned the pamphlet to his pocket and got off at Charles. He walked across the overpass toward the hospital, to see his arthritis man. His bones ached at night. He had friends who were

dying, who were dead; it no longer seemed incredible
that he would follow them. The first time he had visited
this hospital, it had been to court Joan. He had climbed
this same ramp to the glass doors and inquired within,
stammering, for the whereabouts, in this grand maze of
unhealth, of the girl who had sat, with a rubber band
around her ponytail, in the front row of English 162b:
"The English Epic Tradition, Spenser to Tennyson." He
had admired the tilt of the back of her head for three
hours a week all winter. He gathered up courage to talk
in exam period as, together at a library table, they were
mulling over murky photostats of Blake's illustrations to
Paradise Lost. They agreed to meet after the exam and
have a beer. She didn't show. In that amphitheatre of desperately thinking heads, hers was absent. And, having put
The Faerie Queene and *The Idylls of the King* to rest
together, he called her dorm and learned that Joan Ridge-
way had been taken to the hospital. A force of nature
drove him to brave the receptionist and the wrong turns
and the crowd of aunts and other suitors at the foot of the
bed; he found Joan in white, between white sheets, her
hair loose about her shoulders and a plastic tube feeding
something transparent into the underside of her arm. In
later visits, he achieved the right to hold her hand, trussed
though it was with splints and tapes. Platelet deficiency
had been the diagnosis. The complaint had been that she
couldn't stop bleeding. Blushing, she told him how the
doctor and interns had asked her when she had last had
intercourse, and how embarrassing it had been to confess,
in the face of their clinical skepticism, never.

The doctor removed the blood-pressure tourniquet
from Richard's arm and smiled. "Have you been under
any stress lately?"

"I've been getting a divorce."

"Arthritis, as you may know, belongs to a family of complaints with a psychosomatic component."

"All I know is that I wake up at four in the morning and it's very depressing to think I'll never get over this, this pain'll be inside my shoulder for the rest of my life."

"You will. It won't."

"When?"

"When your brain stops sending out punishing signals."

Her hand, in its little cradle of healing apparatus, its warmth unresisting and noncommittal as he held it at her bedside, rested high, nearly at the level of his eyes. On the island, the beds in the log cabin set aside for them were of different heights, and though Joan tried to make them into a double bed, there was a ledge where the mattresses met which either he or she had to cross, amid a discomfort of sheets pulling loose. But the cabin was in the woods and powerful moist scents of pine and fern swept through the screens with the morning chirrup of birds and the evening rustle of animals. There was a rumor there were deer on the island; they crossed the ice in the winter and were trapped when it melted in the spring. Though no one, neither camper nor counsellor, ever saw the deer, the rumor persisted that they were there.

Why then has no one ever seen a quark? Remembering this sentence as he walked along Charles Street toward his apartment, Richard fished in his pockets for the pamphlet on the forces of nature, and came up instead with a new prescription for painkiller, a copy of his marriage license, and the signed affidavit. *Now come. . . .* The pamphlet had got folded into it. He couldn't find the sentence, and instead read, *The theory that the strong force becomes stronger as the quarks are pulled apart is somewhat speculative; but its complement, the idea that the force gets weaker as the quarks are pushed closer to each other, is better established.* Yes, he thought, that had happened. In life there are four forces: love, habit, time, and boredom. Love and habit at short range are immensely powerful, but time, lacking a minus charge, accumulates inexorably, and with its brother boredom levels all. He was dying; that made him cruel. His heart flattened in horror at what he had just done. How could he tell Joan what he had done to their marriage license? The very quarks in the telephone circuits would rebel.

In the forest, there had been a green clearing, an eye of grass, a meadow starred with microcosmic white flowers, and here one dusk the deer had come, the female slightly in advance, the male larger and darker, his rump still in shadow as his mate nosed out the day's last sun, the silhouettes of both outlined by the same light that gilded the meadow grass. A fleet of blank-faced motorcyclists roared by, a rummy waved to Richard from a Laundromat doorway, a girl in a seductive halter gave him a cold eye, the light changed from red to green, and he could not remember if he needed orange juice or bread, doubly annoyed because he could not remember if they had ever really seen the deer, or if he had imagined the memory, conjured it from the longing that it be so.

"I don't remember," Joan said over the phone. "I don't think we did, we just talked about it."

"Wasn't there a kind of clearing beyond the cabin, if you followed the path?"

"We never went that way, it was too buggy."

"A stag and a doe, just as it was getting dark. Don't you remember anything?"

"No. I honestly don't, Richard. How guilty do you want me to feel?"

"Not at all, if it didn't happen. Speaking of nostalgia—"

"Yes?"

"I went up to Cambridge City Hall this afternoon and got a copy of our marriage license."

"Oh dear. How was it?"

"It wasn't bad. The place is remarkably the same. Did we get the license upstairs or downstairs?"

"Downstairs, to the left of the elevator as you go in."

"That's where I got our affidavit notarized. You'll be getting a copy soon; it's a shocking document."

"I did get it, yesterday. What was shocking about it? I thought it was funny, the way it was worded. Here we come, there we go."

"Darley, you're so tough and brave."

"I assume I must be. No?"

"Yes."

Not for the first time in these two years did he feel an eggshell thinness behind which he crouched and which Joan needed only to raise her voice to break. But she declined to break it, either out of ignorance of how thin the shell was, or because she was hatching on its other side, just as, on the other side of that bathroom door, she had been drawing near to marriage at the same rate as he, and with the same regressive impulses. "What I don't understand," she was saying, "are we both supposed to sign the same statement, or do we each sign one, or what? And which one? My lawyer keeps sending me three of everything, and some of them are in blue covers. Are these the important ones or the unimportant ones that I can keep?"

In truth, the lawyers, so adroit in their accustomed adversary world of blame, of suit and countersuit, did seem confused by the no-fault provision. On the very morning of the divorce, Richard's greeted him on the courthouse steps with the possibility that he as plaintiff might be asked to specify what in the marriage had persuaded him of its irretrievable breakdown. "But that's the whole point of no-fault," Joan interposed, "that you don't have to say anything." She had climbed the courthouse steps beside Richard; indeed, they had come in the same car, because one of their children had taken hers.

The proceeding was scheduled for early in the day. Picking her up at a quarter after seven, he had found her standing barefoot on the lawn in the circle of their driveway, up to her ankles in mist and dew. She was holding her high-heeled shoes in her hand. The sight made him laugh. Opening the car door, he said, "So there *are* deer on the island!"

She was too preoccupied to make sense of his allusion. She asked him, "Do you think the judge will mind if I don't wear stockings?"

"Keep your legs behind his bench," he said. He was feeling fluttery, light-headed. He had scarcely slept, though his shoulder had not hurt, for a change. She got into the car, bringing with her her shoes and the grassy smell of dawn. She had always been an early riser, and he a late one. "Thanks for doing this," she said, of the ride, adding, "I guess."

"My pleasure," Richard said. As they drove to court, discussing their cars and their children, he marvelled at how light Joan had become; she sat on the side of his vision as light as a feather, her voice tickling his ear, her familiar intonations and emphases thoroughly musical and half unheard, like the patterns of a concerto that sets us to daydreaming. He no longer blamed her: that was the reason for the lightness. All those years, he had blamed her for everything—for the traffic jam in Central Square, for the blasts of noise on the mail boat, for the difference in the levels of their beds. No longer: he had set her adrift from omnipotence. He had set her free, free from fault. She was to him as Gretel to Hänsel, a kindred creature moving beside him down a path while birds behind them ate the bread crumbs.

Richard's lawyer eyed Joan lugubriously. "I understand that, Mrs. Maple," he said. "But perhaps I should have a word in private with my client."

The lawyers they had chosen were oddly different. Richard's was a big rumpled Irishman, his beige summer suit baggy and his belly straining his shirt, a melancholic and comforting father-type. Joan's was small, natty, and flip; he dressed in checks and talked from the side of his mouth, like a racing tout. Twinkling, chipper even at this sleepy hour, he emerged from behind a pillar in the marble temple of justice and led Joan away. Her head, slightly higher than his, tilted to give him her ear; she dimpled, docile. Richard wondered in amazement, Could this sort of man have been, all these years, the secret type of her desire? His own lawyer, breathing heavily, asked him, "If the judge does ask for a specific cause of the breakdown— and I don't say he will, we're all sailing uncharted waters here—what will you say?"

"I don't know," Richard said. He studied the swirl of marble, like a tiny wave breaking, between his shoe tips. "We had political differences. She used to make me go on peace marches."

"Any physical violence?"

"Not much. Not enough, maybe. You really think he'll ask this sort of thing? Is this no-fault or not?"

"No-fault is a *tabula rasa* in this state. At this point, Dick, it's what we make of it. I don't know what he'll do. We should be prepared."

"Well—aside from the politics, we didn't get along that well sexually."

The air between them thickened; with his own father, too, sex had been a painful topic. His lawyer's breathing became grievously audible. "So you'd be prepared to say there was personal and emotional incompatibility?"

It seemed profoundly untrue, but Richard nodded. "If I have to."

"Good enough." The lawyer put his big hand on Richard's arm and squeezed. His closeness, his breathiness, his air of restless urgency and forced cheer, his old-fashioned suit and the folder of papers tucked under his arm like roster sheets all came into focus: he was a coach, and Richard was about to kick the winning field goal, do the high-difficulty dive, strike out the heart of the batting order with the bases already loaded. Go.

They entered the courtroom two by two. The chamber was chaste and empty; the carved trim was painted forest green. The windows gave on an ancient river blackened by industry. Dead judges gazed down from high on the walls. The two lawyers conferred, leaving Richard and Joan to stand awkwardly apart. He made his "What now?" face at her. She made her "Beats me" face back. "Oyez, oyez," a disembodied voice chanted, and the live judge hurried in, smiling, his robes swinging. He was a little sharp-featured man with a polished pink face; his face declared that he was altogether good, and would never die. He stood and nodded at them. He seated himself. The lawyers went forward to confer in whispers. Richard inertly gravitated toward Joan, the only animate object in the room that did not repel him. "It's a Daumier," she whispered, of the tableau being enacted before them. The lawyers parted. The judge beckoned. He was so clean his smile squeaked. He showed Richard a piece of paper; it was the affidavit. "Is this your signature?" he asked him.

"It is," Richard said.

"And do you believe, as this paper states, that your marriage has suffered an irretrievable breakdown?"

"I do."

The judge turned his face toward Joan. His voice softened a notch. "Is this *your* signature?"

"It is." Her voice was a healing spray, full of tiny rainbows, in the corner of Richard's eye.

"And do you believe that your marriage has suffered an irretrievable breakdown?"

A pause. She did not believe that, Richard knew. She said, "I do."

The judge smiled and wished them both good luck. The lawyers sagged with relief, and a torrent of merry legal chitchat—speculations about the future of no-fault, reminiscences of the old days of Alabama quickies—excluded Joan and Richard. Obsolete at their own ceremony, the Maples stepped back from the bench in unison and stood side by side, uncertain of how to turn, until he at last remembered what to do; he kissed her.

The Fairy Godfathers

"OH, PUMPKIN," Tod would say. "Nobody likes us."

"That's not quite true," she would answer, her lips going cloudy in that way they had when she thought.

They were lovers, so the smallest gesture of hers flooded his attention, making his blood heavy. He knew exactly whom she meant. He objected, "But they're paid to."

"I think they would anyway," she answered, again after thought. She added, "Oz *loves* you."

"He doesn't love me, he just thinks that my self-hatred is slightly excessive."

"He loves you."

Oz was his psychiatrist. Rhadamanthus was hers. Tod had met Rhadamanthus but once, in the grim avocado hall outside his office. Pumpkin had gone in, as usual, flustered and harried, self-doubting and guilty, and had emerged flushed and smoothed and cheerful. Behind her, on this one occasion, loomed a shadow, but a shadow Tod could no more contemplate than he could look directly into the sun. He knew that, via her discourse, he dwelt, session after session, within this shadow, and as he took the man's unenthusiastically offered hand Tod had the strange sensation of reaching out and touching, in a sense, himself.

After her next session, Pumpkin said, "He wondered why you wouldn't look him in the eye."

"I couldn't. He's too wonderful."

"He thinks *you're* wonderful."

"The hell he does."

"He does. He loves what you're doing for me."

"I'm ruining your life."

"He thinks my life was very neurotic and I'm incredibly stupid to grieve the way I do."

"Life is grief," Tod said, tired of this conversation.

"He thinks my life was very neurotic," Pumpkin told him, "and I'm incredibly stupid to grieve."

"She repeats herself," Tod told Oz. Oz rustled in his chair and touched the fingertips of his right hand to his right temple. His every gesture, however small, won Tod's full attention. "That doesn't seem to me so very bad," the psychiatrist said, with the casual power of delivery attainable at only the highest, thinnest altitude of wisdom. It was like golf on the moon; even a chip shot sailed for miles. Oz's smile was a celestial event. "You spend so much of your own energy"—he smiled—"avoiding repeating yourself."

Tod wondered why Oz was so insistently Pumpkin's champion. Through the tangle of his patient's words, Oz seemed to see an ideal Pumpkin glowing. They looked rather alike: broad pale faces, silver hair, eyes the no-color of platinum. Unearthly personalities. Whereas Rhadamanthus, in Tod's sense of him, was subterranean in essence: there was something muddy and hearty and dark and directive about the man. Pumpkin would return from her sessions as from a cave, blinking and reborn. Whereas Tod descended from a session with Oz giddy and aerated, his blood full of bubbles, his brain intoxicated by its refreshed power to fantasize and hope. Oz was, Tod flattered himself, more purely Freudian than Rhadamanthus.

"Oz says," he would say, "I shouldn't mind your repeating yourself."

"Rhadamanthus says," was her answer, "I don't repeat myself. At least he's never noticed it."

"You trust him to hear you the first time," Tod theorized. "He's realer to you than I am. You repeat yourself with me because you doubt that I'm there."

"Where?"

"In the world your head makes. Don't be sad. Freud says I'm not really real to anybody." It was seldom out of Tod's mind that his name in German was the word for death. He had been forty before this had really sunk in.

In those days, their circumstances were reduced. He lived in a room in a city, and she would visit him. From the fourth-floor landing he would look down, having rung the buzzer of admission, and see her hand suddenly alight, like a butterfly in forest depths, on the stair railing far below. As she ascended, there was something sinister and inexorable in the way her hand gripped the bannister in steady upward hops. After the second-floor landing, her entire arm became visible—in fur or tweeds, in cotton sleeve or bare, depending on the season—and at the turn on the third landing she would gaze upward and smile, her face broad and luminous and lunar. She would be coming from a session with Rhadamanthus, and as he embraced her on the fourth-floor landing Tod could feel in the smoothness of her cheeks and the strength of her arms and the cloudy hunger of her lips the recent infusion of the wizard's blessing. She would go into his meagre room and kick off her shoes and tell him of the session.

"He was good," she would say, judiciously, as if each week she tasted a different wine.

"Did he say you should go back to Roger?"

"Of course not. He thinks that would be terribly neurotic. Why do you even ask? You're projecting. *You* want me to go back. Does Oz want me to go back, so you can go back? He hates me."

"He loves you. He says you've done wonders for my masculinity."

"So would weight-lifting."

He paused to laugh, then continued to grope after the shadow of himself that lived in the magic cave of her sessions with Rhadamanthus. He flitted about in there, he felt, as a being semi-sublime, finer even than any of the approbation Pumpkin reported. "He thinks," she would say, wearily, "one of my problems is I've gone from one extreme to the other. You sound just utterly lovely to him, in the way you treat me, your children, Lulu . . ."

The mention of Lulu did bad things to him. "I am *not* utterly lovely," he protested. "I can be quite cruel. Here, I'll show you." And he seized Pumpkin's bare foot as it reposed before him and twisted until she screamed and fell to the floor with a thump.

"I think it was her foot I chose," Tod told Oz the next Tuesday, "rather than twisting her arm or pulling her hair, say, because her feet are especially freighted for me with erotic import. The first time I was vividly conscious of wanting to, you know, *have* her, I had dropped over at their house on a Saturday afternoon to return a set of ratchet wrenches of Roger's I had borrowed, and while I was standing there in the hall she came up from the cellar in bare feet. I thought to myself, Goes into the cellar barefoot—that's great. The only other woman I knew who went barefoot everywhere was my wife. Lulu even plays tennis barefoot, and leaves little toe marks all over the clay. Then, about Pumpkin, at these meetings of the Recorder Society she would wear those dumb sort of wooden sandals that are supposed to be good for your arches, and during the rests of the tenor part I could see underneath the music sheet her little pink toes beating time for the soprano, very fast and fluttery—eighth notes. Soprano parts tend to have eighth notes. And then, the first time we spent the whole night together, coming back from the bathroom, with her still asleep and feeling sort of strange—me, I mean—here she was asleep with this wonderful one foot stuck out from beneath the blankets. She loves to have her toes sucked."

It seemed to Tod that Oz shifted uneasily in his chair; there was a creak that could be leather or a furtive noise of digestion. Tod's weekly appointment came after the lunch hour, and he had a sensation, sometimes, of being engorged by the psychiatrist, of dissolving, attacked by enzymes of analysis. Tod persisted with his pedal theme. "The winter before last, I just remembered, Lulu took the wrong Wellington boots away from the carol sing, and they turned out to be *her* boots, and they were too big for Lulu, which is surprising, since Lulu is taller. *Her* feet, I should say, Lulu's, are quite high-arched, almost like hooves, which is why they leave such marks on the tennis court. When I met her at college, the soles were so tough she could stamp out cigarettes barefoot, as a trick. The third and fourth toes aren't divided all the way down, and she used to hate to have me mention this. Or anything about her feet, for that matter. Yet she never wore shoes if she could help it, and when we'd walk on the beach she'd always admire her own prints in the sand. For the gap where the arch was." Suddenly the theme was exhausted. "What do you make of it?" Tod asked weakly.

Oz sighed. His platinum eyes seemed to be watering. Tod felt that Oz, gazing at him, saw a deep, though fathomable, well of sorrow—sorrow and narcissistic muddle. "It's a paradox," the psychiatrist said, sadly.

Lulu's attitude toward her own feet, he must mean. Tod went on, "After they swapped the right boots back, Pumpkin said to me at a party that Lulu's had pinched, and I had this odd wish to defend Lulu, as if she had been insulted. Even now, I keep wanting to defend Lulu. Against you, for example. I feel you've undermined her, by giving some sort of silent approval to my leaving her. Everybody else is horrified. Everybody else likes Lulu. So do I. She's very likable."

Oz sighed in the special way that signalled the end of a session. "What's that old saying?" he asked, casually. "If the shoe fits . . ."

"What did he say?" Pumpkin asked anxiously, over the telephone. She had had a bad day, of crying children and unpayable bills. Roger was bombarding her with affidavits and depositions.

"Oz attacked Lulu," Tod told her. "He implied she was a shoe I should stop wearing."

"That's not an attack, it's a possibility," Pumpkin said. "I'm not sure you're quite sane, on the subject of Lulu."

"I'm as sane as you are on the subject of Roger."

"I'm quite sane on the subject of Roger. Rhadamanthus says I was all along, only I doubted my own perceptions."

"I've always liked Roger. He's always been very sweet to me."

"That's one of his poses."

"He loaned me his ratchet wrenches."

"You should hear him go on about those ratchet wrenches now. He calls them 'those wretched ratchet wrenches.'"

"Who do you trust more on the subject of Roger—me who's met him or Rhadamanthus who hasn't? I say he is *sweet*." Whence this irritability and unreason? Tod couldn't understand himself. Once, when Pumpkin had wavered and it seemed she might go back to her husband, he had been in agony. His heart had turned over and over in jealousy like a lump of meat in a cauldron of stew.

"Rhadamanthus," Pumpkin answered, to a question he had forgotten asking.

"He thinks you're his princess," Tod snapped. "He thinks I sully you, no doubt."

"He thinks you're *beautiful*," she said, infuriatingly.

"Who *are* these men anyway," Tod countered, "to run our lives? What do we know about *them*? Are *their* marriages so great, that they should put ours down? From the way Oz's stomach burbles I think he has an ulcer. As to your guy, I didn't like the shifty way he shambled out the door that time. He wouldn't look me in the eye. What do you two *do* in there anyway?"

Pumpkin was crying. "Go back," she said. "That's what you're saying to me you want to do. Go back to Lulu and have pinchy feet." She hung up.

But the next time he saw her, after her Thursday session with Rhadamanthus, the psychiatrist had told her that wasn't what Tod had meant at all; he meant that in truth he loved her very much, and she loved him. She felt all smooth and plumped-up on the fourth-floor landing, and inside his room she kicked off her shoes and told all that had been disclosed in the cave of knowing.

They seemed, sometimes, as they moved about the city enacting their romance, gloves on the hands of giants, embodiments of others' hopes. They had no friends. They had children, but these they had wounded. Tears glistened about them like the lights of the city seen reflected in the square pool beside the round white table of an outdoor restaurant. In museums, tall stainless-steel constructs probed space to no clear purpose, and great striped canvases rewarded their respectful stares with a gaudy blankness. In movie houses, her hair tickled his ear as pink limbs intertwined or Sherlock Holmes stalked through the artificial mist of a Hollywood heath. They liked revivals; Esther Williams smiled triumphantly underwater, and Judy Garland, young again, hit the high note. Outside, under the glitter of the marquee, ice glistened on the brick pavements, and chandeliers warmed the bay windows of apartments whose floors and furniture they would never see. They were happy in limbo. At night, sirens wailed lullabies of disasters that kept their distance. Traffic licked the streets. Airplanes tugged snug the blanket of sky. They awoke to find it had snowed through all their dreaming, and the street was as hushed as a print by Currier & Ives—the same street where in spring magnolias bloomed first on the sunny side and then, weeks later, on the side of constant shade. They walked enchanted, scared, unknown but for the unseen counsellors whose blessings fed the night like the breathing of stars. Then the world rotated; the children stopped crying, the pace of legal actions slowed, the city lights faded behind them. They bought a house. He built bookshelves, she raised flowers. For economy's sake, they stopped seeing psychiatrists. Now when she said to him, "You're beautiful," it came solely from her, and when he answered, "So are you," it was to quell the terror that visited them, stark as daylight, plain as the mailman. For Tod was death and Pumpkin was hollow and the fairy godfathers had vanished, taking with them the lovers' best selves.

The Faint

FREDDY PYTHON was a well-known developer around
Boston, always putting together real-estate packages that,
though they seldom came to anything, somehow kept
him in sports cars, tailored suits, and attractive women.
He lived with his mother and a Filipino servant in a
choice slice of house on the good side of Beacon Hill. His
first and only marriage had ended quickly, without children. In the decade since, he had almost forgotten this
wife; she was the most distant figure in a long line of
women he had escorted and seduced, enjoyed spats and
vacations with, got sunburned and frostbitten with, loved
and forgotten each in her turn. In his memory, the succession was clamorous and indignant, like the Complaints
line in a department store, with a few conspicuously silent, sullen sufferers hoping to make their case that way.
Freddy had finessed them all: the weeper, the screamer,
the tedious reasoner, the holder of heated silences. At the
end of a date, however fraught, he would skillfully sail his
Porsche through the bright morass of Park Square and the

erratic rapids of Charles Street traffic, tack uphill into his narrow alley, and nose the car to safety in its space below his mother's window. He would let himself in softly and ascend the carpeted stairs to his bedroom, a vast master bedroom that floated, all puffs and pillows and matching satin, like a dulcet blimp above the contagion of the city and its dreams. The Filipino would have turned his coverlet down. His mother would have left him a note, saying, "The mayor called," or "Don't forget your lecithin." Freddy would undress, checking his gym-hardened body for signs of wear in the full-length mirror before unfolding his pajamas. Composing his pajamaed self for sleep, he closed his eyes and folded his mind around the evening's seized pleasures. His trophies were about him, from the framed citation of the Charlestown Realty Board to the plated statuette signifying second prize in the Malden Teens Tennis Competition for 1956. His schemes for tomorrow were in order. The Hill was quiet but for the burst of a muffler or the scampering footsteps of a mugging. Corinna (or whoever) lay alone in her (rumpled) bed. Freddy was alone in his. What a life.

Corinna. Perhaps they had played out their string. He was of two minds about her, and she was of two minds about everything. A tallish, staring blonde of at least twenty-five, with an ass like two moons, she looked good with Freddy in public, yet she avoided going out. She said she hated crowds. He would appear at her apartment in flared chalk stripes and polished Guccis and find her in the bathtub, drugged by the steam. Around midnight, he would manage to organize her into walking over to Boylston Street for a cheeseburger. Or they would wind up sharing a sweet-and-sour-chicken TV dinner by the fireplace—she had no wood, so they set a reluctant blaze

of rolled-up newspapers kept compact with rubber bands
—while old jazz singles tumbled from WGBH on her bedroom radio. She took dictation all day and after work
seemed to need to express herself, to rotate languidly
through her two rooms, shedding clothes and emptying
ashtrays in a kind of monologue of slow motion, developing her own space. Freddy tossed the theatre tickets they
didn't use into the greasy blue flames and announced,
"There's twenty-two bucks up the chimney."

"Did you really want to go? Wasn't this nicer? Just us?"

"We can be just us any time. We can only go to *The
Belle of Amherst* this week."

"Freddy, you really *did* want to go. I'm sorry, I was
just so tired, I still haven't recovered from that all-male
As You Like It."

"You loved *Equus*."

"I didn't love it, I just loved the way it was only two
acts."

"You said you liked the horses' heads."

In mock consolation, Corinna, clad in only an apron,
bent low over him, her breasts half lit by the same fire-
light that was flickering in the empty compartments of
the tinfoil tray of their TV dinner. "I *did* like the horses'
heads, Freddy. And the way they made the stage spin to
show neurosis. I'll go. Let's go tomorrow night. Can you
get tickets again?"

Actually, Freddy had not planned to see her tomorrow
night. These evenings of a fresh shirt and his suit getting
out of press for nothing were getting on his nerves. There
was a Japanese girl, an assistant to a landscape designer he
was conferring with tomorrow morning, who had given
him the eye at the last conference, though it was hard to
tell with those eyes, those opaque little pools of racial am-

bition, noncommittal as camera apertures. Still, he had
planned to leave things open. Yet if he said no, Corinna
would think he didn't have the pull to come up with the
tickets. "O.K.," Freddy said. "But tell me you mean it.
Otherwise, I'll wear the denim suit and a turtleneck."

At least, when he arrived, she was out of the tub. But
she didn't know what to wear. It was a warm spring
night, windy, ideal for walking to a cheeseburger, but un-
settling otherwise. She padded back and forth from the
living room to the bedroom, saying, "I hate my clothes."
She showed him a wool dress that was too wintry and a
cotton that was too summery. Everything was like that,
nothing was right and never had been, she hated to shop;
if she bought something, she hated it and if she didn't, she
hated herself. When she was a little girl, her mother used
to dress her up in these frilly tight party dresses and she'd
take the neck in her two hands and rip it right down the
middle, *brrruup!* Her tongue was darting about like a rabbit in the headlights; her wheels were spinning. As a boy,
Freddy had had a blue Lionel model train that he loved.
The locomotive sometimes would leave the track, and
when he picked it up, it was surprisingly heavy and
would give a tingle of excited heat to his hand; and when
he set it back on the track, its wheels would spin and the
armature of its heart would whir, the electrical connec-
tion made with magical suddenness. Corinna could be like
that.

From the extreme reaches of her closet she produced a
dress of silvery-blue, patterned abstractly in white, with
a high Chinese-style neck. The Oriental touch chimed
with the Japanese girl on Freddy's mind. More than once,
in conference today, she had referred, with an opaque

glance at Freddy, to her husband, who appeared to be an architect. No commission for him, if that was her thought. On all sides, Freddy was betrayed by hidden loyalties. First the Irish politicians, now the Japanese professionals. Corinna held the dress up against herself. The slim sheath cut of it made her look taller than tallish. As firmly as, years ago, he had set the agitated little Lionel back on its track, Freddy told her to wear that dress. He was tired of babying her. He was no longer of two minds. She had had it.

He scolded her, "You've made us too late to look for a taxi, we'll have to walk." Spatterings of forsythia glowed in the brownstone churchyards of the Back Bay, and spots of daffodils behind the Public Garden fence. The dress's narrow skirt chopped her normally long stride to a hurried clatter. Fragrances of bloom, of car exhaust, of drained wine bottles lived in the warm wind of Park Square. The Colonial Theater lobby was deserted. They took their seats in the dark, disrupting the row. By stage light, Freddy noticed a glisten of sweat on Corinna's upper lip; he touched the silken sleeve of her dress and she pulled her arm away. Gradually, the play absorbed his attention. The brave little female figure, alone on a stage that represented a spinster's house in Amherst, conversed with invisible presences, recited Emily Dickinson's poetry, and called out through a phantom window to the audience. With her dark hair and plaintive, strained voice, she reminded Freddy of someone, someone very distant yet very familiar. It came to him: his wife. Loretta, too, had parted her hair severely in the middle, brushed at her hips to smooth away agitation, called out in a voice of cracked, retracted melody, laughed as if to hint at an inner soreness, been shyly stagy, had a pointed chin, had even written poetry, come to think of it. She inhabited an empty house, however, nowhere outside of Freddy's skull, for she had briskly remarried and borne two children; but this is how he saw her, breathing an aura of desertion, twitchily strumming the filaments of an irrecoverable loss. As the playwright's design proceeded to suggest that Emily Dickinson had triumphed in her loneliness, perversely choosing it, the parallel possibility unpleasantly dawned that he, Freddy, had not so much left Loretta as she had rejected him. *Him.*

The curtain came down; the lights went up. Corinna's face looked round as a moon, though pink, and broadly smiling. "Is it really only two acts? Isn't it stifling in here?" she asked.

"I hadn't noticed."

"You seem so preoccupied. Sad. What are you thinking about?"

The blue of the dress as it enclosed her throat brought out the blue of her eyes startlingly; it thrilled him like a spurt of ice water to realize he must dump her. Nothing to lose through the truth, then. "My first wife," he answered.

"Your only wife, as I understand it," Corinna said. "Let's get up."

He took her into the lobby and bought her a cone of orangeade. Even in this crush, he imagined, she was being admired—her rosy high color, her cool blue stare as she sucked at the straw. Her cheeks dented in, draining the last. The warning bell rang. As they shuffled toward their aisle, she placed her hand heavily on his forearm. "Freddy. I'm going to faint."

"Faint?" It seemed a concept wildly out of fashion, like bastardy or family prayers. "Why would you do that?"

"I feel vomity," she said, staring ahead. Her rosy face had lost its color. The weight of her hand on his arm slippingly intensified and he put his arm around her waist to hold her upright. Her legs seemed to be abdicating responsibility for her body.

"You really want to do this?" he asked, and in the silence of her response, the calm of disaster descended upon him. She mustn't fall to the floor here, to be trampled by Italian leather. He spotted a sign that spelled LADIES at the corner of the lobby, past some pilasters. "Hold tight," he muttered. Corinna was still conscious but leaning against him like a flying buttress. He pulled her toward the archway; there was no door to push through, just a few astonished faces to brush aside. A female attendant the size and age of Freddy's mother, and with the same hobbling thrust, strode forward indignantly. "She's fainting," Freddy called to her, and the indignation on the old lady's face hesitantly dissolved. Corinna's weight went altogether dead, a silken ton of blood.

"Poor thing," the attendant said, and bent to share Freddy's responsibility.

In less than a second, he had appraised his surroundings. That pink door must lead to the toilets. There was no plumbing in sight, merely mirrors and dollops of gilt, as if squeezed from a giant icing tube. So this was a ladies' lounge. Everywhere there were places to sit, sofas and chairs, for ladies to be faint upon. The room, emptying as the second warning bell sounded, still held women, perhaps a dozen; they formed an audience as Freddy and the motherly attendant lowered Corinna's utterly limp and ponderous body onto the nearest receptacle, a chaise longue covered with blue stripes that complemented the skyey pallors of her Chinese dress.

The Faint

She was out cold, and looked grand. Displayed thus on the dainty chaise, her long legs trailing to the floor, she had grown huge in unconsciousness. Bent above her, Freddy felt himself engorged by pride. She was his, his, with her wide hips tugging the dress into horizontal wrinkles and her hands flopped palm up at the end of arms longer than swans' necks and her oblivious face impassive and wide as that of a Mayan idol. Only he, in the audience gathered around her body, knew her name; it, and all of the trivial facts with which she might have described herself, had sunk into the depths of her sudden majestic abdication. He was one of these details and he, too, with his money and his mother and his cunning, his maddening resistance to marriage, had sunk with them, without a trace; he had ceased to grieve her, he was lost within her, as within the universe. How big she was, his doll! How beautiful and mysterious! The inside of his chest felt crammed, scraped, distended. In panic, he wanted to call her back into being, from behind her face —this untouchable mask with a strand of disarrayed hair pasted to one cheek—lest it find peace too blissful and begin to decompose. He was inside her, somehow, every detail of him down to his mediocre record at Colgate and his father's humiliating shoe store. He wanted to see her lips move, her eyelids flutter. He wanted to be allowed to put their lives back on the track.

The attendant thrust some smelling salts under Corinna's nose. The rapt face grimaced and then, in an instant, beaded all over with sweat. The watching women greeted this prodigy with murmurs, and Freddy, as somehow its father, took their applause as a compliment to himself. Exercising his prerogatives, he bent a shade closer, and Corinna's nostrils perceptibly narrowed. The ammonium carbonate was re-applied, and this time her soul pushed through the maze of her physiology and popped her eyes open. "Oh," was her single word. Her eyes in fright searched all their faces until they found his, and closed. Her hand, however, lingered to brush aside the strand now tickling her cheek. In ten minutes, she was ready to walk out into the air.

The second act, he supposed, would have been much like the first.

She said it was the dress; that dress made her feel, the cut of it and fabric both, *closed in,* which is why she had put it, though she knew it was flattering, at the back of her closet.

They were married in the open, on a site where some slums had been cleared as part of one of Freddy's packages.

The Egg Race

OR WAS IT CALLED the Spoon Race? The children lined up, each holding an egg in a spoon, out in front of his chest. The eggs precariously wobbled, of their own semi-liquid, semi-live weight. On your mark, get set, go. Those who dropped their eggs, of course, were out. In that rural green world careless of its produce, nearly forty years ago, there seemed no worry about a mess; the dropped eggs were casually absorbed by the earth of the playground where the race was held, once a summer at some fête when the gods of calendar and nation stooped low over the children, beaming, bestowing prizes as simple as a Hershey bar or a paper kite, furled. Ferguson had not thought of it for years, but lately he was visited, as if grown permeable in middle age, by recollections and premonitions.

His father appeared to him in a dream, with the vividness of living flesh. What did it mean? The man had died five years before, while his son was in Iraq, on a dig. Ferguson was an archaeologist, a seeker of lost cities. Even in dying, he thought at the time, his father had been con-

: 231 :

siderate, sparing him the bedside decisions, the hospital vigil, the embarrassments of parting. The old man's circulation had been failing for some years; death came as a mercy. The burial service witnessed a surprising display of grief and tremulous remembrance from ex-students and colleagues of the dead man. He had been a high-school teacher; his life had been poured into the shifting sands of Hayesville's continual, thankless young. Then, at the funeral, all this outpoured life came gushing back, in the tears of strangers, shaming the son, whose own eyes were dry, and whose dominant emotion was relief. The funeral passed; Ferguson's career continued to take him to the desert and back; he left his wife for another woman. He had long contemplated this last, but would never have done it had his father been alive. Why should this be? In all the years of his growing-up, Ferguson had never heard a paternal reprimand. His father had been encouraging and forgiving, purely. There had been some great unstated sorrow his father had been protecting him from, to the end.

In the dream, they were travelling together, as they had so often done, in a confused but somehow exhilarating manner. Cars broke down, wallets emptied, trolley conductors were rude, yet they went places, father and son, and what blew from the dream, with such shocking freshness that Ferguson awoke, was the *breath* of the trip, a sensation mixed of speed and his father's timid smile, paternally anxious to please. His father smiled over at him from within the vague, low-roofed vehicle in which he was travelling, and his smile said that his son was *with* him, would join him; and Ferguson awoke, shocked, the strange bliss of this lost companionship dissolving about

him in the dawn light, while his second wife slept motionless beside him.

The beloved sensation, of sharing with his father some
ill-starred but merry and illuminating trip, he had tried to
re-impose upon his own children, but their ventures felt
like imitations, lacking not only the authentic late-Chris-
tian flair—stoic yet quixotic, despairing yet protective—of
the dead wanderer but the right threadbare environment.
It was no longer the Depression, trolley cars no longer
swayed through the center of cities, people no longer
boarded railroad trains in their Sunday best, coal no longer
sparkled in the weedy rights-of-way, the next town was
no longer another planet. Ferguson's children graduated
from ten-speed bikes to driver's licenses, and toward the
end scarcely needed him to take them places. He had left
them, he felt, only a little before they would have left him.

Since the divorce, there had been a few trips with his
children. One son, turned seventeen, allowed Ferguson to
escort him on a tour of Midwestern colleges. For a week
they checked in and out of motels overlooking lakes and
cornfields, soared in and out of airfields lightly carved
from the general flatness, walked across campuses Neo-
Gothic, neoclassic, or neo-Bauhaus in style, admired chap-
els and libraries and audiovisual labs, and at night returned
to that day's motel to drink beer at the bar. To Ferguson's
surprise, the boy was never refused service. One night, in
Iowa, on two beers each, they decided to swim in the
motel pool. The pool lay green and still and inviting beneath the dome of stars, amid the alien corn. They were
the only swimmers. While Ferguson tamely crawled from
side to side, the boy did backflips off the diving board. He
had grown big, with a puppyish thickness to his arms and

legs, and each flip precipitated a tumultuous splash. Coming out of the pool, he shivered gleefully, and told his father, "I remember it took a whole summer for me to get my nerve up to do that." The remark crushed epochs together: the child, his shoulders wrapped in a motel towel, seemed poised exactly between boyhood and manhood, between the college student coming to birth and the diapered infant who, in the telescoping of summers, ventured to the end of the diving board and hurled himself backward into watery space. The boy's encouraging, comradely smile resembled, down to its faint blur of fear, his vanished grandfather's. It was a moment of harvest for Ferguson, who felt, momentarily, forgiven.

Business took him to the Smithsonian Institution, where he walked through an exhibit commemorating how Americans once lived. Log cabins, corner saloons, immigrants' apartments—all lovingly reconstructed and mounted behind glass, like mammoth butterflies. He stopped, startled, at an antique classroom. Rows of slant-top desks with inkwells, bolted to the floor; a blackboard bearing large chalked examples of the Palmer penmanship method; George Washington, in Stuart's unfinished version, above the blackboard; and a sepia map of the spice routes on one side, by the windows that would overlook an asphalt playground. Ferguson stood baffled. What was historical about this exhibit? He had studied in such a classroom. If it were not for the glass, he could walk in—a shabby little overachiever, often the first to arrive—and take his seat.

More and more, he visited hospitals. The padded lobbies, the gleaming corridors, the ubiquitous click and bustle of efficient mystery: they, and airports, are our cathedrals. A colleague of Ferguson's lay dying of lung cancer.

Ferguson entered the room timidly, afraid of death, but was relieved to find nothing abstract—rather, the highly specific form of his old associate, the chairman of his department, whose two-volume opus on Toltec temple mounds had won the coveted Schliemann Award. Seven years older than Ferguson, and far more clever, he had been something of a father figure. Now his long brainy head, above the blank neck of a hospital johnny, in the sallow weariness of disease, had become an old woman's, a scold's. "I thought your last paper," he drawled with his drugged tongue, "a little less than rigorous. You posited a new stratum on the basis of a single shard. What does that do to the death pits of Level Twelve? You've displaced an entire population by three or four centuries." Ferguson imagined compounded strata of the dead shifting, clutching their pottery and lapis-lazuli beads and sandstone totems, all because of him. "You know," his critic continued wearily, "a chunk like that could be a sport, a stray copy of a Cretan model or something brought in from Anatolia. The dead were great travellers—never forget it." In a way, Ferguson loved this other man, for knowing what he himself knew, and more; they were, the two of them, split creatures, who in shady universities unloaded the bright, crusted fruit of their raids on lands of sun and sand, amid illiterate hirelings and the threat of banditry. What, then, was this exultant trembling in Ferguson's chest? His voice came out mercilessly crisp and clear, in contrast to the other's drugged remonstrances.

"Only Khirbet Kerak has those grooves," Ferguson said. "I'll bring you back more next summer. Tons of it. I'm sure it's down there."

Next summer. The dying man stared at a blank wall, eggshell in color, and exhaled.

Ferguson changed the subject. He cheerfully admired the room—its size, its view of the soft suburban hills south of Boston.

His colleague sighed in conciliation. "People our age should be restrained. We indulge ourselves. You got your divorce, I'm robbing my estate of two Cs a day for this room with a view."

Ferguson, looking up with a rejoinder on his tongue, saw the other man's face as something already lost in the earth, and an onrush of pity quelled the triumphant racing of his heart; he wanted to save his colleague from the crushing mass of forward time when the man would not be here, he wanted to lift him up from the bed as he would lift the shards of a flattened amphora up from centuries of sedimentation. Forgive me, Ferguson said to himself, in this room that felt already deserted.

From the streets outside, the hospital's gray walls hulked above the sunny neighborhood like an anonymous factory that makes an obscure but widely necessary product. Walking these streets, Ferguson saw how right Shakespeare was: life is a matter of stages. There goes the infant in his carriage, lulled by the swaying, and there goes the schoolboy, slouching with bare legs and baseball bat down an alley toward a playground and one more game amid the long shadows. Ferguson had been there, he could still taste those dusty, infinite afternoons. There goes the young husband, skinny in his shirtsleeves, bending to take his whining toddler's hand while his wife beside him complacently hatches another responsibility in her stomach. The motions of changing a diaper still lived in Ferguson's hands, and the feel of a small child's gritty grasp on a single finger during the bedtime song. And there went the divorcing man, haggard yet lightened, carrying gin and frozen Chinese food back to his apartment, which he has furnished in the same manner, long on posters and short on lamps, as the last habitat of his solitude, his college room. These roles, thoroughly performed, need not be performed again. A paradox: though Ferguson in theory dreaded death, in practice he was glad, relieved, that he would never be asked to be young again.

The stratum of middle age has its insignia, its clues, its distinguishing emotional artifacts: the glaze of unreality, for instance, that intervenes even in moments of what formerly would have been rapture. The middle distance blurs, and the floor appears to tilt, as if in unsteady takeoff toward some hopelessly remote point. New glasses help. The axis of astigmatism is rotating, the world is turning, the soul finds itself locked in a house with smeary windows. Contrariwise, the mail, once so pregnant with mysteries and stimulations, can now be read without opening the envelopes: photographs of the maimed and starving, angry petitions for justice, comradely appeals to the alumni, proceedings of learned societies, advertisements for undesired treasures, scholarly offprints, photocopies of photocopies. Into the wastebasket it can go unopened, cleanly posted to the void. One day, Ferguson rescued an envelope from the trash, noticing that his address had been typed, not stenciled. "Dear Fergy," it began in a serene, trite, Palmer-method hand from the past, and continued with mimeographed exclamations: " C O M E to *Your* Twenty-fifth! Hayesville High Class of '52 wants YOU!!" The underlined, hyper-capitalized "YOU" assigned him the same spiritual importance—feathery, comical, innermost—with which he had awoken from the dream of his father. He would go. The missive was signed by Linda Weed Gottfinger, the class secretary. Ferguson and she had begun kindergarten together. Linda Weed used to steal his book bag on the way home from school and keep it from him until he cried. She had been wonderfully quick, with pigtails and a snub nose, and even when her figure ripened—her breasts overnight become amazing jutting softnesses—her belly had stayed flat and her legs thin and hard. That had been her handwriting saying, "Dear Fergy."

At the reunion, after midnight, while the band played all the old tunes, from "Near You" to "Tangerine," Ferguson through a veil of bourbon perceived that amid these old children, these accents, and these melodies he had experienced Paradise. Nevertheless, he wished he were home. He had come alone. His old role, of lonely grind, was waiting for him like a shabby suit; it fitted perfectly. The band played "Rag Mop," and Linda Weed drifted toward him purposefully. While the others were dancing, or reliving ancient heartbreaks, or helping each other be sick in the motel rest rooms, she was taking a poll for their Quarter-Century Memory Book, to be mimeographed and distributed. She asked him, "Single, married, separated, or divorced?" Her pencil waited, slim and alert. Linda had kept her figure, to the age of forty-three. Some beauties of their class had been utterly swallowed by their own fat, so that in looking at them Ferguson seemed to be witnessing an act of cannibalism or gazing down at a Pharaoh swaddled in a bulky sarcophagus. He looked ceilingwards for an accurate answer. The motel management had hung their ballroom with red and white crêpe paper, though their class colors had actually been maroon and cream. "Maroon and cream, maroon and cream," their class song had gone, and then a murky line that ended with "dream."

Ferguson answered carefully, "All of them. But not all at once."

"What are you now?"

"Homesick."

"I'll put down 'Married.' " From kindergarten on, she had been a hard girl to faze. Cool green eyes, and one false tooth when she smiled. She had fallen skinning the cat on the playground jungle gym. The band shifted to "Across the Alley from the Alamo."

"Profession?" she asked.

"Digger," he told her, and it seemed profoundly true. He tried to tell her how true. "I seek to bring what was hidden back into the light. Last winter I found a single shard that made thousands of skeletons move over."

"Fergy, you're drunk," she told him.

Her breasts had become amazing in the seventh grade, beneath the fuzzy angora sweaters of that epoch. Now, as if to advertise that her breasts had survived two Asian wars, six Presidents, five recessions, and four children, the class secretary was wearing a deeply décolleté bodice of lemon chiffon, in the Fifties' strapless style. Was it her prom dress, miraculously preserved? Essence of Eisenhower and orchid corsage wafted upward from her cleavage. He would never, not in all eternity, see her breasts, Ferguson thought sourly. Linda had married her tenth-grade steady and never left Hayesville; she had never travelled in the land of guilt.

People were dancing, reminiscing, falling down. A confusion as of shards and unstrung beads and retrieved statuettes filled the ballroom and Ferguson's skull. Unhoped for, what had been hidden came to light. Nasty Kegerise, the class pest, waltzed up to them. He owned a million-dollar electronics firm called Xister, Inc., had gone jowly and gray and wore bifocals, but was still the class pest, with the class pest's perennial immunity. He ogled Linda and lightly flipped aside one chiffon leaf of her bodice, with its built-in bra. So for a second her soft conical breast lay exposed upon the glazed platter of Ferguson's vision. His breathing stopped. Her breast was perfect, more candid and ample than he had dreamed, weighty yet buoyant in its shadowy cup of cloth, as perfect as an egg.

Linda slapped Nasty's hand and tugged the bodice back into place, unfazed; her composure hitched only when her cat-green eyes flicked to Ferguson's, where they had not expected to encounter, perhaps, such bliss, bliss like a blossom put forth by a slender branch of yearning thirty years long. "What is your present address?" she asked.

"I forget."

Outside the windows of the little cedar-shingled house in Maine, pine branches breathed of primeval hush, of Indians, of somehow Siberian rocks and moss, before the Bering Straits closed and the continent was cut off with its cruel dream of freedom. There was a creek nearby where he and his second wife and her only child, a boy, could pick up arrowheads right off the silt.

Linda's pencil remained cocked. "How well," she asked, taking her poll, "do you feel America has kept its promises to you?"

"Well enough," Ferguson said.

She snapped shut the notebook.

The band started in on "So Tired," with that soul-chilling wah-wah of the muted trumpets.

Their class giant came up to him, a tackle and a shot-putter. He had gone bald. "You're not the man your father was," he told Ferguson.

"I know. I'm sorry."

"He was so damn encouraging, was the thing of it. I never forget how he used to tell me, 'You're on Fool's Hill now, but you'll come down. What goes up must come down,' he'd say, and throw a blackboard eraser into the air. 'The last mile is the hardest,' I remember he used to say so often, and I didn't know what he meant at the time. Now I do. Now I do." The giant gazed down at Ferguson, where he was sunk in a trench of sadness, of love that had nowhere to flow. If he cried, would he get his schoolbag back?

"Goodnight, Iree-hee-heen," the band played in conclusion, "gooodnight, Irene."

The next day was a Saturday. Hung over, Ferguson prowled the town, his lost city of Hayesville. Except on the fringes, where in his childhood fields had supported corn, and creeks had been choked with watercress that old women would come and harvest, Hayesville had changed little. In the alleys there were curious artifacts, cages of wire and wood, and with some difficulty Ferguson identified these as street-hockey goals. In his boyhood they had played only the games where a ball soared, the baseball a black speck in the wheeling sky and the fat basketball grazing the auditorium rafters and the football finding the fingertips of the galloping end. The old elementary school, a Gothic fortress rising from an asphalt lake, was boarded up, with revolutionary and racist slogans spray-painted across the weathering plywood. They had sold the classrooms to the Smithsonian. There had been a little candy store the children would sneak to during recess, Boonie's, and this, Ferguson was surprised to find, was still there and still open. He entered the crypt and bought a dime's worth of the old candies—jelly hats, licorice pipes, nougat in waxed paper, coconut strips dyed to resemble bacon. The wizened, arthritic old man behind the blackened, cracked glass case patiently filled a little paper bag piece by piece. He pressed Ferguson's change back into his palm, making the fingers close like a child's around the coins. "Now hold tight, Fergy," he crooned. "Don't drop any pennies now." So this was Boonie, a living fossil. On all sides, Ferguson was known. The tilting front porches knew him, and the twitching window curtains. The horse-chestnut trees would have known him, had they not been cut down. The alleys seemed brighter, the sky barer, since the days when he had sneaked the back way home from school to avoid bullies. No bullies approached him now—just old people who said, "I bet you don't remember me." It was true, he didn't, but he remembered the style—the striped shirts and suspenders, the baggy cotton smocks, the suety skins, the loose elbows, the enfolding warm voices, with yet a pinch of something sardonic in the intonation. Like the salt machine at the bottom of the sea, Hayesville had continued to turn out Hayesville people. He had been one of them. More than once, he was mistaken for his father. The town, the houses thinned. On the athletic fields be-yond the high school, where the crones of Hayesville in his childhood would circle stooping, gathering weeds for dandelion stew, a little stadium had been erected. Gazing into the barred cement portals, Ferguson glimpsed an acre of Astroturf.

The old playground still stood on the embankment above the baseball diamond. It suggested a Hopi village on a mesa, a skeletal village of swing sets and jungle gyms. Huffing, sweating in his gray suit, wishing for a pith hel-met to shelter his headache, Ferguson climbed the embank-ment and found himself, amid the rotting box-hockey frames and the rusting, buckling slides, looking down into the grass, as if for traces—shards of shell, bits of dried yolk—of the Egg Race.

He had never won. No doubt he had been too intent on finishing with his egg intact to move very fast. A brisk heel-and-toe walk was the fastest one could do, and it was a revelation how much this simple locomotion jarred the body, how alarmingly the egg bobbled and lurched in its spoon. The sensations returned to Ferguson, unlabelled, whenever he drove down a treacherous highway, or walked across the carpeted lobby of a hospital to visit an acquaintance, or boarded an airplane. Travel generated smooth motion only in his dreams, when his father beckoned. The Egg Race, meant to be festive, had struck him as tragic, as one of those tough things, like the beheading of chickens and the swatting of flies and the overworking of adults, that went on around and above him in the grown-up world. And he wondered now, while his airplane ticket burned in his pocket, and the bandits of Iraq swabbed their guns, and his first wife slept alone, if this premonition of the tragic had not functioned as a limitation upon him, so that to this day he crouched within his life as within a fragile shell.

Home, Ferguson read in the paper that his colleague had died. Sitting at the breakfast table, he battled down the exultation that rose in his breast, a jubilant trembling that made his hand shake as he lifted egg on his fork to his mouth. The child he lived with called imperiously from upstairs. He had awoken with a sore throat and stayed home from school. Ferguson, turning the newspaper pages, heard the child's mother mounting to him with breakfast on a tray and remembered those lost mornings when he, too, stayed home from school: the fresh orange juice seedy from its squeezing, the toast warm from its toasting and cut into strips, the Rice Krispies, the blue cream pitcher, the sugar, the japanned tray where his mother had arranged these good things like the blocks in an intelligence test, the fever-swollen mountains and valleys of the blankets where books and crayons and snub-nosed scissors kept losing themselves, the day outside the windows making its irresistible arc from morning to evening, the people of the town travelling to their duties and back, running to the trolley and walking wearily back, his father out suffering among them, yet with no duty laid upon the child but to live, to stay safe and get well, to do that huge something called nothing. The house in all its reaches attended to him, settling, ticking, clucking in its stillness, an intricately worked setting for the jewel of his healing; all was nestled like a spoon beneath his life, his only life, his incredibly own, that he must not let drop.

Guilt-Gems

FERRIS, a divorced, middle-aged man, discovered in the blue ground of his midnight brain certain bright moments that never failed to make him feel terrible. Guilty. The treasure was of inestimable value.

One gem showed his younger son, at that time about fourteen, in tearful exasperation throwing two cats down the cellar stairs. The enveloping situation was this: Ferris's doctor had strongly advised him, for the sake of his asthma, to get rid of the cats. "But they're the children's pets," Ferris had said. "We can't just get rid of them."

"Get rid of them," his doctor had said. "Those cats are suffocating you."

"They don't mean to," Ferris had pointed out. "They can't help making dander."

"Tell Eileen to get rid of them. Tell Eileen it's either you or those cats."

"I've told her, and she says the children love the cats. She's right. She's always right. What can we do?"

His doctor then had peered at him through the upper half of his bifocals. Returning his eyes to the record he was making of this visit, he muttered, "It would help to keep them down in the cellar."

But the cats had been used to the run of the house and always found ways to evade their confinement. They would writhe out through a loose cellar window and come in through the kitchen door with the milkman, or a visiting child, or with Eileen when she had her hands full. Ferris's asthma continued bad. He was clogging his lungs with the Medihaler; his hands always trembled. Only his younger son recognized the emergency: it was his father or the cats. Since the cats could be neither killed nor controlled, Ferris would have to leave. He had already made his decision when, one day otherwise altogether forgotten, he saw the boy so desperately trying to keep the animals in the cellar and his father in the house.

Had Ferris imagined his son's tears of despairing fury? He thought not; there has to be some shine of the extreme, to make a guilt-gem.

Months later, he had left, and one of the duties that had fallen to him in the breakup was the driving of his older son back to his boarding school, in southern New Hampshire. It was usually a Sunday night, and the night he remembered must have been in winter, for there seemed to be ice everywhere. In the car, they had tried to talk; Ferris had tried to thank the boy, for continuing to go to his classes, to pass his exams, to play on the hockey team, to grow. For Ferris's dereliction loomed to him so large that he saw it as a blanket permission for all the derelictions in the world. The boy had listened in a silence that became wet and warm and heavy-breathing, and when

Ferris began to touch, he thought delicately, upon the reasons that had led him to leave the child's mother, the boy said "Yeah" with the quickness of a sucked breath. He knew enough and wanted to know no more: it was the kind of signal one man gives another.

Yet at the destination, in the dark cold spaces of the campus, after unloading from the car some piece of the bulky equipment—ski boots, or a guitar—essential to an American male adolescent, his son kissed him goodbye. The lit windows of the dormitories glowed all about them. The kiss was like a little spot warmed through a frosty windowpane. Through it Ferris saw how the boy's room felt to him, as haven—haven, amid the Escher prints and motorcycle posters, the hi-fi sets and horseplay-scarred walls, from the horror of having parents, of family.

Also in this period, his younger daughter, his baby, announced across the net from him at tennis, as she hit the ball with a clumsy forehand, "I think you're very *self*ish." The "self" stood out twangingly in the memory, the sweet spot of the sentence. The ball was out. He called it in. It was this false call, oddly, that had crystallized. Her accusation had the flaw that it was *meant* to make him feel guilty; and such a moment is to the real thing as a cultured pearl is to the found pearl.

His older daughter had married soon after his divorce, as if to keep a marriage in the family. She had been his child longer than any; she had taken the full brunt of his parental ineptitude. Once, he had twirled her by the hands so hard that her little wristbones audibly snapped, though X-rays at the hospital showed no fracture. On another occasion of acrobatic foolery, she had bitten him on the leg to get him to stop holding her upside down. Worse than

these shameful incidents, however, loomed a childish softball game he had played as pitcher for two teams of children, his own and a neighbor's. For some reason, the
neighbor's children feasted off his underhand offerings,
pounding hit after hit into the tall grass of the outfield.
His own children chased the ball until they were red in the
face, while those loathsome little opponents jeeringly
rounded the bases.

When at last the young Ferrises' turn at bat came, the
very intensity of their father's wish to serve up fat pitches
must have put something baffling on the ball, for they unaccountably hit pop-ups and dribblers. A ball bounced
out to the mound and Ferris had no choice but to field it
and chase down his older daughter as she raced from first
to second. The child didn't have a chance; his legs were
longer. He could think of no way not to make the play.
In the moment before the tag, she looked at him with a
smile, a smile preserved as in amber by a childish wild
plea on her face. She was out.

And now, though all the other players of that day had
grown much larger, and whatever expression *he* had worn
in that moment had faded forever from his daughter's
mind, her bright helpless face hovering above her hur-
rying body had lost none of its lustre for Ferris, none of
its edge, and immutably invested him with shame, with
an urgent futile need to *undo,* whenever he held this moment up against the blue light of midnight.

Guilt, for those prone to it, need not attach to conduct
generally judged reprehensible. Had Ferris deliberately
dropped the ball, had he *not* tagged his daughter out, that
would have been reprehensible. In himself he detected,
like the background radio noise that underlies the universe

and apparently is still transmitting the big bang of its creation, a pervasive ceaseless guilt in regard to his children for having called them into being at all. Just to see one of them walk across a high-school stage to receive a diploma, or up a church aisle to get married, or into the thick of a college soccer game on an overcast November Saturday, was to spangle his insides with terror.

Contrariwise, while it was widely agreed he had treated his ex-wife reprehensibly, her image shed his guilt as a seal sheds droplets of water. In his dreams she floated lithe and uncomplaining, and about ten years younger than she really was. He did remember this: at some point in their separation, Eileen had put her arms around him in their old kitchen, overcome by the sight of him once more leaving, and had sobbed; and by sympathetic pumping action her belly beat against his like a heart. Like a heart: more background noise, momentarily amplified by a defect in his automatic deafener.

His mother, now old, and he, now single, had flown to England together for a trip; she had always wanted to see Tintern Abbey. But she lived in southern New Jersey and he had holed up in Boston, so from Kennedy Airport she had to drive home alone, while he took a shuttle flight in the opposite direction. Worse, he drove himself in her car to LaGuardia, giving her the wheel with all of Queens and Brooklyn between her and the route home. Could she make it, in the Sunday traffic of megalopolis, tired as she was from the trip? As when he had fielded the softball and his daughter was racing from first to second, he couldn't think what else to do. But tag her. But abandon her.

It was a darkling spring evening in the eastern United

States. Rain bejewelled the windshield and there was just enough light left for her to make the Verrazano Bridge. Ferris studied the map. "278, Mother," he said. "Just stay on 278 South, no matter what."

"278 South," she said faintly, from a great distance away, behind the wheel. The distance between them, after their week together, had suddenly become the distance between one who must fly and one who must drive, between one who must submit and one who must steer. She was seventy-two. A sea of damp metal surrounded her. It had been sunny—that golden, almost mintable sunshine of poems—at Tintern Abbey.

"Stay in your lane," he told her. "If anybody honks, ignore them."

"They might be trying to tell me something."

"They have nothing to tell you," he told her. "Don't change lanes without looking, is all."

"Once I get to the turnpike, I'll be all right," she insisted.

"278 South will take you there," he said. "Mother, maybe you should stay in a motel. Maybe I should drive with you and fly from Philly."

"Don't be silly," she said. "The light's fading. I can do it. My goodness. I just stay on 278."

"South," he said.

Sitting behind the wheel, she was trembling; more than trembling, she was filling the interior of the car with the anticipatory vibrations of a girl before a dance—a prom, the dance of a lifetime. He imagined a corsage on her chest. Her cheek, as he leaned over to kiss it, was stretched smooth by fear, and he could smell perfume, the perfume our nerves give off above a certain pitch of tension. He pulled his suitcase out of the car and slammed the door.

As she haltingly pulled into the roadway, in the dusk, in the rain, a car honked, and then another.

How young her face had become at the last! Smooth and oval, with a half-laugh on her lips. That same half-laugh was in her voice when, three hours later, she had called Boston. "No mishaps," she told him. "Just a thunderstorm over Newark. It got so dark I thought my eyesight was failing. I felt my age."

"How do you like it?" Ferris had asked, of feeling one's age. He was genuinely curious. He saw her now as his forward scout in the wilderness of time.

With a lilt quite unexpected, dipping into some spring of girlish enthusiasm predating his birth, she answered, "I *hate* it!" and did laugh.

Her face, the parting kiss, his sense of perfume remained to torment him. His constant guilt had here compressed, her about-to-be-abandoned face a crystallization of the seducer's shame he had failed to feel on other, more appropriate occasions.

A guilt-gem is a piece of the world that has volunteered for compression. Those souls around us, living our lives with us, are gaseous clouds of being awaiting a condensation and preservation—faces, lights that glimmer out, somehow not seized, save in this gesture of remorse. Sifting them through his brain, Ferris would grow dulled to their glitter, indifferent to life and able to sleep. He had been a bully since his first cry for milk, and had continued a tyrant. He had tripped an infant playmate so the boy's head struck a radiator and gushed blood. He had told lies, about an imaginary pet dog, in Sunday school. He had teased his father, once pretending to start the car while the old man was putting a tire in the trunk, making the crowd of kids on the luncheonette steps laugh. Lord, what a treasure! Greater than Fafner's, a lode that goes down and down. Ferris was further soothed by this discovery: in amassing these guilt-gems, in reducing the matrical terror and grave displacement of his existence to a few baubles he could, as it were, put in his pocket and jingle, he was, doubly, guilty.

Atlantises

AT BREAKFAST, seeing on the front page of the local newspaper a photograph of a sweet-faced mass murderer, Mr. Farnham said to Mrs. Farnham, "Doesn't he look like Mr. Ciemiewiscz?" Then he realized, with a sinking feeling, that it had not been she who had known Mr. Ciemiewiscz; it had been the *first* Mrs. Farnham with whom, on the vanished continent of Atlantis, Farnham had known Ciemiewiscz, the "super" for the building containing the first apartment he and his former wife had occupied, over twenty years ago. It had been a basement flat. Cats had crept in the window at night. More than once, he had awakened with a cat purring on his chest. He and his wife had begged Ciemiewiscz in vain for screens. Looking out at the street, the Farnhams' young eyes had been level with a bed of lilies of the valley, the little white waxy bells hanging down like old-fashioned lampshades in miniature. Ciemiewiscz had burned the building's trash in the incinerator just outside the Farnhams' door (B-1), cursing loudly to himself over the incombustibles that found their way into his collection. His face had not been sweet, exactly, but soft, with curved lips and mild wide Polish eyes behind which—who knows?—may have hung murderous dreams. Farnham had not thought of this man for years. His thoughts of him now had taken less than a second.

His wife, glancing upward from the "Living" section at the photograph he was displaying to her, perhaps had not heard his slip of misplaced nostalgia. "Incredible" was her simple response, answering to many situations. Her lovely eyes lowered and returned to "Living."

The Farnhams lived inland, in a state people confused with Ohio; the fertile flatness, the tall skies, the way the trucks rolled day and night made them happy, because these things were theirs alone. They had both been Easterners. He had lived (it seemed incredible now) all his life, in one city or suburb or another, within a few miles of the sea. He had got out just in time. Atlantis was now sunk beneath the sea. It had been sandy, marshy, permeated by glistening water like something very rotten, and doomed. Odd moments of his life there, as detailed and difficult of explanation as religious visions or archaeological finds, returned to him: he saw himself, *was* himself, walking on sand, with a lame and swollen foot, down to the salt water, arm in arm with a woman with whom he had never had an affair. Their one moment of intimacy, of contact, had been then. He had stepped on a nail in his basement; it had gone through the sole of his sneaker and an inch of his foot with a brutal, buttery ease. Incredible! Had he stepped a little to one way or another in the dark, had his son or whoever was to blame not neglected to pick up the board, or had some carpenter at a majestic remove of contingency not driven that nail through that board at all, his foot would not have been pierced. But pierced it had been, forcing Farnham to perceive what a second-rate club actuality is. Membership in it is secured through a mix of mediocre credentials and fortuitous qualifications, while a host of preferable possibilities vainly clamor outside for admission. The nail through his foot, once admitted into actuality, brought with it a tetanus shot, a cancelled golf game, a spat with his son; thus this event, which so easily might have missed occurring, dubiously enriched reality. Of all these consequences, none endured now but the somehow uneradicated image wherein, at sunset, at one of those typical Atlantan beach parties, with their poignant intersections of childhood and adulthood, conjugality and infidelity, this woman in no way especially dear to him had taken pity on his buffoonishly displayed discomfort and led him to the water, on the theory that the cold brine might ease the swelling. As he took his halt steps in her embrace, they both seemed enclosed in a bubble of white-wine, with its illusory shimmer of well-being. The sand as they approached the water's edge became smooth and cool. Their friends from beside the bonfire of driftwood called after them jokes, of the sort that fall so flat on television commercials for beer or Coke but that in reality do live, do echo, do knit us one unto the other. The woman's waist felt solid under his hand. His foot hurt. The scent of woodsmoke was eclipsed by the great cold salt breath of the sea. The jokes fell away, and there was silence, except for the timeless slip-slapping of the wavelets and his anticipatory sigh of relief as the bitter summer Atlantic embraced his wound. That was all. The memory, now sunk so deep in the currents of time, had invested itself with an idyllic grandeur, magnified like a plaster castle in an aquarium and perhaps lent a touch of eternity by the uninvited kindness of the woman. On Atlantis, every woman was a priestess.

On Atlantis, Farnham recalled with wonder, people never tired of parties. There were beach parties, lawn parties, housewarming parties, office parties, birthday parties, post-party parties, all with "something of the barbaric," as Plato relates, though the temples, with their walls and pillars "variegated with gold and silver and orichalcum," were seldom visited by Farnham, his wife, and their friends. In their suburb, it was true, "of the buildings some they framed of one simple color, in others they wove a pattern of many colors by blending the stones for the sake of ornament so as to confer upon the buildings a natural charm." Flowering shrubs were cultivated, pools were dredged, and such industry as was needed to fuel the game of life was hidden behind tall fences. The terrain supported hosts of children, innocent bystanders bored yet glued by dependence to the constant festivities, bitten by mosquitoes at the edge of the volleyball court, crankily falling asleep on the sofa as cocktail hours stretched into pickup suppers and beyond. "When darkness came on and the sacrificial fire had died down, all the princes robed themselves in most beautiful sable vestments, and sate on the ground beside the cinders of the sacramental victims throughout the night." The children, as the seasons turned, enlarged gradually in size, spiked the volleyball, drank all the beer in the refrigerator, vied for the family chariots, and cultivated an illegal weed in corners of their parents' estates. Unnoticed by all but a few, the tides were seeping higher, as could be confirmed by the rings of barnacles on the old pilings, and the mussel flats gleamed blue under only the fullest of moons. Rather suddenly, it seemed, all was sunk beneath the water; temples, gardens—all was lost, though an occasional Christmas card floated to the surface, and the gaze of some vanished child, wanting to be taken home, would well up from the sparkle of a flat sidewalk and break Farnham's expatriate heart.

Mrs. Farnham said, "Don't blame me," setting aside "Living."

"For what?"

"For not knowing who Ciemiewiscz was. Or remembering how you all used to stay up all night eating mussels on the beach and then going to somebody's house for scrambled eggs."

"Did we use to do that?"

"Rodney and I used to do it, too. We'd stay up till four in the morning playing Botticelli and then be up for church at eight."

"Incredible," Farnham said.

"Oh, he was fanatic about not missing church. Yet I could never get him to explain to me what it meant to him."

"We used to go to church fairs," Farnham said. "Then they built an A-frame parish house and there wasn't any church lawn anymore."

"After church," she said, "all the husbands would play touch football while we sat on the cold grass reading the damn Sunday paper. Or softball, depending on the time of year. Once we even had a track meet."

"God, the energy," Farnham conceded. "God, we must have been young."

He sometimes forgot she was an Atlantan too. She too

had seen the walls of orichalcum, and the great moat of which Plato admitted, "It seems incredible that it should be so large as the account states." Now, bored with reminiscence, she turned her blue eyes to the window, where they could see corn. The Farnhams floated here in corn like angels in a cloud—corn planted, corn sprouting, corn greening, corn ripening, corn as high as an elephant's eye, corn harvested, corn stubble.

"We're not young now," she told him. "Your little girl is living with a boyfriend in Bridgeport. Your little boy is making three hundred a week in data control in Worcester."

Farnham stopped himself from saying "Incredible," though he felt it was. The way his wife's face caught the window light reminded him of another woman, who for a time he would visit in her house by a tidal river, and who in remissions of their passion might lightly gaze out at a passing rowboat, its oar plodding, or at some sudden wheeling outcry of gulls. Or else she was listening, through the tremble of elm leaves proximate to her window, for a repetition of a sound downstairs that made her fear that her husband or children had returned prematurely. The very atmosphere of Atlantis, in such moments, seemed a shimmering fabric that might tear. On the sloping banks of the river, dark mud mixed with granite and clamshells, an old man would be tying a dinghy, or some children might be skipping stones, to the admiration of a pet dog. The innocence of the scene would flood up to their windowsill, and tremble through, it seemed in memory, while their breathing stopped and their hearts thundered on.

"You're thinking about your old girlfriends," Mrs. Farnham accused.

"How can you tell?"

"By the light in your eyes. They get green."

The same light, sea light, had trembled through and saturated the skin of the priestesses as they lifted on an elbow and listened for that which was forbidden to be discovered. The sacred laws of Atlantis were written on golden tablets. The tidal world outside creaked, as with a complexity of winches—gulls, oarlocks, children's voices. And the alien corn outside his window dimmed, became husky, negligible, permeated by the memory of Atlantis, its curving waterways, its towering cities, its endless parties. A whiff of salt water wakened him to present reality; he looked across the breakfast table and said, "Don't cry."

The child who had been living with a man in Bridgeport was getting married, unexpectedly, to another man. The wedding was to be in Westerly. Mr. and Mrs. Farnham flew East, into the past, against the course of the sun, and rented a car. The industrial haze, the crowdedness, the cornlessness moved him keenly, even in the airport parking lot. They drove east, along the coast. In the words of Plato: "It was possible for the travellers of that time to cross from it to the other islands, and from the islands to the whole of the continent over against them which encompasses that veritable ocean." Norwalk, Fairfield, Milford. On a high bridge, they passed above a river and a helicopter plant. They left the Merritt and drove due east, along the coast. New Haven, New London. To their left loomed gray structures of amphibious intricacy, and Mrs. Farnham was reminded of a story.

"You see that tall tower, way over? That's full of water, and they use it to train people to get out of submarines without panicking. A guy I once knew, between Rodney and you, was a frogman, and his job was to hang inside the tower on a wire and watch the guys going past to make sure they were blowing enough bubbles."

"Going past?"

"Going *up*, from the bottom, where they'd put you in. You had to keep blowing air out of your lungs. Otherwise you'd get an embolism and die. Some guys did die. My friend's assignment was to grab you if you weren't blowing out enough bubbles."

"Grab you?" Farnham was distracted by a sign to Mystic. Did he want to go to Mystic? Did he want to go to Old Mystic?

"And pull you into a kind of compartment until you'd get up your nerve and start blowing out bubbles again."

"Is there that much air in your lungs?"

"There is when you begin at the bottom of the sea."

"I think I'd panic. This guy, he must have been some guy."

"He had his points."

"Name some."

"We didn't work out, though."

"Did—how well did you know him?"

"Pretty."

He looked over; her eyes were green.

Farnham, heading toward his daughter's wedding along the mazy coast, prayed: O rise, frogman, smoothly and without panic, up from the depths, trailing your train of air; bring us news of sunk Atlantis, our fabled pasts. Keep us in touch.

A Note About the Author

John Updike was born in 1932, in Shillington, Pennsylvania. He was graduated from Harvard College in 1954, and spent a year in England on the Knox Fellowship, at the Ruskin School of Drawing and Fine Art in Oxford. From 1955 to 1957 he was a member of the staff of *The New Yorker*, to which he has contributed short stories, poems, and book reviews. *Problems* is his sixth collection of short fiction; his other books include nine novels, four volumes of poetry, and two of criticism. Mr. Updike lives in Massachusetts.

A Note on the Type

The text of this book was set on the Linotype in Janson, a recutting made directly from type cast from matrices long thought to have been made by the Dutchman Anton Janson, who was a practicing type founder in Leipzig during the years 1668–1687. However, it has been conclusively demonstrated that these types are actually the work of Nicholas Kis (1650–1702), a Hungarian, who most probably learned his trade from the master Dutch type founder Dirk Voskens. The type is an excellent example of the influential and sturdy Dutch types that prevailed in England up to the time William Caslon developed his own incomparable designs from them. The italic is taken from a font of Electra, a typeface designed by W. A. Dwiggins.

The book was composed, printed, and bound by
American Book-Stratford Press, Inc.,
Saddle Brook, New Jersey.